FIRST STRIKE!

"Boss," the workman yelled, "you'd better get out here fast."

Matt, Teddy, and Moore all came running out immediately. The workman who had called Moore raced ahead toward the bank of the river, and they followed as quickly as possible.

When they got there, they could see that a cut had been started in one of the native trees. The long blade of an impulse cutter was still caught in the shallow cut, the weight of the power head causing it to vibrate slightly. At the foot of the tree lay a mass of yellowish-white powder over which two men were working frantically, colored to the elbows by the powder. The mound was heaving frantically, and, with a gasp of horror, Teddy realized that within that mound of yellowish-white was a man. . . .

Zach Hughes has also written:

SUNDRINKER

LIFE FORCE
ZACH HUGHES

DAW BOOKS, INC.
DONALD A. WOLLHEIM, PUBLISHER

DAW Book Collectors No. 757.

First Printing, September, 1988

1 2 3 4 5 6 7 8 9

PRINTED IN CANADA

COVER PRINTED IN THE U.S.A.

"And God said, Let the earth bring forth the living creature after his kind, cattle, and creeping thing, and beast of the earth after his kind: and it was *so.*"

—*Genesis 1:24*

Chapter 1

At one with the soughing wind and the moon-gleaming, ripening grass nuts of the browned plain, the presence drifted, lowered into the soft, murmuring song of summer, falling with a seeding pod as it expelled new life for the rich earth. From afar came the song of a fellow presence, steeped in jungle-moist richness, and a call of wonder from a young one high in the snowed, timberless mountains. All was one, all was contentment.

It rose now on a thermal as the sun-blessed plain gave back to the upper darkness the gift of the day, and the rustling grasses flashed past into a region of thinly treed, rolling ridges—a conversion zone—and as it moved over great distances, there was always the work. A flowering tree emitted a rush of perfume, feeling the brush of the presence, and that unseen one was dusted with minute pollen spores that seemed to drift upon the cooling night wind until, in another rush of perfume, flowers of a like kind were brushed. Ah, to watch the land renew itself and bring forth fruit, that was the wonder, and the work and the reward.

A new sound, the awareness of intrusion, a measurement of molecular movements led its attention high, high, where, in a blaze of red, something falling slowed, steadied, swam with graceful precision through the night sky.

Chapter 2

Tinker's Belle came out of transdrive just where Matt Tinker and his trusty Lamda 201 had pointed her, inside the orbital paths of two gas giants and three smallish, frigid planets and less than half an astronomical unit from the astral pathway of the target, detected for its blue tinge from not a few light years away. *Belle* was singing sweetly. Matt's ears, tuned to her moods after just over two years of seemingly peripatetic but actually well-reasoned wanderings in her, noted and were pleased. Way to hell and gone back toward the periphery, in the old neighborhood where mother Earth spewed out her deluge of humanity, a sour note in *Belle's* song might or might not have been panic-producing. Out here Matt wanted her to be purr-fect, and she was, odd little systems ticking and humming and the soft flow of air from the vents sweet.

"Hey, Teddy," Matt yelled, "you wanta look before we go in, or are you gonna take all day getting dressed?"

"Coming," said a very nice feminine voice, and there she was in the hatch that separated *Belle's* bridge from crew's quarters.

"Looks good," Matt said. "Instruments registering fine. Lots of water. Oxygen. No bad stuff so far."

The planet was magnified on *Belle's* viewer. Tedra Tinker saw the hint of blue seas, the whiteness of clouds. She hadn't spent too much time dressing, since it took only a couple of seconds to slip into her favorite shipboard wear, plain, loose-legged shorts and a frilly little shirt. She had spent some time on her hair. She wore it not quite shoulder-length: in all its auburn glory. And, as always, she had taken time to touch her face with a hint of color, her lashes just enough to enhance the natural impact of her huge, green eyes.

"Let me take her in?" Teddy asked, as she bent to plant a warm pair of lips on Matt's neck.

"Okay," he said, "but no showboating, hear?"

"Coward," she said, seating herself, beginning to punch buttons even before she'd plopped down into the contour chair for which she had modeled, quite bare, when the ship was being customized to its new, two-man crew just over two years ago.

Matt watched closely. In deep space it was hard to screw up when using the transdrive. Space, in spite of its white, pretty glow of stars, was largely an emptiness, and some fine-tuning to Andrew Reznor's engine—the invention which opened the age of interstellar space—had built-in safeguards against a careless pilot programming in a trans that would end up at the core of one of the nuclear furnaces called stars. Inside a solar system, with a few odd planets swimming around and with the possibility of floating scrap left over from the planet forming process, it was a bit more tricky. He nodded as he saw Teddy make the right observations, the right adjustment, the perfect programming, and then he blinked and below, or out there, or up there, depending on how one wanted to think about space, was a beauty of a world, blue and bright, with weather and seas and brown-green land areas.

"Hey," he said, as *Belle* dived like a bullet toward the planet.

The Reznor transient-drive functioned in two modes, deriving its motive energy from an eerie sub-elementary particle that Andrew Reznor, its discoverer, called the "transque," pronounced with a "k" sound at the end. At sublight speeds the transdrive called for a redefinition of several formerly inviolate laws of physics and the nature of energy and matter. And what it did when it was kicked into FTL mode was a clear aberration that defied all known logic. All laws of physics became void, and parsecs could be covered without measurable loss of time.

Of course, the relatively short distance to be traveled from *Belle's* point of emergence from subspace or, as Reznor himself said jokingly, Alice's Wonderland to planetary atmosphere did not allow acceleration to that point where Einstein was proven somewhat right, when ship's mass began to increase and time to be altered, but the distance was enough for *Belle* to gain more speed than Matt liked.

"Teddy, you wanta slow down?" he asked mildly, as the good old Lamda 201 clicked and counted rapidly multiplying molecules of atmosphere.

"Slow it down, Teddy," he said, his voice a bit stronger, as *Belle* began to transmit through her hull the rush and whine of air.

"Teddy," he yelled, as a mighty sonic boom thundered behind them and he could see the red-yellow glow of heated air through the front ports.

"You're no fun at all," Teddy said, even as she began to slow the ship, and the heat flares started to dim and the hurricane of wind sound outside began to fade.

"Kick in the G.D.," Matt said calmly.

Teddy's long, slim fingers barely moved. The Reznor G.D. rumbled. That was the only trouble with the old man's Gravitational Deflection Planetary Engine. It growled. The sound was in the ship and from the ground it sounded like steady, distant thunder. The G.D. did interesting things with a planet's own force, its gravitational pull, and used that power to soar, dart, hover, land, or orbit within atmosphere. In an emergency the trans could be used, but *Belle* wasn't stressed for continuous use of that drive in atmosphere.

Belle was flying into the dawn at eighty thousand feet. Sunlight sparkled on her hull, making her a daytime star.

"Wow," Teddy said, as the planet moved slowly underneath, revealing everything that a planet should have—seas, land masses, mountains, rivers, lakes, vegetation. They were too high to see details of the greenery.

"What shall we call it?" Matt asked. He felt fine. It wasn't every day, or every year, or every lifetime that an explorer found a new life-zone planet.

"Do we get to name her?" Teddy asked eagerly, her green eyes wide, making Matt almost forget his excitement at finding a new world.

"We can submit suggestions."

"Beauty," Teddy said.

"We need a name, not a description."

"Can you think of anything better?"

"Just Beauty?"

"As in Beauty and the Beasts," Teddy said.

"That's singular, beast."

"Not in this case," she said.

"Point taken," he said, as he watched a new sea edge into view past a line of snowy, rugged mountains. "But we need to submit more than one suggested name."

"Tinker's World," Teddy said.

"That would be rejected offhand," he said. He grinned. He'd taking a lot of ribbing after having the

name, *Tinker's Belle* etched onto the ship as she was
being reworked in the Reznor Yard, even though
most of the men who snickered didn't know the reference hidden in the name. They just thought it was
cute, maybe a little too cute, but it was Matt and
Tedra Tinker who would be off in the great dark in
that little teapot of a ship, and, since it was company
policy, they could damned well name her what they
wanted to name her.

"Let's not think about it now," Teddy said.
"Let's land."

"Whoa," he said.

"Matt, it's just what we've been looking for, just
what the old man wants."

"You know we have to check it out before landing. Want a screaming alien virus to fly up your
nose?"

"Now how many life-forms have been found on
the fifty explored worlds?" she asked, sniffing.
When she sniffed, her nose tilted just a bit more and
warmed Matt's heart. He had fallen in love with that
tilt of nose five years before when she first appeared
at the Reznor complex with a brand new degree in
Terraforming from M.I.T.'s School of Space Sci-
ences, and that love had quickly spread from nose
to eyes to mouth to long, slim legs and the interior
works, too, all that made up Tedra. If anything, he
was more in love five years later.

"Matt, it'll be months before they can send out
an analysis team. We won't be the first to walk on
our world if we don't land."

"No," he said. "Gimme." He took the controls
and sent *Belle* shooting down, down, until, at hovering speed, he opened test vents and collected air
that read so pure and sweet that he whistled. To Teddy's credit, she never sulked. Nor, in actuality,
would she have opened the *Belle's* outer hatches on
an untested new world. She buckled down to work,

although in five years of exploration she had not previously had the opportunity to use the various tools of analysis that gradually built up a picture of a perfect world, a world so fresh and pure that it was unbelievable. On six out of every ten of the new habitable planets discovered and settled in the past three decades there had been some imperfection, perhaps just a trace of some noxious gas, or over-acidity of ocean to discourage the growth of those wonderful little plants that were the base of the food chain and producers of sweet oxygen.

"It's too damned perfect," Teddy said, after the third work day, after two nights spent in low orbit with *Belle* muttering and clicking and looking after herself while Matt and Teddy slept, limbs entwined, always touching. "Let's find something wrong, so that the Bureau of Colonization won't grab Beauty away from us."

But try as they might they could find no wrong on Beauty. Nor did they find anything other than plant life. Little plankton plants ruled the seas. A pleasing variety of vegetation owned the land, and in that Beauty was like other worlds discovered in the past three decades.

"Plants rule the galaxy," Teddy said.

"Be more peaceful if they did," Matt said.

"We're freaks. Us and all the other animals and bugs and creepy things on Earth," she said.

"There may be bugs," Matt said. "There were on other worlds with rich and varied vegetation. I'd guess there'd have to be. How else does everything get pollinated?"

"They're all like oysters, both male and female, producing both male and female pollen?"

"Could be," he said. "Let's leave such weighty questions to the eggheads."

"I'm an egghead," she said. "You love me only for my body—"

"Grrrr," he said, making a move on her that she avoided by slipping to one side.

"—and you forget that I am a legitimate—"

"So am I, my mother was married."

"—sigh-an-tist," she said.

"Let's take a break and set a nice, smooth orbit and go to bed and make us a little sigh-an-tist," he said, leering.

"That makes you look rather youthful, that expression," she said.

"I feel youthful, and I am youthful."

"You're not bad looking for a space jock," she said. In fact, she liked looking at him. He was an even six feet tall, just slim enough, just muscular enough, and he had the softest black hair. His brown eyes were rimmed with healthy white, his nose sort of short and cute, his lips curled upward at the corner and— "Now, Matt, we have work to do."

"There's always work to do. It can wait."

And so, because things of more immediate import occupied the discoverers of the world to become known as Beauty, the question of vegetative propagation on the world was left to others. After all, how exciting can the sex life of a tree be when two people are young, parsecs away from other human beings, and almost disgustingly happy to be alone, just two unique bipedal, at least semi-intelligent animals from an odd planet that seemed to be a freak? For their home planet was so packed with life that it took one hell of a lot of computer space simply to catalog it. It was a world where the life force was so persistent that life existed in the most inhospitable places—in the depths of the seas where no light penetrated, in the air, on the surface of the earth, in the soil itself, in deep, dank caves that had never seen the sun, and even within the pores of frozen rocks in the dry valleys of Antarctica where it lay dormant for three hundred sixty days a year, living and procreating during the five brief days of its summer. Life. Never fully understood, never explained. Life dear, however, to even the most minute living thing, and each living thing endowed with the instinct to fight to survive, and to reproduce and go through eonic changes in order for its species to continue to survive.

It was strictly against company policy and common sense, but *Belle* grumbled down and landed. Cautiously, Matt chose a torrid, barren desert on a large land mass. He ran a couple of tests, detected no danger in the form of microscopic alien villains, and, with Teddy's eyes glowing with excitement, cracked the hatch. The air was hot and dry, but sweet.

The sun was low in the morning sky and the desert was just beginning to warm, the night-cooled rocks making odd, cracking sounds as they expanded with the growing heat. They walked no more than a hundred feet from the ship. In the shade of jagged, wind-exposed boulders Teddy saw tiny crimson flowers on low growing, gray, bristly plants.

"There's vegetation, even here," she said, bending to look more closely at the flowers.

"Look but don't touch," Matt warned.

She smelled a faint aroma, a scent that would, she felt, be an instant best seller as a perfume.

"She is a Beauty," she said, standing, looking off into the shimmering, barren, rapidly heating wastes. "I wish we could stay longer, get to know her."

"Let's let the eggheads see if there's anything with teeth first," Matt said.

Tinker's Belle flew low, once more, over the largest land mass, sleek hull only feet above a smooth and endless plain of deep grasses and quiet, clear streams.

"Isn't it odd," Teddy said, in a quiet voice.

"I'm sure it is," Matt said.

"He worked a short week on all planets but Earth."

"I guess I know what you're talking about."

"Day and night on the first day; the firmament the second day; earth, grass, the herb yielding seed, the fruit tree yielding fruit after its kind on the third day; the stars on the fourth day."

"Yep," Matt agreed. "Four days for that and then all the fowls and fishes and beasts and man in three days."

"But the last three only on Earth," she said.

"It's a big universe, and we've seen only a half-block neighborhood so far," Matt said.

"I think it's going to be the same everywhere," she said seriously. "I think we are unique, Matt. I think it's our work to take over, on all the other worlds, where He left off."

"I hope Reznor pays overtime, then," Matt said, and she hit him in the shoulder and the mood was gone. *Belle*, after one last look, soared and the muted thunder of her G.D. faded into the upper reaches of the atmosphere and was gone, as was the ship when Matt engaged the trans.

Beauty was once again silent, save for the winds, and the life-bringing rains, and the rolling of her oceans.

Chapter 3

"A man," Andrew Reznor was fond of saying, "is as young as his newest part."

Part of Reznor was just past twenty-four—his heart. His left kidney was forty-four and his left hand, indistinguishable from his original right hand, had been a part of him for three years. Reznor himself had to think a bit to remember his actual age, the age of those parts of his body that had not been replaced with younger material from organ donors who had met accidental death at an early age, but when he did remember he was more pleased than dismayed. He was just past his first century of life and had more good years ahead.

Reznor had been in his mother's womb when Air Force Major Lynsey Paige Collier opened the hatch and let the near vacuum of Mars pull air from the lock of the *Mars Explorer* to be the first woman, the first human, to set foot on the red planet. He'd been a teenager when the second Russian Revolution ended forever the threat of communism and led to the formation of the Pax Of Five, that combination of world powers which outlawed war, cleaned up all the little brushfires, at the cost, some historians said, of neocolonialism. Reznor, sometimes a conservative, sometimes a flaming radical, felt that the overpopulated nations were one hell of a lot better off under the control of the world's five big powers than they'd been fighting each other over religion or grazing ground or skin color or whatever other silly reason they could find, even if, in a Malthusian snit, he regretted the loss of the process of natural selection for population control.

He had seen space exploration grind to a halt, for with power came responsibility, with peace came the need to do *something*, something to feed the billions of Africa, Asia, and South America. That something took the growingly meager resources of the developed nations and squeezed them as dry as Saharan sands. The bellowing, beautiful, awe-inspiring, fire-breathing monsters stopped climbing the gravitational slope heavenward and left space to the imagination and to the necessary communications satellites that still went up occasionally, from places like Vandenberg.

Now *that* irked Reznor no end. He lived for the exploration of space. He'd cut his teeth on the classic stories of science fiction, graduated to scientific studies, sharpened his wits as he breezed through Cal Tech in two years, and devoured the embryonic space studies programs in two other tech schools. Then he invented a desalinization process that, within a decade, had the lower parts of the Sahara blooming again, got filthy rich and retired to his well-equipped laboratory in the Arbuckle Mountains of Oklahoma, where God had left His tracks in the form of exposed rock strata. Here Reznor proceeded to make it possible to end dependency on fossil and nuclear fuels with his development of the principle that had one offshoot in the G.D. system. Next he proved Einstein wrong by sending a small probe from an orbiter—powered with his G.D. Transdrive—four-plus light years to return with close-up pictures of the nearest star.

With sixteen billion mouths screaming for food,

and even with use of desalinated sea water, demand
was straining supply. The Five Powers began to
build starships. By the time Andrew Reznor was
fifty, a half billion of Earth's surplus population,
most of them the cream of the crop, were in space,
planting Earth wheat on distant planets and doing
their best to make Reznor a god. Of that last he was
having no part. He was, after all, just a working man
who'd come up with a few new ideas.

Reznor, at fifty-two, took a vacation and traveled
on a ship equipped with transdrive and the G.D. to
one of the newly settled planets, there to see men
and women working, happy, optimistic, ambitious,
and breeding like midges. He saw, quickly, that the
metallic resources of Earth would not stand the drain
of building enough ships to meet the growing clamor,
coming now from the backward peoples as well as
the so-called not so backward ones. He used most
of his not-too-inconsiderable fortune to build an industrial complex on a new world and thus began to
drain the resources of that world while ships leaped
spaceward from his new shipyards, went to Earth,
and groaned back spaceward laden with humans and
all their needed paraphernalia, their poodle dogs and
pussycats, their children, their milk cows and the
assurance that they alone owned the stars and their
planets.

True, no intelligent species stood between man and
his apparent destiny. There were bugs on the new
planets, some of them rather evil bugs that took an
instant liking to human blood—and thus had to be
exterminated, not a difficult task for a race that had
eliminated the screwworm fly, the disease vectors of
all insect classes, and the cockroach—except for a
few, perhaps, living deep in the dampness of the
South American and African jungle preserves. Man
had the power. The species had gone quickly through
a period of development that saw man fly in a

cranky, almost uncontrollable airplane one instant in time and walk on the moon in the next. Now, thanks to the Reznor miracles, humans had the ability to not only negate gravity but to use its force, and the ability, too, to bring two points in space in conjunction in a nanosecond.

Reznor Galactic Enterprises developed a method to deacidify oceans, purify planetary masses of atmosphere. Reznor, it was said, was the Michelangelo of twenty-first century science, the savior of mankind.

He had not, as a young man, set out to save mankind. He'd been interested only in following through on the tickling images of a couple of interesting ideas, and he, like most, had wanted to make a dollar or two. He was still an unassuming man, his natural friendliness not affected by his multi-trillion dollar empire on several planets, and he took every opportunity to state that he knew full well where credit was due for his achievements and his success. In Reznor's Top Secret file held by only two governmental agencies, was a personality profile drawn up by a highly respected psychiatrist in which the opinion was stated that Andrew Reznor represented the almost perfect product of the spiritual revival movement of the late 1900s. This movement was brought about, explained the learned psychiatrist, by a slightly insecure feeling in mankind due to the presence of thousands of nuclear warheads, intricate delivery systems, and Star Wars hardware floating around in the sky above them.

"All I am and all I have achieved," Reznor often said, in public and in private, "I owe to my God."

Once, on a public forum television show, that same learned psychiatrist had tried to belittle Reznor's faith in an old-fashioned, all-powerful God. "You credit your health to God, Dr. Reznor," the psychiatrist had said, "and yet you are alive and almost one hundred years old because of medical science. So is your faith in God or in medical science, for if faith in God alone could do it, how do you explain the early deaths of all those who have gone before us, even those with a strong faith in God?"

"Doctor," Reznor had said with a smile, "I settled all those questions over the coffee table when I was a freshman in college." He held up a hand to halt a quick reply from the psychiatrist. "I know what you're going to say. You're going to say, for I have read the paper you published on the subject, that the miracles that some of us believe in, miraculous healings for example, are explained by our new understanding of the body, and all its complicated systems, and the fact that we have the ability to cure ourselves by positive imaging. True. I agree. However, isn't it just possible, Doctor, that our Maker built this ability into us, and we're just now beginning to understand it? Doctor, if you can look me in the eye and tell me that you honestly believe that life is an accident brought about by the coincidental combination of various amino acids, carbon molecules and the like—if you can explain the termite, for example—he's a miraculous little creature that can digest totally indigestible cellulose only because he harbors another life form in his body, a little microbe that can break cellulose down into the sugar that the termite uses as his fuel—if you can explain how a few molecules got together in some primordial sea and said, 'Hey, fellows, let's combine our talents and make ourselves into a termite'—then I'll listen to you, and that's not even taking into account the amazing variety of life-forms on our Earth, nor the human brain."

Oddly enough, that profession that knew the inner workings of the human body best, the medical profession, showed statistically fewer believers in religion than any other. Among physical scientists, those who were coming nose to nose with the mysteries of the universe, there had been a new and often private questioning leading to an incontrovertible conclusion. It, meaning everything, could not have been an accident. There was a purpose. Man had purpose. Since exploration of a rather large volume of space had turned up nothing like man, no life other than plant life or insects, it seemed, in the opinion of many, that man's purpose was to take dominion of the universe, just as he'd been given dominion over the Earth and all that flew, crept, crawled, walked, ran, slithered, or swam. Since the universe was older than man, and since the definition of purpose indicated that it was something set up as an object or an end to be attained, who had originally set the purpose? Not early man, for he had had no conception of distant stars, of other worlds like the rather dangerous one on which he had had to fight to survive.

God lived. His book was on board every ship that left the Earth, beginning with the first exploration ships. A man who is venturing out into the big black had to have something, and that something, for the majority of space explorers, was faith in something greater than themselves. Generally it was not a militant faith, not a faith that spouted the type of religious jargon which alienated many. It was a quiet, sure, rather beautiful faith and it was strong enough to overcome the early tragedies when ships failed to return.

Still, in spite of his sincere faith, Andrew Reznor had not set out to save mankind. He thought it was rather neat that God had inspired him to invent gadgets that were rapidly relieving the intolerable overcrowding of Earth, and he was thankful for the opportunity to serve his fellow man. But deep in his heart—although, mind you, he obeyed the biblical injunction to love his fellows—he believed that love

and like were two different things and that it was not
necessarily a sin to think that, in general, mankind
was a sorry lot. In short, the older he got the more
sure Reznor was that most dogs were nicer than most
people.

On Reznor's office wall, directly in front of his
desk so that he could see it day after day, was a
quotation from a poet who had died before the twentieth century began.

> I think I could turn and live with animals, they are
>   so placid and self-contain'd.
> I stand and look at them long and long.
> They do not sweat and whine about their condition.
> They do not lie awake in the dark and weep for their
>   sins.
> They do not make me sick discussing their duty to
>   God.
> No one is dissatisfied, not one is demented with the
>   mania of owning things.
> Not one kneels to another, nor to his kind that lived
>   thousands of years ago,
> Not one is respectable or unhappy over the whole
>   earth.

One of Reznor's greatest sorrows was the knowledge that he belonged to a species that had been
directly or inadvertently responsible for the elimi-
nation of thousands of species of animals. He didn't
concern himself with amoebas, paramecia, mesozoa
parasites (some species, such as the malaria para-
site, deserved extermination), with flat worms, comb
jellies, ribbon worms, spiny-headed worms, the
Rotifera, Nematoda, Nematomorpha, Entoprocta,
Annelida. He knew the Class Insecta was man's only
possible rival for continued domination of the uni-

verse. He did question the wisdom of the almost total extermination of several species of mosquito not only on emotional grounds—God had created the mosquito, too, and who was to know whether the lowly mosquito had a purpose? He was not on firm scientific grounds when he wondered if the mosquito just might have had some part to play in the miracle of evolution, somehow contributing by his habit of biting warm-blooded animals, thus spreading blood and those more minute and mysterious things that make up a living cell from animal to animal, but he questioned it.

Generally, although he found certain species of Mollusca to be admirable, and edible, Reznor's favorite creatures fell into five classes, the conglomerate of classes that took in all fish; the Amphibia; Class Aves; Class Reptilia; and, of course, Class Mammalia. He admitted that he was not totally rational in preferring something that flew or had warm blood, hair, and mammary glands, but that was the way it was. He couldn't begin to name all three thousand, five hundred or so species of Mammalia, but he could thrill to an old documentary showing a cheetah in pursuit of prey, even while sorrowing for the terrified, defenseless, sweet-fleshed little antelope or wildebeest calf that was trying so desperately to live, to delay for a little longer its inevitable contribution to a food chain that had, long since, been totally disrupted by man.

When he had been twenty-one, Reznor had married a certain member of Class Mammalia, who, incidentally, was equipped with one sweet set of the glands that shared the class name, and she had given him five sons and two daughters, all of whom had gone into the family business in various capacities. Andrew Reznor, Jr. was now in titular control of all Reznor enterprises, and he was a chip off the old man's unquestioningly superior DNA block, running the complicated operations as if he were playing a noncompetitive game of chess.

Yes, God had been good to Reznor in the matter of children. Not a dud in the whole lucky seven, and the girls had chosen well, both marrying men who held responsible positions in the family business. With things running so smoothly, and with the assurance that the prolific Reznor clan would do its share of that odd and mysterious reproductive ceremony of the Mammalia, Reznor, at the age of one hundred and two, was, at last, free to devote himself to a project that had been forming in his mind since his early years. In those days he had witnessed—via television—the death of the last California condor in the wild, and the whooping crane, and on and on through species after species. He had begun even while in college, when money was definitely scarce, to contribute to organizations which defended wildlife. As his fortunes grew, he had become the owner of no less than eleven U.S. Senators and a bevy of Congressmen who liked Reznor money well enough to divert themselves from such important activities as giving away money created by producers to nonproducers long enough to, among other things, establish the International Gene Bank. Here were stored the materials necessary to imitate God—but not equal, of course, for twenty-first century science had yet to create so much as a termite, or a blade of grass—by recreating from frozen sperm and eggs nearly all of the three thousand five hundred species of Mammalia, over eight thousand species of Aves, some six thousand Reptilia, over two thousand Amphibia, and a representative portion of the twenty thousand (plus or minus a few thousand) species of fishes.

"Great God-a-mighty, Dad," Andrew, Jr. had said. That was when the old man had revealed, now that the family firm was in good hands, that he intended to withdraw from day to day decisions and devote the remaining years of his life to a pet project he'd been thinking about for eighty years or so. "You're talking billions."

"I don't see you or your kids or your kids' kids going hungry," the old man had said.

"Actually," Andrew, Jr. had said, after thinking it over, "I think it's sorta neat. Maybe you can get your name legally changed to Noah Reznor."

Chapter 4

Tinker's Belle had a lovely trip home. Matt and Tedra had spent a lot of time studying the vision tapes taken by *Belle's* cameras, and Teddy was more sure than ever that there was only one name for their planet.

Belle growled down to the Earth on G.D. after more than two years away. When they landed near the Arbuckle complex, Teddy was dressed in a sweet little one-piece shift dress. Fashions during the past decade had done one of their periodic flip-flops, reaching back into the middle twentieth century for simplicity of line and designs that emphasized the feminine figure. Matt put on a fresh set of white company coveralls, decorated with the various brightly colored patches which symbolized his position and service. He was at the console, bringing *Belle's* systems down to shutoff in preparation for the usual all-over maintenance received by any ship just in from transing among the far stars. *Belle's* systems purred and whined and clicked and quieted.

"Matt," Teddy said, "the old man's out there."

"Who? Reznor?" Matt asked.

"Himself," Teddy said. "He's riding a goat."

"Naw," Matt said.

"Come see for yourself."

He stood beside her at one of *Belle's* ports and,

sure enough, there was the old man sitting on the padded seat of a little hydrogen-powered vehicle used for handy transportation around the complex. It was called a goat because it could go just about anywhere on or off road. Reznor had one leg pulled up and crossed over the seat and looked quite at ease, his spectacular white hair blowing in a slight Oklahoma breeze.

They had each seen Andrew Reznor face to face only when they were hired. Matt had wondered, at the time, how a man as important as Reznor had time to personally interview all new employees. Although he hadn't actually asked the question, he'd gotten the impression that he was to take part in a special project under Reznor's personal supervision. In that he'd been right.

They had sent a signal ahead of them from Earth-zone space, using a company code that, it was said, could not be broken even by the Pax Five spy shops.

"Is he that interested in our planet?" Teddy asked.

"Who knows?" Matt said. "Let's go find out."

When the *Belle's* hatch opened, Reznor threw his leg down off the seat, dismounted, and walked spryly to meet the two returning space explorers, hand outthrust, taking Teddy's hand first and then Matt's, making small talk as he welcomed them home. Then he looked into Matt's eyes with his own startlingly clear, amber ones and said, "I want to know all about this planet of yours."

"Yes, sir," Matt said.

Reznor turned, motioned to a crew chief. "Have all this ship's data brought over to my office as quickly as possible." He smiled at Teddy. "You two have done well. Do you have any idea of how much your bonus is going to be if this planet is all you say it is?"

In fact, Matt had some idea. That had been one

of the fun things they did, just one, on the way home, figuring the bonus about eleventeen different ways and making it come out bigger each time based on habitable land areas, land productivity, the potential usefulness of Beauty's vegetation, etc.

"Well, sir," Teddy said, "we'll leave that up to you."

"You people tired or anything?" Reznor asked.

"No, sir," Matt said.

"Hungry?"

"I could use some planetside food," Teddy said, "after two years of ship's rations."

"Grab a couple of those mules and follow me," Reznor said.

Reznor drove into an open bay, up a ramp, parked on a landing and waited while Matt and Teddy joined him, then he led them into a maze of corridors and emerged into a living complex where a dining room looked out on the little sea of grass that flowed down from the complex to Sheep Creek. The view included a little clump of American bison, a few pronghorns, a tall and stately giraffe, and a pair of cute little South African springboks. Two girls started putting food on the table the minute Reznor entered the room and soon the three of them were seated, Matt and Teddy side by side across the table from Reznor.

"I don't care if you talk with your mouth full," Reznor said. "Tell me about it."

"Sir," Teddy began, "I think I can best give you an idea by telling you what we'd like to name it. We want to call it Beauty.'

Reznor's amber eyes seemed to look into far distances.

"We tried our best to find something wrong with it," Teddy said, "so that they wouldn't try to claim it for colonization, and we couldn't."

Matt spoke then, giving some facts and figures as

he remembered them. Reznor forked a bite of sliced, barbecued pork and chewed thoughtfully. "That good, huh?" he asked, as Matt paused.

"A habitat for almost everything," Teddy said. "Jungles and deserts, forests and plains, mountains, lakes, streams, oceans."

"I wanta see it for myself," Reznor said. "How soon can you have your ship ready for a turna-round?"

Matt looked at Teddy. They'd been talking about spending some of their wages and bonus money in Rio de Janeiro, where there was a current revival of an old musical form that featured soft guitars, a catchy, running rhythm, and soft voices singing of love. Matt thought that Rio might be a very good place to do the pleasant groundwork leading to the first of what they had agreed would be three chil-dren.

"Oh, sorry," Reznor said. "I have been ground-bound for so long that I forget how one looks for-ward to some ground time after two years in space. I imagine you have made plans. I can take another ship."

"No." Teddy said quickly. "I mean, sir—"

"Wanta call me Andy?" Reznor asked, grinning at her, having anticipated just that reaction. He knew that the discovers of a planet had a proprietary in-terest.

"What?" Teddy asked, confused.

"Call me Andy. If we're going to spend time to-gether on a small ship, we need to drop the formal-ities. I'd like for you two to take me there because I want to keep this hushed up as long as possible. As you indicated, the colonization boys like to get their grubby paws on any life-zone planet, and one like Beauty would drive them into a frenzy of pos-sessiveness."

"You like the name then, sir?" Teddy asked.

"Andy. Call me Andy. Yes. It has a certain simplicity, a nice ring. That's your first choice, right?"

"Yes, sir—I mean, Andy," Teddy said.

Reznor snapped his finger and a girl put a portable keyboard beside his plate. He pushed his plate to one side, centered the keyboard and his fingers moved rapidly, the artificial ones on his left hand as dexterous as the flesh and blood fingers on his right. "Okay. Done. When the claim is filed with Pax Space Central, she'll be called Beauty."

"Thank you," Matt said.

"Thank *you*, for finding her," Reznor said. "Now you'd better eat."

The food was delicious. Teddy tackled a cold appetizer first, a meaty salad. "Delicious," she said. "Crayfish from Louisiana?"

"From Sheep Creek," Reznor said, "crawdads. I pay some of the kids to catch them for me. Any nice little clear creeks on Beauty?"

"We didn't have time to do a total small area scan," Matt said, "but we did see a few nice little creeks in low flyover."

"Good," Reznor said. "A world without crawdads would not be complete."

Matt looked at Teddy and winked. It was his way of saying, "Hey, how about this old man?" He found himself feeling totally at ease, his awareness of Reznor's wealth, fame, achievements, and power fading in the face of down-to-earth friendliness. It would be much later, when he was older, that Matt would recognize that Reznor was an artist in exercising that one absolutely vital element of success, people skills. As for Reznor, he was simply being himself, as he could be with few people, mainly those many called the space jock type, those usually young people who dared fling themselves into the far places for the kind of pay not often matched by Earth's industro-space complexes.

Matt found himself talking, sometimes, with his mouth full. Teddy, excited that Reznor had so easily accepted her name for their world, ate little, and alternated with Matt in singing the praises of Beauty. Serving girls cleared the table. One was Asian, the other Caucasian. Teddy wondered about the Asian, but there was no chance to talk with her, for Reznor was intent on drawing forth every morsel of information about Beauty.

"While we're waiting," Reznor said, "there's something I want you to see. You've probably seen such films before, but bear with me." He motioned and a slim, dark skinned young man entered, carrying a control box. The lights faded. An old-fashioned screen was revealed when panels of a wall opened.

"Ready, Dr. Reznor," the dark man said. He was relaxed, at ease. Teddy, subconsciously aware of his skin pigmentation, would not have thought of him as being black. If questioned, and such questioning would have been unlikely, she would have spoken in terms of race and the genetic diversity that made mankind such a driving force in the world and now in the near galaxy. Nor, questioned, would she have shown the slightest wonder or discomfort at having been served by females. The servers might well have been male in other places, and there was no hint of animus in her toward any person who was doing a job, nor was there subservience involved on the part of any worker. In a world of some sixteen billion people it had been a vital necessity to return to what some conservatives called "individual responsibility," and what any casual student of ancient literature knew as Paul's doctrine on industry as written in the second epistle to the Thessalonians.

The screen came to life. "These pictures were filmed in the late 1980s," Reznor said.

The scene was an African plain teeming with life. Vast herds of grass eaters grazed, flurried as a fat

and sassy lioness walked, unhungry, among them.
In quick succession the film showed the intriguing
variety of African wildlife—hyenas and elephants,
small, nervous antelope and bucolic buffalo, graceful
cheetahs, a tree swarming with raucous monkeys.

That plain, both Matt and Teddy knew, without
knowing its site, was probably under the plow, irrigated with desalinated sea water delivered by pumping systems powered by Reznor's G.D. power. At
best, it had become grazing grounds for domestic
cattle or one of the few species of originally wild
grass eaters which were now bred for meat.

When the film ended, Reznor turned to face them
as the lights came up. "Do you understand?"

"I think so," Matt said.

"We crowded them off this planet," Reznor said.
"Yard by yard and square mile by square mile we
usurped grazing grounds and habitats that had been
theirs from, in many cases, before the time our first
ancestor stood on his hind legs to look over the tall
grass for the telltale movements of a predator. We've
confined the poor remnants of an astoundingly rich
diversity of life in tiny preserves. Thousands of species now exist only in zoos. Thousands are lost forever. I'm not going to preach to you, but can anyone
imagine that man, or the lion, or the termite is the
end product of evolution? We've short-circuited a
vital process. We've been on this planet for what is
only the blink of an eye in geological time. The
cockroach was here over a billion years ago."

"Ugh," Teddy said.

Reznor laughed. "We won't be putting cock-
roaches on Beauty just now. But he's a good illus-
tration of what I'm getting at. What was his purpose?
Is he really as obnoxious as you feel, Teddy? Before
man inserted himself into the cockroach's habitat
he went about his business, whatever that was.
He didn't evolve too much, except in smartness. He

learned to adapt to man, to live in his buildings, to eat his leftovers. But what was his purpose? Has it been fulfilled?

"If your plan is to recreate Earth's ecosystem in detail, bring your lunch," Matt said.

"Well, we won't be able to do that, will we?" Reznor said. "We'll have to start and work backward. There'll be as many decisions to make as there are species on Earth. I'm sure we'll make mistakes, and I'm equally sure that I won't live to see the end of the work. But, with God's help, we're going to give back to the animals what we have taken from them."

A chime sounded. Reznor motioned and his assistant went to the door. Two men rolled in a cart laden with *Belle's* carefully gathered horde of data on the new planet. Reznor had the visual tapes run first. He watched leaning forward in his seat, a look of musing pleasure on his face.

"You named it," he told Teddy. "It is Beauty." He rubbed his hands, and his face was animated. He motioned to his aide, said, "Call communications. Tell them to give the go signal." When the man was gone, he said, "In a matter of hours, ships will lift off from Earth and several other planets nearer to Beauty. As soon as we get the all clear on health hazards and all the necessary testing is complete, ships will land and begin to build facilities in places to be selected by my animal folks. We'll build in unobtrusive places, and the facilities will be designed to blend with the natural landscape. After they're built, we'll remove the workmen, and the human population of Beauty will be limited to no more than a few hundred people, just those necessary for the seeding programs: veterinarians, animal behavior specialists, ecologists, and the minimum number of support personnel."

"Sounds like it's going to be a lonely post," Matt

said. His plans very definitely did not include a long
stay on Beauty, nice as she was.

"It won't be all bad," Reznor said. "We'll go
first class, the best of everything for everyone. Basic
salary will be augmented by isolation post bonuses.
The company will be good." He grinned. "Because,
after a while, the company is going to include me.
I'd like to have a few people out there that I can talk
with other than scientists who get pretty involved in
their work, Matt. I've taken a good look at your file
folder in the last couple of days. You're an academy
man, excellent service record, and you've shown me
that you are persistent and consistent, loyal, not
afraid of work or hardship. As a part of the support
personnel of Beauty I'm going to need a security
force. We'll not want unauthorized visitors for a
while until we learn something about what it's going
to take to recreate the complicated food chains of
land and ocean from scratch. I'd thought to offer you
the job of sort of planetary boss."

Matt cleared his throat and started to speak. Teddy
put her hand on his arm and Reznor spoke before
Matt could. "Teddy, you're overqualified for a two-
man exploration ship. I understand why you were
willing to take on the job, to be with your husband.
You've had a nice five-year honeymoon off to your-
selves, transing around space. I think it's time you
got to work on your specialty. I've looked over your
file folder, too, and I'm impressed. Top two percent
of your graduating class, honors in grad school, a
thesis that got comment outside the academic world.
It doesn't look as if Beauty will need much physical
terraforming—" He paused, scratched his chin. "By
the way, I suppose you know the origins of that
word, terraforming."

"Yes," Teddy said.

"No," Matt said, shaking his head.

"Correct me if I'm wrong, Teddy," Reznor said.

"It's an Amenglish word, and it appeared for the first time in the fiction stories of the mid-twentieth century futurists who described themselves as Science Fiction writers. It's based on the Latin word terra, meaning land. So to terraform means to alter a land to make it Earthlike. Teddy's thesis, Matt, in case you haven't read it—''

Matt looked at Teddy sheepishly. She'd never mentioned her thesis and he'd never asked.

"—concerned itself with the theoretical terraforming of a planet much like Earth during an ice age. She had some rather ingenious ideas about changing the climate to make it warmer, and thus more hospitable for settlers."

"By using G.D. power," Teddy said.

Matt was beginning to worry. Teddy was looking quite interested, and he was trying to envision how it would be, living on a planet where there were only a few other people, a planet teeming with a zoo of animals.

"As you said, Beauty doesn't need terraforming," he said.

"Well, not in some spectacular physical way, not the major alteration of the chemical contents of sea or air," Reznor said. "But won't we be terraforming her, using as a pattern the Earth of a few thousand years ago, before man bred himself into pesthood?" He smiled at Teddy. "We need you on Beauty."

Teddy looked at Matt. He could see she was damned interested. "Matt—" she said.

"Sir," Matt said, "we'll have to have some time to consider this. We appreciate the offer, and I'm flattered that you consider me capable of doing such an important and responsible job. But we'll have to—" Teddy dug her fingernails into his arm. He flinched. "—have some—" Teddy's pressure increased. "Ouch," he said. "—have some time to think—"

"Matt," she hissed.

"—it over. Teddy."

"Fine," Reznor said. "I'd like to leave for Beauty in a couple of days. We'll make the decision point the time when your ship is ready for space again. Okay?"

"Maaaaatt," Teddy whispered.

"That's quite fair, sir," Matt said, rising and half-dragging Teddy out of the room.

Chapter 5

Each time Davis Conroy had to leave either his quarters or his offices in the penthouse of the soaring Bureau of Colonization tower he questioned the wisdom of politicians. For all the technological advancement of the twenty-first century, there still was no method for preventing sweat. For Conroy, it began first in the tight and secret places of his body and then on his back, so that even five minutes in the equatorial heat of Africa required a bath and fresh clothing.

It was Pax Five policy to build new facilities in underdeveloped countries, and those countries of equatorial Africa certainly met the definition. If one adhered to the belief that one way of sharing the wealth with those who had never created their own was as good as another, it made sense to put a multi-billion dollar complex in the jungle, for the Bureau poured a lot of Pax dollars into the region. Ten thousand natives were employed. Imported executive and technical level personnel poured more money into the local economy. Yet ten miles away, people still lived in mud huts and practiced slash and burn agriculture. In many ways, Conroy felt, Africa had not changed in hundreds of thousands of years. The principal changes were readily evident to one flying over the continent, however. Each time Conroy trav-

eled he felt that he could look down and see a sea
of upturned, multihued faces, billions, for Africans
of all hues practiced intently that most common of
human pastimes—breeding.

Conroy, at fifty-five, was not old enough to remember the old Africa where vast areas were given
over to animal life and there had been thousands of
square miles of unpopulated, or, at best, thinly populated land.

It was one of the Deputy Director's duties to bid
official farewell to colonization ships lifting off from
one of the several spacepads within the Bureau's one-
hundred-square-mile compound, and it was that duty
which had brought him out into steaming heat and
moist, heavy air redolent with the aroma of the remnants of the jungle. His words of Bureau blessing
had been broadcast throughout the great starship, but
he wasn't sure how many of the passengers had understood, for this was a local load. Teeming Africa
contributed, it seemed, more than its share of people
who wanted out, who wanted to leave this crowded,
tiresome world for an ideal, a heaven in space. And
the almost completely African load aboard the ship
illustrated one of Conroy's private concerns.

He had, just a few days past, voiced that concern
to Angus Meade, Director of the Bureau, a political
appointee, naturally. "Angus," he'd said, "we're
polarizing space. We have Bureau embarkation facilities in the wrong places. When a ship lifts off
from the main complex here, the people aboard are
almost all black, or some shade of brown or tan.
When one lifts off from the Columbia Complex in
South America, the cargo is mainly Indio brown."

"Mr. Conroy," the director had said, "such
things are not our concern."

What the hell, then, was their concern? And if the
creation of black, brown, yellow, and white ghettos
in space was not the Bureau's concern, whose con-

cern was it? Not the concern of the politicians in the
Pax Five capitals. Not the concern of the industri-
alists who profited from the expansion, whose plants
on several planets built the ships, supplied the basic
necessities for beginning a new life on a new planet,
counted their profits in the billions. Whose, then?

Conroy stayed in the open-air observation shelter
until the latest in the growing fleet of colonization
ships roared upward and puffed away into the bright
blue of the African sky. Then he hurried to his
closed, air-conditioned vehicle and gave the black
driver orders to deliver him to the tower, quickly.
He removed his supposedly lightweight formal
jacket, loosened his tie, wiped sweat from his face
with a white handkerchief and looked forward to a
quick shower, lunch, and a quiet afternoon. He had
not too much hope for the latter. Every one except
the director knew who ran the Bureau, and it was no
small job.

In an age where drugs could melt away fat and a
man had to be mentally disturbed to eat enough to
be five pounds overweight, Davis Conroy attracted
stares from those who did not know him, for he was
a solid chunk of a man, shorter than the general population, thick of chest, equally thick of belly—although not one ounce of fat had accumulated on his
frame—treelike of thigh and leg. In spite of his so-
lidity, he moved easily and with a certain grace. His
hair was just beginning to gray, and he disdained any
artificial method of preventing this natural occurrence. He refused to wear some contraption in his
eyes, and so his nearsightedness was corrected by an
anachronistic pair of horn-rimmed glasses. Glasses
were so rare that he had to go to Geneva for fittings,
but he didn't mind anything that got him away from
Africa's heat.

The ground vehicle delivered him into Siberia, so
called because the lower levels, parking areas, and

service areas of the tower were something of a sump for the tower cooled air. He stepped out into the glacial temperature—or so it seemed after the outside—and felt his clothing grow quickly clammy and clingy. He almost ran to the lift and was stripping out of his shirt, his jacket thrown aside, even as he moved past the reception area into his private preserve, his office and his home, for he was a bachelor and conscientious about his job, and saw no reason why he should live outside the tower away from his work.

With his sodden shirt flying into a corner, his thick chest bare, he noticed that his office was not empty. He halted in mid-stride to glare somewhat angrily at the trim woman who sat in a chair in front of his vacant desk.

"The girl said you'd be back shortly," the woman said, "and that I could wait in here."

Conroy didn't like being caught bare-chested, and especially not by Genna Darden, pristine in white, blonde hair seemingly molded into place, makeup meticulous.

"Damnit, Genna, I'm soaked. Whatever it is, it'll have to wait until I shower." He plunged into his own living room and was a bit pissed to hear Genna's voice as she followed him. He slammed into the sanitary area, ripped off his pants, stepped into the shower, and was luxuriating in cool, clear water when he heard the door open.

"Genna, damnit, can't a man have privacy in his own shower?" he bellowed.

"I won't peep, Davis, I promise," Genna said. "I have a little something from Intelpax that I think will interest you."

"Wait in the office," Conroy yelled over the drumming of the shower.

"Reznor's found another life-zone planet," Genna yelled back.

The cool water suddenly seemed less seductive. Conroy slid the door open and stuck his dripping head out. "The hell you say."

"No official report yet. Intelpax decoded a burst from a homeward bound ship to the Reznor complex in Oklahoma."

"Indeed," Conroy said bitterly, "for unto every one that hath shall be given." He shook his head. "Would you *please* wait in the office so that I can get dressed?"

"Why, Davis," Genna smiled, "I've been waiting for years to find out just what it is about you that is so different you keep it entirely to yourself."

But she left, closing the door behind her, and Conroy dried off quickly, aided by the blowing of air as dry as the Sahara. When he went back into the office he wore fresh clothing topped by the waist-length official uniform jacket of the Bureau.

Genna Darden was the Bureau's Interagency Coordinator in Africa. No Pax Five agency or office was without someone like Genna. The Bureau, a Pax entity, was not, in theory, accountable to any one of the five individual member nations, but any Pax entity constantly came into contact with agencies of the various governments and with other Pax agencies, and the result, often as not, was total chaos. Interagency Coordinators were originally placed in all offices in an economy move, after Pax auditors found that in many cases several agencies were pouring millions or billions down the same rat holes, often to the enrichment of local officials.

"So tell me," Conroy said, taking his seat safely behind his desk.

"The planet is in a zone far off the beaten path," Genna said. Conroy nodded. When the starships had first begun to reach out into the darkness they had, quite naturally, headed for the nearest stars. Once habitable planets had been found, they made perfect bases for further exploration so that, to date, settlement of space had proceeded in a regular pattern. On a star map, a line encompassing the populated planets formed the shape of a fan, with the stem on old Earth.

Genna walked to a starchart on the wall behind Conroy's desk, and pointed. "Here."

There were no laws restricting exploration ships to any given volume of space. Privately owned ships could go where they pleased in the galaxy, but it was just plain bad economics to go jumping off into the wild black without planning or pattern. No matter how fine this new planet was, it would be isolated. To get there a ship would have to be intent on going there, and there alone, with no intermediate stops on settled planets.

"What's the old bastard up to?" Conroy asked. He'd worked with Genna Darden long enough to know that she didn't carry gossip, and that her views, sometimes shared over dinner, were much like his own on things political and economic.

"No report yet, you say?" Conroy asked, when Genna made no answer to his rhetorical question involving Reznor's ancestry.

"None. The burst message was intercepted at Intelpax three days ago."

"Plenty of time for an official report," Conroy mused.

"I don't think there'll be an official report," Genna said.

"Oh?"

"Reznor spent a couple of billion dollars perfecting a communications system that was considered to be totally inviolable. His codes rival those of the big powers. It cost Intelpax more to break the code than it took Reznor to develop it."

Conroy made a face. He didn't particularly want to know any more than he already knew about Intelpax, or any other Pax Five or national spy shop. The Peace of the Five was secure. Why was there a need to spy?

"For some reason the old boy wants this one kept quiet," Genna said. "When the burst was decoded, Intelpax put out a few feelers. I'm sure they have someone planted in Reznor's Arbuckle facilities. They have sleepers in just about every important industrial complex. No one at Arbuckle knows about the planet except Reznor and the man and wife team who discovered it."

"Odd," Conroy said.

"The burst message was rather rhapsodic," Genna said. "They're apparently quite confident in their code. The brief description, if you'll read it—" she put a sheet of paper on Conroy's desk "—makes it sound like one very fine planet. To quote, 'no anomalies,' meaning that it's as hospitable to human life as Earth."

Conroy read the material quickly and looked up. "And on a dozen planets settlers are sniffing sulfur or otherwise being patient as the planets are being slowly terraformed."

"Exactly," Genna said. "Now the question is this: here's a planet that would mean billions to Reznor. Land grants, discovery rights, all that. In spite of the fact that Reznor's is still family owned, they seem to be in business to make money. Why hasn't he reported this one and started the process of getting his grants and discovery money?"

"Why don't you go and find out for me?" Conroy asked.

"Davis, I'm a paper-pusher and a glad-hander, not an explorer or a spy."

"Then find me someone who can find out."

"Is that bureaucratic greed I see in your eyes?"

"Maybe it's the faces of a few billion people who

need living space, good air to breathe, a place to call their own.''

"Ah, the idealist," Genna said.

"You can be a nasty woman," Conroy said.

"Only when I play tennis and sweat like a hog," she said, standing. "I'll do some digging. First I'll see if I can pry the name of the sleeper in Oklahoma, if there is one, out of Intelpax. Failing that, I'll put someone on it."

Alone, Conroy sat with his hands on his desk, staring. Andrew Reznor was one of the world's most powerful men, but not even Reznor was immune from the control of government. He had no desire to get into a toe to toe fight with the man who was, perhaps, the richest man in the galaxy, but there was a limit to free enterprise. Each citizen of the galaxy had his duty, and that duty was, in the final analysis, to the common cause, to the good of the maximum number of people. It was early yet. The burst message was less than a week old, and maybe Reznor would make his report and file his claims, but, like Genna, Conroy didn't think so. The old man was up to something, and it was up to Davis Conroy to see to it that the masses of mankind were not deprived of what just might be the most desirable planet yet discovered.

Chapter 6

Andrew Reznor proved to be a genial and unde-
manding companion during the days aboard ship.
Belle had not been designed for three, but when Reznor insisted on taking the improvised bunk hastily
installed in the engine space one problem was solved.
When Reznor demanded he stand his share of the
watches, he quickly proved that he had done some
time on a transer. His help gave Matt and Teddy
more time together in their private little quarters.
This quickly engendered, Reznor noticed, a change
in Matt's attitude.

It was no secret to either Reznor or Tedra that
Matt was, at best, a doubtful member of the enterprise. On that day when he and Teddy had left Reznor's offices, Teddy looking pleadingly up at him,
the discussion had extended far into the night, not
always in quiet voices.

"I want a baby," Matt had said.

"There's plenty of time for that. We're not even
thirty yet."

"I want a baby, and another one, while I'm young
enough to remember how it was to be a kid."

"When we're settled into life on Beauty," Teddy
had said, "we can have a baby. I wouldn't be the
first woman who has continued working while she's
pregnant."

"A planet with nothing but animals isn't the place to raise kids."

"We're not signing on for life. A little boy would thrive on such a planet. He'd be able to lead a healthy, outdoor life."

"Unless he got eaten by a lion," Matt had said.

"Oh, shoot. Matt, give it, say, five years. We'll have our baby. When he's school age, we'll come back to a developed planet, maybe even Earth."

"We were going to Rio," Matt had said sadly. "Soft music, rum drinks with fruit in them, beaches."

"We'll go after we take Reznor to Beauty. There'll be a period of time while the facilities are being constructed when we'll have nothing to do on Beauty."

Now Beauty was ahead of them, again. There were, of course, no visible changes from near space, although Matt was in communication with Reznor's men planetside. He took *Belle* down himself. He felt just a bit sad when he saw that Beauty was getting her first man-made scars. Earth movers were working on a little plateau, a rather arid, barren, useless plateau overlooking a seasonally arid plain of grass. As *Belle* lowered, he saw the construction underway, low buildings, a landing pad, the beginning of an irrigated lawn around other buildings that had the look of separate quarters.

Reznor couldn't take his eyes away from the ports, bending this way and that to see more. Off toward the ocean the green of jungles. Mountains inland. Endless, grassy plains underneath.

"It's everything you said it was," he whispered. He pointed. "That looks like elephant country up there, toward the hills. Can't you see them there? And herds of wildebeest, zebra, buffalo, gazelle, giraffe."

Matt was looking only at *Belle's* instruments and

the landing pad. He put the ship down so lightly that Reznor had to be told they had landed. They were met on the pad by a man and a woman, the man tall, balding, mild looking, the woman short and vivid, dark and full of nervous energy. After politely worded, and rather wordy, greetings and welcome to Reznor, the man looked at Matt and Teddy for the first time. The little woman, and she was little, under five feet, had been examining Teddy with interest.

"This is Dr. Cassie Frost," Reznor said, "and Dr. Jackson Frost. I stole them from the International Wildlife Conservation Organization. Jack, Cassie, this is Matt Tinker. He's going to be the honcho here. The pretty one is his wife, Tedra, and it's going to be her responsibility to see that we stay on the straight and narrow toward terraforming, at least as far as animal life is concerned."

"It's nice to have another woman aboard," Cassie Frost said, taking Teddy's hand. Cassie had the huge, dark, eyes of an endearing little monkey, a face that most often looked very serious, and a nice smile.

"You've got to be called Jack," Matt said, taking Frost's hand.

"What else?" Frost asked.

"I want Jack and Cassie to give me the grand tour," Reznor said. "If you two are tired—"

"Now why should we be tired?" Matt asked. "Just because we've traveled a few trillion miles and haven't had a full night's sleep in a week?"

"You'll find a vacant suite down toward the west end of that building," Cassie said, pointing to a low, graceful, long building whose color matched the arid plateau. "Housekeeping has it all set up for you. If you take a shower, don't let the color of the water put you off. The engineers tell us that it'll clear up after we've pumped a bit more water through the system.''

"I had to go to work for a macho old man," Matt said, rolling his eyes. "We'll go along."

"You wouldn't be the first younger fellow I've worked right into the ground," Reznor said.

Frost wondered how one got to be so casually familiar with a man like Reznor. He wondered what Reznor had meant by calling Tinker "the honcho." It worried him a bit. The project on Beauty was a technical and scientific challenge made no less so by the fact that the integrals would be flesh and blood. He knew every man of reputation working in any field relating to zoology or wildlife management and he'd never heard of either of the Tinkers.

The tour of the physical plant didn't take long, since most of it was still under construction. The sun was hot, the climate, Jack Frost explained, very much that of the Serengeti Plain. The region was coming toward the end of its dry season, but the construction people promised to have all facilities complete, with the exception of the huge animal nursery, before the rains came.

Matt was beginning to think longing thoughts about a cold shower, even with slightly muddy water, but Teddy was all eyes and ears. The group of six ended up in an office-lab-living complex in one of the finished buildings. The walls were covered by maps, climatological charts, and other information. The large room contained two desks, several chairs, a refrigerator—from which came cold glasses of tasteless, distilled ship's water—computers, screens, and things that Matt didn't even recognize.

Jack Frost had been talking a steady stream, with Cassie feebly trying to get in a word now and then. In the office, Jack continued. Matt, seeing that he was stuck with trying to keep up with a one-hundred-year-old man who never seemed to tire, decided that he might as well begin to pay attention and get some idea what sort of task he faced.

"As I understand it, I'm going to be sort of a planetary sergeant at arms," he said, and with that statement put some of Jack Frost's doubts to rest.

"More than that," Reznor said. "You're to be the glue that holds us together."

"An interagency coordinator," Matt said, grinning. "I guess I'm to keep wolves out of the fold and keep things running smoothly." He winked at Cassie. "But I refuse to become involved in any family quarrels, and the first one who asks me a scientific question gets two demerits."

Frost was feeling much better. Administrators were necessary.

"So, if it's not too much trouble, Jack, maybe you can tell me why you picked this particular spot for the main facility on this continent, and just what I can expect to happen here."

Frost looked at Reznor, who nodded. "We're here because this is the best place we've found to recreate one of the most prolific areas of wildlife in history."

"Yes, I've seen pictures of the Serengeti before it ceased to be a wildlife preserve," Matt said. "But why start with Africa?"

"Because we have more living animals of Africa available to us," Frost said. "Africa was one of the last places on Earth to be put to the plow, and by the time most of the more spectacular species, such as the rhino and the elephant, were threatened with extinction a few people on Earth were aware of the great potential loss we were facing and began to do something about it. Zoos all over the world are over-populated with some species. They'll be happy to sell them to us, and we'll have a natural breeding stock. Since Beauty's grass is much like the grasses of Earth, and quite nourishing for herbivores, we can show progress immediately. We'll have calves on that plain down there in a year.''

For once, Frost listened as Cassie spoke. "It's logical to start with African wildlife, too, because in Africa were found thirteen of the seventeen recent orders of mammals, just for a start, not that we'll stop with the more attractive mammals. We'll begin with grazing and browsing herbivores—"

"Like the wildebeest," Matt said, just to show that he was listening to Cassie's rather soft and monotonous voice.

"Oh, yes, the common ones, but we'll be giving special care to such things as the rock hyraxe, the okapi—"

Jack Frost, unable to resist any longer, took over, "hartebeest, waterbuck, gemsbok, gazelle, giraffe, zebra, Cape buffalo, antelope, deer, wild sheep, wild goats—"

"And to the south, in the jungles, all the monkeys," Cassie said, "and—"

"Aardvarks," Jack said, "and mongeese—" He paused to see if anyone had caught that, grinned when Matt nodded, "golden moles—"

"Shrews and hedgehogs," Cassie said.

"Apes and peacocks," Teddy put in.

"Of course," Jack said, smiling at Teddy.

"In short," Reznor said, "of fowls after their kind, and of cattle after their kind, of every creeping thing of the earth after his kind, two of every sort shall come unto thee, to keep them alive."

"The grass forms the basis of the food chain," Cassie said, "so we start with the herbivores and get them well established before we bring in the jackels and hyenas."

"To begin to educate the grass eaters to the facts of life," Frost said. "And then the big guns, the cheetahs, leopards, lions."

Teddy had been staring out the window at the

grassy, browned plain below, imagining it to be filled
with life, with animals of all shapes and colors, with
little calves cavorting and chasing their mothers'
udders for a midafternoon snack. Then, suddenly,
images were in her mind. A cheetah, a graceful but
somewhat ugly animal—with that hulking stance and
his long, powerful rear legs—dashing into a peaceful
herd to single out some young calf which, in its desire to live, ran and swerved. Then it was lying on
the brown grass, fertilizing the dry dirt with its
blood, big, doleful eyes open in terminal agony,
tongue lolling. She shuddered.

It was Teddy who gave up first, saying that it was
all very interesting but it was time for a shower.
Matt was involved in a discussion of further plans
with the Frosts and Reznor. It was after dark when
he joined her in their new quarters. She had put on
a new and excitingly brief sleep garment and was
sitting propped up on pillows watching an old documentary about whales when Matt entered.

"The water is a little muddy," she said, "but
cool."

Matt was standing just inside the door, having
closed it behind him. He always liked looking at
Teddy, but now, with her auburn hair freshly washed
and dried, full and loose, *wow*. He felt a pang of
regret. "Oh, rats," he said.

"Well, if you're going to have a complete ecosystem you have to have rats," she said, although
she knew that something was bothering him.

"No, Rio," he said.

She pushed a button and the screen went blank,
sound ceased, and a nicely finished wooden door
closed off the screen.

"Things are going to be happening too fast," Matt
said. "There'll be a tech ship here tomorrow to begin installing eyes in the sky. It'll have three fast
patrol ships aboard, along with their pilots. More

construction crews coming. And Reznor has sent orders back to Earth to start loading the *Ark.*"

"The *Ark*," Teddy said.

"What else would you call an interstellar cattle boat?"

"Take a shower and come to bed."

"How did I get myself into this?" Matt demanded.

"I'll put on some soft music, we'll open the skylight so we can see if Beauty's moon is up, and we'll pretend it's Rio."

"A zookeeper," Matt moaned. "I'm going to become a bloomin' zookeeper."

Chapter 7

In particularly bitter moments, of which there were a few, Denise Reznor had been known to state that her husband, Andrew Reznor, Jr., had the mentality of a bookkeeper. This puzzled the son of the great inventor, who was called Andy by most and Junior by some, for he knew from Denny's tone of voice and her obvious agitation during those bitter moments that she was trying to insult him. He did not, however, feel insulted by being called a bookkeeper. Someone had to have some idea of the assets and debits, the cash flow and liquidity, the immediate demand for money and the future demand, the profit and loss column which, in Andy Reznor's mind, was the bottom line. Secondly, it took one helluva fine mind, an excellent bookkeeper to keep track of the hundreds of sets of books kept at hundreds of different sites on several different planets.

"Of course I have the mentality of a bookkeeper," he'd tell Denny, puzzled, and he'd become more puzzled when she would do something silly like bury her face in a pillow and scream.

Andy Reznor was quite a handsome man at six feet and two inches, with bushy eyebrows over a sharply cut but strong face, and penetrating amber eyes like his father's. He was most at peace in the privacy of his office, surrounded by his efficient staff of wardens—those people he, himself, had assembled to guard the Reznor empire's assets—and by rows of computers and data banks interconnected with Reznor facilities all over the galaxy.

Andy didn't look like a bookkeeper. He looked more like a man who would be cast to play the hero in a period piece, a saga of the American West, or the wielder of a broadsword in an effort drawing deeper from man's sometimes inaccurate history. Andy was most uncomfortable in the kind of situation he found himself to be in now, on a particularly nice May morning in Washington, D.C., acting on his father's orders sent from a new planet called Beauty. His discomfort didn't show to the half-dozen men and two women who were gathered in the penthouse suite of a hotel that just happened to be owned, at least temporarily, by the Reznor interests. If anything, it was those who faced Andy as he supervised a barman in mixing a little picker upper before the meeting began who were a bit uneasy.

The six men and two women represented only the leaders among that contingent of American lawmakers who wore the invisible but very persuasive Reznor brand. Being a very good bookkeeper, Andy knew the price of each of the senators and congressmen present. The Reznor name never, never appeared on a check made out to one of the people who helped direct the financial and social and foreign policy actions of the most powerful nation in the galaxy. In fact, such business was never, never done by check. But Andy knew to the dollar the amounts delivered at regular intervals in a variety of secretive ways to members of what an ancient writer of the nineteenth century had called America's only native criminal class. The fact that most of the actions taken on behalf of the Reznor interests by a bevy of pet senators and congressmen were in a good cause—all the Reznors were honorable men, and it was, after all, not immoral to make a profit—did not make Andy feel any better about doing business with such people.

There was a buzz of friendly and often animated conversation while each of the members of the group got his or her little picker upper, although it was just ten a.m. Then the barman departed, leaving ample supplies for refills, and Andy cleared his throat.

"Ladies and gentlemen," he said. "I suppose you're wondering why I called you here." That, with a half smile, was the nearest Andy Reznor ever came to a joke.

The distinguished legislators soon found out because Andy Reznor was not a man to waste words. Less than half an hour after the barman left the suite Andy had been assured that his latest request would be no problem. In fact, since his request did not involve any expenditure of federal money, nothing more than a simple little innocuous amendment to the next bill that went through both the House and the Senate, he was assured that he could consider it done.

And it was, just three days later, and the routine bill that had to do with some simple mechanism of the day to day running of the vast bureaucracy, was signed the very next day by the president, into whose campaign coffers the Reznor enterprises had poured a bundle.

An aide of Andy Reznor's called his attention to the fait accompli. Andy nodded, included the information in the daily briefing messages he had sent, at considerable expense, to Beauty, where, hopefully, his father would take time to look at them.

Chapter 8

Davis Conroy had spent a valuable hour in an unsuccessful effort to explain to the hereditary chieftain of the Hadendoa group in Ethiopia why those who had signed up to emigrate aboard the *Hope Of The Nile,* a colonizer that ran regular shuttles from the Bureau's Khartoum exit port to a newly opened planet in the Vega sector, could not take all of their personal wealth with them, since that wealth was counted in goats. The chief had left in a snit, not at all convinced that it would be unsanitary, and perhaps a bit noisy, to allow the settlers to house their goats with them in *The Hope Of The Nile's* cabins. It was difficult, Conroy understood, for pastoral nomads to conceive of starting a new life on a new planet with nothing more than frozen goat embryos.

Usually such pedestrian interviews were handled by someone of lesser rank, or by field workers as they traveled the teeming human slums of Africa with the message of heaven among the stars. The old chief, however, had pulled strings all the way to London, and had come to Conroy with a letter of introduction from the Prime Minister himself, not that that amounted to much in an age where the British Commonwealth was the weak sister of the Pax Five. Conroy, however, just happened to be British, a Londoner, and there was such a thing as tradition.

Nevertheless, he was not much in the mood to talk with Genna Darden when his secretary announced her. He sighed, checked to see if he'd sweated through his shirt under the arms even in an office that had been cooled to the blue lip stage in accordance with his personal preference.

Genna looked, as usual, almost edible. She was an artist with makeup, able to give her cheeks the peach bloom look on a consistent basis. Of all things, she was an Icelander, although one would never guess it from her Oxfordian English accent. It had occurred to Conroy several times that he'd heard—from some source long forgotten—that Icelandic women were notoriously independent, sexually and otherwise. Perhaps it was his mood of angry frustration engendered by his hour-long argument with the wizened old Hadendoa chief that sent his eyes first to Genna's face—all peach blooms and apples—then to her splendid torso and her smooth, long legs extending from beneath a neat little silken skirt. He had not had an ongoing relationship with one particular woman in a decade, and he found himself wondering how Genna would look first thing in the morning.

"I'm having dinner tonight at the executive lounge. Are you busy at eight?" he found himself asking before thinking it through.

"That old sonofabitch is going to reserve an entire planet," Genna said, her voice showing agitation for the first time since Conroy had known her, "for animals."

"Animals?"

"Elephants and other odd sorts," Genna said. "The finest, most hospitable planet yet discovered. And for animals."

"First, I will ask you the source of your information," Conroy said, "before saying, somewhat archly, he can't get away with that.'' He was only a bit hurt that she'd ignored his invitation.

"My source is, as before, Intel,'' Genna said, seating herself and crossing one shapely leg. "A series of messages. The intent is clear. Reznor is going to make the planet a zoo, to—and I quote him—give back to the animals that which we have taken from them. There will be no settlement. It's to be a closed planet.''

"Impossible,'' Conroy said. "He has not, as yet, I take it, filed a claim through the Bureau?''

"Not yet.''

"Then he is acting illegally, making plans for a planet without Bureau participation.''

"You can expect him to file soon,'' Genna said. She opened her small briefcase and extended a sheaf of papers toward Conroy. He took them. "The pertinent information is on page two hundred and seven, one small paragraph at the end.''

Conroy saw that the papers were copies of sheets from the American *Congressional Quarterly*. He thumbed through the pages and found the proper page, read the last paragraph.

"The amendment was offered by a senator known to be friendly to Reznor,'' Genna said. "The reference is to a very obscure provision buried somewhere deep in the treaties that made the Bureau of Colonization a Pax Five agency.''

"I know,'' Conroy said. "That obscure provision, as you call it, was insisted upon by my own government.''

"Whatever for?'' Genna asked.

"At the time, we were in a rather xenophobic state,'' Conroy said. "We had seen our former glories usurped by wogs, American and otherwise. Russian, Brazilian, Chinese, European, American and other exploration ships were transing all over the near stars. We had two exploration ships in space. The

white races were grossly outnumbered on Earth, and
we Britishers—that includes the Commonwealth—
were tiny pockets of what we liked to think was genteel civilization in a world on the verge of—well,
who knows. So, at our insistence, this little clause
was inserted.''

"The discovering nation can choose at its own
discretion as many as one out of ten newly discovered planets of habitable characteristics for its own
national uses, that selection not dependent on
whether the chosen planet is the first or the tenth to
be discovered,'' Genna sighed.

"And so the United States has given Andrew Reznor a planet,'' Conroy said.

"With a brief little amendment to a housekeeping
bill,'' Genna said. "The American media didn't even
pick up the story.''

"How did you?''

"Intel.''

"Oh.''

Genna sighed again. "Animals, Davis. Billions of
people eating soya bean meal on this planet, and he's
going to take an entire planet for animals.''

"I'm rather partial to koala bears,'' Conroy said.
"I wonder if there are eucalyptus trees on Reznor's
planet?''

"You're not at all concerned?'' Genna asked.

"Well, yes,'' he admitted, "but, my dear, I just
spent an hour with a rather smelly gentleman of color
from Ethiopia who kept yelling at me that goats had
as much right as people. Do you agree?''

"Davis, you are going to do something about this,
aren't you? You're not going to let him get away
with this?''

Conroy shrugged. "There is no budget here for
bribing American congressmen.'' Then he smiled.
"Yes, I will *try* to do something. Even if the Hadendoa of Ethiopia say no goats no go, there are those

who want and deserve a chance to live and breathe free on a new world. Yes, I will try.''

"Good," Genna said, rising.

He watched the sway of her as she went out the door, sighed, and picked up his dictatape, already composing in his mind a series of messages. The Asians, with their huddled masses yearning to be unhuddled would resent giving a planet to animals. The South Americans, as well. The Africans? Well, perhaps a few of them. He had opened the switch to begin talking when Genna opened the door and stuck her smiling, blonde head in.

"Eight o'clock, did you say?"

"Well, yes."

"Do you like red? I have this smashing red cocktail frock."

"I love red," he said.

It was some time before he got back to dictating his messages of concern.

Chapter 9

Matt was aboard *The Reznor Developer*, a space-going electronics laboratory and miniature factory, when she put into place the tools without which no planet could function, the satellites, weather satellites and geophysical satellites, satellites with infrared eyes and clear vision eyes so sensitive that Jack Frost and his people would be, later, able to count heads among the growing herds of animals. The big weather satellites, in geosynchronous orbits that covered every inch of Beauty's surface and atmosphere, carried small hitchhikers, sensitive little instruments oriented toward space that could detect the approach of anything down to a baseball-sized chunk of space rock.

The eyes toward space were soon tested by the arrival of Reznor ships carrying construction materials and instrumentation for The Shop, where banks of equipment allowed technicians working shifts around the clock to monitor the information being sent down from the orbiting satellites. The Shop was underground simply because it made it easier to maintain the constant low humidity and sixty-eight degree temperature optimum for the electronics. Beauty's satellite communications system occupied one room in The Shop. Early on there was no one to talk to except pilots flying low photographic and survey runs, but, since there would be a place on Beauty for reindeer, polar bears, penguins, the fauna of North America, the panda, and a few thousand other species of animals not to be located on the continent that was to be host to the African species, there would be, later, a string of facilities much like, if smaller than, the initial installation.

There were goats on Beauty, not the four-legged variety, and not the domestic goat that had been so responsible for the defoliation of huge tracts of semiarid and arid lands on Earth, but the four wheeled variety that seemed made to order for Beauty, which would never see a network of hard-surfaced roads, never even so much as an old-fashioned railroad track.

Matt and Teddy, riding their own personal vehicles—men in the mechanical shop had painted their names on the frames of the goats—took time to venture out onto the plain to watch the *Ark* make the first of its many landings. No hot rod approaches for the *Ark*. She came in from the east, slow, ponderous, a tub-shaped mass that, on high, seemed insignificant but grew into impressiveness as she swam slowly, slowly, enlarging until she seemed to blank out the sky. She settled into the knee-high grass without so much as a thump.

The first animal cargo had come from Reznor's own game preserves. The original seeding of Beauty reversed Genesis. Only females emerged from the *Ark's* hatches, blinking at the bright sun, wildebeests, zebras, gazelles.

Teddy pointed to a particular zebra who had darted down the ramp and run a few yards away from the huge ship before stopping. "Either that one ate a lot on the trip or there'll be young on the plains sooner than we thought."

"Some within a month or so," Matt said. "This is the test bunch. Jack wants young as fast as possible, so they brought as many pregnant females as possible. The others will be artificially inseminated as they come into season.''

''It's going to be a long process, isn't it?'' Teddy asked.

''I think it's safe to say that we won't be around to see it completed,'' Matt said. He had no intentions of spending the rest of his life on Beauty. He was more conversant now with Andrew Reznor's plan, and he simply was not interested in becoming an old, old man waiting for nature to take over and make Beauty teem with life as the Earth had. The enormity of the task Reznor had undertaken was intimidating, and, after all, it was not Matt's dream. It was pleasant, he had to admit, to see the animals emerge from the ship and, after a bit of breeze sniffing, rolling, and tentative darting runs, spread out. Aboard ship a few hundred good sized animals had been impressive. As they began to browse and graze, spreading in groups of like kind, the plain swallowed them, and that was just one plain on one continent, and only a handful of varieties had made up the *Ark's* first load.

He didn't envy the crew of the big ship. He had met her in orbit, boarded, and even with the ship's scrubbers and purification systems going full blast there'd been the faint smell of manure. Nor would there be any respite for the crew on Beauty, for any ship coming to Beauty could expect no layover time, no break from shipboard life while the ship received servicing and attention. There would be only emergency repair facilities on Beauty, no big yards as on other civilized planets. In fact, within an hour after the last nervous antelope scampered down the ramp to stand, trembling, belly-deep in rich, sweet grass, the ship had closed hatch and lifted with that deep, low, thunderous sound of a G.D. at full pitch.

They were away from the facility, and it was a

lovely day. With the sun warm on Teddy's bare legs, Matt led the way across the plain toward a rise where Beauty's bones were exposed in a line of tortured strata telling of some long ago upheaval. The goats could go faster than the terrain warranted, so Matt held his speed down, with Teddy pacing him, a few yards off to his right.

As they approached, they could see that the ridge before them rose in an escarpment of barren rock to a height of around two hundred feet. Matt steered into the shadow of the cliffs, turned south, moving back toward the facility.

It was some minutes before he noted a change in the sound of his goat's engine. It was not practical to use G.D. engines on a vehicle so small, so the goat was powered by a combustion engine using hydrogen for fuel. The series of small explosions that gave the goat its motive power, muted by a not too efficient muffler system, sounded like a high-pitched purr that rose to a snarl when the engine was at speed. Riding along at over twenty miles an hour the sound of the engine was scarcely noticeable above the sound of the wind, but Matt was hearing the snarl of the engine clearly, much more loudly than usual. It didn't take a genius to realize that he was getting an echo effect, with the sound of the engine bouncing off the face of the cliff. He pointed to his ear and to the engine and then the cliffs and nodded, yelling to Teddy, "Interesting echo effect."

"What?" she yelled back.

Matt slowed, stopped. She pulled up close. "We're getting quite an echo off the cliff," he said.

"Oh, yes. I noticed," she said. She revved the engine of her goat until it snarled at high pitch. The echo came back, and grew. Teddy looked toward the cliff, puzzled. She held the engine at high speed, and the snarl of the echo became a roar, like that of a giant cataract, with overtones that began to hurt her ears.

"What the heck?" Matt said, his words lost in the pulsing roar of sound.

Teddy eased off the engine. The echo died away. "Wow," she said. It had been as if the engine's snarl had been amplified many times.

"Now that's interesting," Matt said.

"It's almost as if Beauty is protesting the intrusion," Teddy said, looking, head back, toward the top of the cliff, then out onto the plain where she could see a few tiny dots, the animals left behind by the *Ark*.

"Just an acoustical freak," Matt said, as his communicator chimed and he reached for it.

"I've never heard anything like it," Teddy said. "We'll have to ask some of the engineers to find out why it happens."

Matt's attention was on the voice now issuing from his communicator.

"Let's go," he said, kicking his goat into gear. "We've got company. There's an unidentified ship, small, fast, trying a variety of approaches to the planet." He sped toward the facility, and neither of them thought again about the odd echo from the cliffs.

Chapter 10

Jake Jordan had found several ways to compensate for the fact that nature had shorted him, literally, making him five-feet-eight-inches tall in an age in which six feet was the average height for men and that ancient and honorable sport of basketball now was played with seven-footers at the guard positions. The ultimate macho compensation had been to become a modern mercenary. With no wars to be fought, being a mercenary wasn't always exciting. Mostly, since his was a one-man business, it was lonely and often boring, for it involved doing a lot of traveling in a neat little ship that had been altered from a luxurious space yacht into an overpowered, secretly armed bomb. Although her name did not appear anywhere on her black hull, Jake knew her as the *Can Do*. She was a sweetheart. Internal stressing enabled *Can Do* to use sublight trans in atmosphere, and extra shielding prevented her hull from ablating in the extreme heat of such travel. Her G.D. was monstrous, large enough for a small freighter. Her computer power was such that she could trans with a loading time of mere seconds, which is what she was doing when Matt and Teddy arrived at The Shop to lean over the shoulders of the duty man.

"What the hell?" Matt asked, as a blip appeared

near one of the eyes into space and immediately disappeared.

"He's been at it for a couple of hours," the duty man said. "That's one helluva little ship up there." He pointed. The blip had appeared again, near another satellite, and, as quickly, was gone. "He's just about completed a survey of the sphere of space down to about twenty miles."

"A survey?" Matt asked.

"What else? He's pinpointed every eye we've got up there except these two." The duty man pointed to the screen. "He'll come out right here." There it was, the blip, and then it was gone to appear again near the last uncharted satellite. "Okay, that's the lot. He'll probably make a few more trans just to be sure."

"He moves," Matt said.

"If I didn't have an exact read on his mass, I'd swear he was a Defense Force destroyer. I mean, that's some souped-up ship up there."

"Why is he here?" Teddy asked. "Why is he locating all our eyes?"

"If I were going to make an unauthorized approach, or attack some point on the planet, I'd first find out the planet's alert capacity," Matt said.

Jake Jordan made a couple of high speed circumnavigations of the globe, all his specialized search instruments at max, and, satisfied that he had located all the eyes, zapped *Can Do* out past detection distance and suspended her in space. The long eyes and sensitive ears he then brought to bear on the planet had Chinese markings. They'd been part of a deal that had turned out to be very profitable, one of the few times he'd chosen to do business with a governmental agency. He didn't trust bureaucrats. He liked to work for the private sector, where there were men who had a cash incentive to keep secrets. But the Chinese gig hadn't been bad, involving nothing more than a courier run. Of course, if the materials he'd been carrying in *Can Do's* safe had fallen into the wrong hands, say into the hands of a captain of a Defense Force warbird, things would have gotten a little sticky, which is why Jake had demanded as prepayment the state of the Chinese art in long-range eyes and ears.

"I've got to be able to spot a warbird before they spot me," he'd insisted, and he'd gotten what he demanded.

Beauty was revealed to him as being largely empty. One sprawling facility was well advanced, another was just getting underway on another continent, and there were three small ships cruising in atmosphere on G.D.

After being nothing much more than a high-priced messenger for years, moving items too secret or too valuable to be trusted to regular milk runs between planets, Jake welcomed the challenge he'd discovered way to hell and gone out in unexplored space. Someone had buttoned a sizable planet up damned tight. He'd never seen a better positioned set of detectors. He ran the picture on the computer, got the graphic of the globe and put in the detection zones, using U.S. standard, since the power signals from the satellites indicated U.S. manufacture, and whistled. There wasn't a hole anywhere in the envelope.

Jake dressed neatly, even when he was alone in space. He favored black, and his most worn costume was a modification of Academy in-space wear, black, seamless slacks with an expanding waistband and a comfortable black pullover shirt in silkweave Chinese material, light and uninhibitive of quick movement. He had a shock of black hair and wore a neat, equally black beard. He had a pleasant expression around his eyes, the effect heightened by the grin lines that come to a man who spends a lot of time in space.

The challenge was to find a way past the electronic eyes and ears. That's all that was being asked of him on this trip. But there wasn't a way in. The only way a ship could get through that envelope of protection without being detected was to wait until one of the eyes malfunctioned, and that could be a long, long wait. He didn't have time for that, nor was that a viable alternative for anyone who wanted to approach the planet at a specific time.

There was one other possibility. Among hot pilots everywhere there were tales about some hotshot transing directly into planetary gravity and atmosphere. He'd never met anyone who had done it personally. The teller of the tale was always a fellow who had known a fellow who did it or had known a fellow who had known a fellow who definitely saw old so-and-so trans from space down to within a few thousand feet of the surface. The technique was simple enough. You just measured and entered the readings and pushed a button. The problem was that both atmosphere and a strong gravitational pull could affect the readings and with such small tolerances if a man goofed he would trans into the ground and cause one very nice explosion when the ship materialized in solid rock. Even transing perfectly and coming out in air would be no assurance that one had not been detected, because when a ship came out of trans it became solid and since two things cannot occupy the same space at the same time the air would be displaced, and displaced explosively. Probably, it was thought, the sound would be like thunder or a sonic boom, but no one really knew.

On the ground, meanwhile, The Shop was a busy place. The encroaching ship had disappeared from the eyes in space, but a technician was cranking up long-range detection, that just happened to be the state of U.S. art, and slightly superior to the Chinese long eyes and ears on board Jake's *Can Do*.

"There he is," a technician said. "About ten thousand miles. He's stationary."

"Let's go," Matt said to Teddy, who followed him, on the run, to the pad where *Belle* lay sleeping, dreaming, perhaps, of far-flung flights into the neighboring galaxies. "Keep me posted," Matt said, on the run, his communicator open. "Figure me a trans vector from one hundred thousand feet so that when I come out I'll be nose to nose with that dude."

It took five minutes to get *Belle* humming and ticking, and by then the trans vector was programmed in. Matt took her up easy. It was very dusty there on the plateau and the technicians complained if a ship was careless. Clear, he juiced the G.D. and listened to Teddy call out altitude. The computer took over and counted down and then *Belle* transed and there was a black ship with silver trim, no name, lying nose to nose not over fifty feet away.

"Now that's cutting it too damned close," Teddy said.

Matt could see the bearded face of the black ship's pilot. He nudged *Belle* and she snuck closer until no more than five feet separated her from the black ship and Matt could see the startled look on the dark man's face when he looked up and out the port and saw Matt's face.

Jake's hand shot out to the console, his finger on the beam's safety button, then he relaxed. The lad out there was damned good, damned good. It served him right to get caught napping, without even having turned on the ship's detectors. Detectors send out a signal and that signal can be detected, so he'd been running without them while making his survey and had not thought to turn them on when he was finished. Yes, the pilot of that ship sitting five feet from his nose was damned good. He raised one hand, gave a smart academy style salute, and then transed the hell out of there.

"There were no markings on the ship," Teddy said.

"Let's see the tape," Matt said. Teddy pushed buttons and the image of the black ship appeared on a screen, grew, until, on full magnification, the face of the black ship's pilot was larger than life-size.

"Not a bad looking guy," Teddy said.

"If you like woolly boogers," Matt said.

"Sometimes a beard can be a mark of distinction."

"Well, he's gone," Matt said. "I doubt if he'll hang around, now that he knows we've spotted him." He let *Belle* edge over and nudged her just a bit to put her into free fall toward Beauty.

There were two levels of emotion in Jake Jordan's head as he halted *Can Do* half a light-year from the planet. He was chagrined to have been caught out so easily by some dude in a gold and white exploration ship with nowhere near the guts of *Can Do*. On that level it was his pride that was hurt. On a deeper level, there was a chilling realization that he had goofed rather badly, a goof so flagrant that, had he committed it under other circumstances, he would most probably now be a few scattered molecules being swept slowly down into the planet's gravitational well to burn up on contact with the atmosphere. True, this job didn't have the built-in peril of some he'd done, but he had no way of knowing when he'd be back in some situation where letting a strange ship come nose to nose with him would do greater damage than hurt pride. For example, about once a year he made a run out past Valhalla to the asteroid belt where certain entrepreneurs saw no reason to pay heavy export duties on some very high grade diamonds being mined from an asteroid that contained the core of an ancient volcanic pipe. With the help of Jake Jordan and *Can Do*, they bypassed both the German officials of Valhalla and the Pax Five

customs gentlemen. The squareheads on Valhalla, a
poor planet, would have taken a dim view of such
activity and would, no doubt, use the state of the
German art weaponry on a black and silver ship
without markings coming from a known jewel producing belt without Valhalla clearance.

Perhaps, Jordan felt, the smiling pilot of that pretty
little exploration ship with the quaint name had done
him a favor by reminding him that even in loose
situations one could not afford to get slack. On the
other hand, who did that smiling son of a bitch think
he was, sticking his nose right into the port housing
a beam that could have melted him at two hundred
miles?

Hot pilots of all eras, from the time of the Wright
brothers, have had their pride, and Jordan had his
share. It was pride that sent him to the computer,
pride that programmed a small trans. It was pride
that pushed doubt away and sent Jordan's fingers flying over the console. The computer kicked back his
first three calculations as being potentially disas-
trous, and grudgingly accepted the fourth set of figures with a yellow warning light that showed a
marginal safety factor. *Can Do* transed.

The small black ship came back at just over thirty
thousand feet over the southern ocean of Beauty. Her
instantaneous appearance pushed air out in all directions with explosive force, but the thunder in the
reaches of the southern ocean rumbled over the ice
sheets and the faceless waters.

So it could be done, and had been done, transing
into atmosphere. He'd come past the planet's eyes
and ears, and he doubted if there was a surface detection system. No need for it since the gates were
closed so tightly on the near fringe of space. It didn't
matter, because now he wanted them to know that
he'd breached their guard. It was a matter of pride.
He consulted the graphics he'd built of the planet

during his survey and his fingers gave *Can Do* her orders.

Tinker's Belle had made a leisurely descent and had landed on her assigned pad. Matt and Teddy, having shared wonder about why the black ship had been surveying Beauty's defenses, were in no hurry to get back to work. It was a fantastic day, the afternoon having spent its heat and the cool of evening to be sniffed on the slight breeze.

Teddy saw it first. It came from the south, seeming to curve up from the horizon with a speed that made her gasp. By the time she'd called Matt's attention to it, it was growing larger and appeared to be higher.

"Ho—lee," Matt gasped, as the fireball seemed to be coming directly toward him, orange-red at the front, tapering with flames reaching backward like the tail of a short comet.

The thing moved at an incredible rate of speed, flashing over the Reznor complex at an altitude of less than eighty thousand feet, and with its passing— so fast was it moving that the sound came only after the fireball had seemed to climb directly toward the sky and dwindle—came a mighty sonic boom, a heaving, thunderous concussion that rattled windows, sent the few herbivores grazing on the plain into panicked flight, and thundered back from the rocky escarpment to the west.

"A meteor?" Teddy gasped.

"Going straight up?"

There were no human ears to hear the low, moaning sound that came from the escarpment in the wake of the sonic boom. From the southern ocean, from the southern end of the continent, to the north and away the thunderous announcement of *Can Do's* trans-powered atmospheric flight battered the quietness of Beauty.

Teddy was just behind Matt when he burst into The Shop. "What the hell was it?" Matt asked.

"It was making power enough to drive a colonizer ship," the duty man said. "Trans."

"That was a ship?" Teddy asked, not really believing it.

"She'd have to be stressed stronger than a ship of the line, and have a power plant that was something else," the duty man said, "but it was a ship."

Matt looked at Teddy with a wry smile. "He didn't like our sneaking up on him." He turned. "Where did he come in?"

"He didn't," the duty man said. "No detection."

"Impossible," Matt said.

"He came up from the south," the duty man said, "and he kicked in the trans and went just outside atmosphere."

"That leaves us with a lot of unanswered questions," Teddy said. "Why was he here in the first place, and why would he so blatantly announce that he has a way to evade the eyes and ears?"

"You tell me," Matt said.

The *Can Do* would need a new paint job. She'd lost only a tiny layer of shielding in the showboat flight as a burning fireball through atmosphere, so a coat of paint or two would do it. It was no big deal, since the cost of the repair could be added to Jake's bill. He took her transing as fast as the computer could figure to Earth orbit, sent a coded recognition signal and went down under power, making a splashy landing, coming from free fall to a powered halt two inches off the pad, at a military field tucked almost unseen into the side of a mountain in the Italian Alps. Serious faced, armed men, all taller than he, escorted him across a short area of nonreflecting surface hardener. A long ride on a fast elevator and he was several hundred feet into the bowels of the

mountain, sitting down without being asked in front
of the desk of a grizzled, unsmiling man in the uniform of the joint intelligence agency of the Pax Five.
In his report, made orally—there was to be nothing
in writing—he left out his last flight at fireball speed
less than fifty thousand feet over the planet Andrew
Reznor had named Beauty.

The grizzled, unsmiling man in uniform listened,
nodding occasionally, and then he had a look at the
printouts from *Can Do.*

"Animals?" he asked, staring into Jake's intense,
dark eyes. "Nothing but animals?"

"You see it," Jake said.

"A planetary alert system to guard animals?"

"A very good system," Jake said. "Anyone who
visits that planet will not come as a surprise to those
on the surface."

"You have done well," the grizzled man said.
"As agreed, the designated sums will be deposited
in Pax Five dollars to your numbered account."

Chapter 11

After a few weeks, the test animals on Beauty didn't even bother to run when vehicles approached. When they heard the snarl of approaching goats or vans they would raise their heads, switch their tails and—if you were one of those people who attributed humanlike emotions to animals, as Cassie Frost was—say to themselves, *oh, well, here we go again.* Having been bred and reared on Reznor's game farms, the animals were already accustomed to being pampered, pawed, pricked, and force-fed by humans, but on Beauty the testing seemed to be endless.

His conversational style came, Jack admitted, from what he termed to be a grasshopper brain, meaning that he jumped from subject to subject and competed fiercely for vocal time as if there had been given to each only a limited number of minutes to talk and he wanted his share and someone else's too. But Jack Frost was all business, direct, efficient, when it came to his work, which was and had been since he was a teenager, animals. When personally recruited by Andrew Reznor, Frost had been teaching and doing research at the Auburn School of Veterinary Medicine. In addition to being the finest diagnostician in the field, and very handy as a cutter, he was recognized as one of the top experts in the field of animal behavior. He'd had one big decision to make, for there were to be no domestic animals on Beauty, no pussycats, tweety-birds, puppy dogs. That meant leaving behind a menagerie acquired over years, built of the cringing, bone-protruding, heart-breaking pup abandoned by the roadside, the stray kitten, the unwanted mama alley cat whose stomach protruded with life. It had taken Andrew Reznor exactly five minutes to overcome that objection. He'd merely put a few million dollars up to establish the Jackson Frost Animal Shelter, purchasing a hundred acres of used up cotton land in Alabama as a start. Strays and discards now had a home, scientifically balanced diets, gentle if effective sterilization, and they poured in from all over Alabama and parts of Mississippi, Florida, and Georgia.

Cassie, on the other hand, had been holding her breath all through the discussion of the possibilities of Reznor's plan. She and Jack had met twenty feet below the surface of the sea, atop a dying coral reef in the Bahamas. However, marine life was not her main interest. In conservation circles she was known as the monkey woman, not because of her petite frame or her large, somewhat simian eyes, but because of her interest, which was anything with four legs and a tail that climbed trees and belonged to the orders that included all apes and monkeys. She'd been vacationing in the Bahamas when she swam up over a dying reef, where life was being slowly exterminated by the sewage dumped into the sea from the booming resort towns, to see, first, a balding head, a long, lanky body, and then two curious eyes staring at her through a diving mask.

During their brief and not too exciting courtship—doing a census of howler monkeys in the dwindling rain forest of the Amazon basin was one of their romantic interludes—Jack had been on his best behavior, listening with interest as Cassie, who'd published several papers not only on animal behavior but on anthropology as well, voiced her theories, beliefs, and dreams. It was only after the wedding that Jack's **Hy**de overpowered his Jekyll and he showed himself to be the conversational monster that he was, except when they were actively working together.

Still they made a good team. Cassie's theoretical flights often sent Jack to the lab, sometimes, true, in an effort to prove her wrong, but most often with a bit of excitement.

It was fine with both of them that Cassie could not have children. They had enough babies, every animal with which either of them came into contact. From Jack's teaching base at Auburn—his reputation and the credit he brought to the school assured that he got anything for which he asked and was allowed to come and go as he pleased and to choose his own research projects—Jack and Cassie collaborated on *the* definitive study of the lack of gene diversity in the dwindling population of cheetahs. They crowned that achievement with the most complete documentation of a subsidiary form of DNA to corroborate a theory which had first surfaced in the 1980s that seemed to indicate that all people, whether brown, black, yellow, tan, red or white had a common mother. Although both, like most who had been exposed to the endless individual miracles of life's diversity, were firmly convinced, as was Andrew Reznor, that it could not have been an accident, they had not set out to prove Genesis. Their work, complete as it was, still left open the old, old question of the sudden appearance of Cro-Magnon man. It was their study of that form of DNA that can only be transmitted by the female of the species that had attracted the attention of Andrew Reznor. Any scientist who could explain where Cain got his wife was Reznor's kind of scientist.

"You see," Reznor explained, while Cassie looked back and forth from Reznor's intense face to Jack's frosty one, "God made Adam and Eve, a new breed, Cro-Magnon, if you like, and Eve bore Cain and Abel. Cain killed Abel, leaving three human beings alive on Earth, then Cain went out into the land of Nod and *knew* his wife. So who was Cain's wife and where did she come from? She was *there*, in her hulking, apelike, pre-Cro-Magnon form, and that's where a lot of the world's troubles started."

Although Cassie did not often live up to her name and did not like to cry bad news, she wasn't quite sure that she would be able to work with a man who used science to rationalize what, to her, was an old myth recorded by the scribes of a primitive tribe at the beginning of the historical era. The opportunity to be involved in conducting the ultimate experiment, not only returning animals to the wild and the life for which nature had created them, but having a chance to recreate at least major portions of Earth's ecology ante-Homo Sapiens, overcame her doubts about Reznor's not always rational, to her, beliefs.

Cassie and Jack had stood by to witness the first animal birth on Beauty. They didn't interfere, even when the zebra mare seemed to be in difficulty, because the animals of Beauty would be on their own as the project advanced, and it was a part of the plan to allow nature's laws to operate. (Of course, if the mare hadn't overcome her difficulties and given birth naturally to a healthy, wobbly-legged little female colt, Jack would have intervened.) They stood a few feet away and held hands as the beautiful event transpired and then swooped down, after the newborn calf had found its legs, had been licked clean by the mother, had had its first meal, to draw blood from the startled colt.

The first animal born on Beauty was pleasingly normal, healthy, and developed quickly into a frisky, lovable little beast that kicked up its heels in play and attracted an audience, at one time or another depending on duty times, of every man and woman in the Africa facility. And all of the animals were thriving. Belatedly, some flora experts had arrived to work with the fauna experts who were already in place, and their initial analysis of Beauty's grass proved that Cassie's lab work had been accurate in showing high nutritional value with all of the odd little trace elements needed for animal life.

The botanists began a study estimating the effects of large numbers of herbivores chomping contentedly on Beauty's grass, and a couple of them voiced doubts about the project. They had no solid ground, in the minds of Reznor and Jack Frost, because everyone knew that grass grows healthier when cropped, and that the droppings of grass eating animals enrich soil and that which grows in it.

Only one person, a feisty, rather attractive blonde named Kerry Hertz, known for her catalog of the flora of the Germanic planet, Valhalla, persisted. "There is a balance on this planet," she insisted. "Not enough study has been done to determine what effect the insertion of herds, droves, gaggles of animals will do to that balance."

Kerry found one person who would listen, and that was Cassie Frost, perhaps because she'd developed such patient listening habits during her years of being married to Jack. Then again, perhaps Cassie listened because she'd requested a botanist to catalog and test tropical fruit from the jungles to the south in preparation for beginning the establishment of those favorite animals of hers, the monkey family.

Kerry quickly proved that almost all the varieties of fruits and vegetation were potential monkey food and in the process continued voicing her doubts. "Had I suspected that we would move so fast," she said, "I would have reconsidered Reznor's offer.

There was a common plant on Valhalla that was so virulent, so poisonous that merely breathing the aroma that it excreted during its blooming cycle caused severe vomiting.''

"We've found nothing like that here," Cassie said.

"How do we know?" Kerry demanded. "Dangerous plants aside, how do we know that turning a—what do you call a group of monkeys?"

"A group of monkeys," Cassie said.

"No, as in a pride of lions, a murder of crows."

Cassie had a protective habit of going off into a little world of her own thoughts when a current conversation did not interest her. At such times a vague look came into her eyes and she was capable of looking directly at someone without seeing him. Kerry had become invisible.

"I don't know," Cassie said.

"So, how do we know that turning a bunch of monkeys loose won't violate some critical balance, some interdependence among species of plants?" Kerry went on. "We don't. One thing I learned on Valhalla, in an alien environment one can assume nothing. For example, just because animal manure is good for the soil of Earth doesn't mean that it's good for the soil of Beauty. There hasn't been enough work done on soil bacteria. What if Earth manure kills it and stops the vital process of decay of dead vegetation?"

"A chatter," Cassie said, coming back to reality, but at a point a few paces behind Kerry's rapid-fire talk.

"What?" Kerry asked. She was unfamiliar with another habit of Cassie's, the habit of selecting one statement from a conversation, chewing on it for a while while not hearing a further word and then coming back into the conversation with her conclusions.

"A chatter of monkeys."

"Oh? That's good."

"I made it up."

"Good for you," Kerry said. "Now about what's happening here. Do you know there are no beelike insects?"

"A buzz of bees," Cassie said, smiling happily.

"No insects at all to pollinate thousands of species of plants," Kerry said. "Now how has that happened? How is it possible? There should have been intense work done on that question alone—"

"A macho of men," Cassie said.

"—before anyone set foot on this planet."

"A welcome of women," Cassie said, having a wonderful time.

"One quick, low flyover with close scan showed me that the vegetation of Beauty cannot be self-pollinating," Kerry said.

"I ate one of the yellow, mangolike fruits yesterday," Cassie said.

"You what?" Kerry exploded.

"It was delicious."

The lack of scientific method, in Kerry Hertz' opinion, and, just perhaps, Cassie Frost, was making Valhalla and her teaching job there seem very attractive. But, day by day, she decided to stick it out one more day, one more week. Things were beginning to come together. She was enjoying field trips to spots on Beauty where hers was the first human foot to come into contact with the soil.

The *Ark* was making round trips to Earth as quickly as she could be turned around. A rotation system had been worked out to give her crew respite from the smell of animal dung and endless transing in space. The African herds were growing and new species were being added at what Kerry Hertz was convinced was a reckless pace. Still, the animals continued to thrive, the rains came and the plain

greened and bloomed. The fresh green made the animals fat and sassy. Birth became a daily occurrence,
and Jack Frost's assistants were kept busy inseminating various female animals with sperm gathered
from as many different sources as possible in order
to get as much genetic diversity into the herd as was
possible, lest all the species continue down the track
toward extinction, as the cheetah seemed intent on
doing. The cheetah, at some distant time in Earth's
past, had, it was thought, come close to extinction,
perhaps during an ice age, so that there had been
extensive interbreeding among a relatively few individuals. Now, with extinction threatening again,
the cheetah had a long way to go. The DNA molecules of all living cheetahs, and those in the sperm
taken from males long since dead, was so similar
that it was possible to graft skin from one animal to
the other without witnessing the rejection syndrome
with which an animal's body protected itself against
invasion by foreign bodies or infections.

More was known about the cheetah's immune system than that of most animals, except man, since the
twentieth century battle against a disease called AIDS
had been won with an antiviral agent developed
through the use of cheetah blood. The outgrowth of
the AIDS battle had been, in the end, positive, add-
ing greatly to man's life expectancy, since one spin-
off of the research had allowed organ transplants
without the massive chemical poisoning previously
necessary to defeat the rejection syndrome. The
cheetah had benefited, if only briefly, through con-
certed efforts to maintain a wild population and
through intensified research into the cheetah's main
problem, a lack of virility in the male's sperm,
thought to be a result of that lack of gene diversity
that so concerned all those involved in turning Beauty
into the new garden of Eden minus Adam and Eve.
However, the last cheetah in the wild had been shot

by a native poacher in 2025, leaving that splendid animal's survival in the hands of a few wildlife parks and the zoos.

Fittingly enough, the first large carnivore to be introduced into the expanding animal population of Beauty was scheduled to be the cheetah. They would come soon after hyenas and jackals, before the lions and wild hunting dogs, leopards and panthers. But it would be a long time before the peacefully grazing herds on the plains would be reminded of their racial past by the terrifying dash of a hunting cheetah or the roar of a hungry lion. Now each newborn animal was too precious to take its place in the ancient food chain.

The first step toward establishing that interesting area of life known as the treetop zone began on the cluttered floor of the jungle with the release of a few thousand queen termites along with their necessary males and workers.

"Termites?" Matt Tinker questioned. "Whose crazy idea was that?"

"You wouldn't call it crazy if you tried to make your way through the jungle, through any forest on Beauty," Teddy told him. "It's a mess. Leaves and fallen limbs don't decay properly."

"Beauty got along all right without termites for a few billion years," Matt said.

"They serve a definite purpose," Teddy assured him. "They'll clean up the jungle floor."

"With no natural enemies they'll take over," Matt said. "We'll all have to learn to eat termites or be swarmed over by them."

"I hear they're delicious sautéed and dipped in honey," Teddy said. "But we'll bring in the various anteaters rather quickly now. Right after we bring in a shipload of Cassie's relatives."

"Meow," Matt said.

"No offense meant," Teddy smiled.

"I'm flying up to America today," Matt said, still not sure he approved of termites. For lack of other plans, the various land areas of Beauty had been given the names corresponding to the types of wildlife that would be implanted into them. Thus, home base was in Africa and the western continent—west from Africa—was America. It was not a double continent, as were North and South America on Earth, but it was big, had climate ranging from Arctic tundra to tropical jungle, and would have to accept all the implants from both American continents.

Building had begun on America, preparatory to bringing in American bison, pronghorns, various deer, bighorn sheep, caribou, moose, elk, all the North American grass eaters.

Teddy joined Matt aboard *Belle,* sighing with contentment as she settled into her form-fitting seat. She almost wished that they were setting off on an exploration trans, far away from people and work and responsibility, but she dared not voice that particular little mood to Matt, because she knew it would pass. Things were just too interesting on Beauty, the work too rewarding, to think about leaving now.

Teddy had helped select the building site for Buffalo House. It was in a plains area less arid than the home base in Africa, and she'd chosen a knoll on the bank of a very pretty little clear-water river. The tall trees alongside the river were dwarfed by the rolling plains extending seemingly forever on either side, and by the faultlessly blue vault of sky. *Belle* landed on the temporary pad beside a large construction ship from which workers were removing materials. Matt and Teddy were greeted by Sandy Moore, the architect and construction boss who had built Africa House.

"Good to see you, Matt," Moore said, extending a hand that showed by its hardness that Sandy was not a hands-off supervisor. "And you, especially, Teddy. I need a policy variant from you."

"Tell me about it," Teddy said.

"It'll wait. Come take a look and have a cool one," Moore said.

Buffalo House was taking shape rapidly. It was tucked among trees with leaves like dinner plates, huge, round, and fleshy. Both Teddy and Matt accepted a beer from a portable cooler and sat down with Sandy Moore on a freshly dried foundation to appreciate the warmth of the sun, the sparkling water of the river, the soft song of the big leaves of the trees as they kissed each other in the light breeze.

After a bit of small talk, Teddy said, "What's this policy variant you need?"

"Well, I hate to admit that I need it because of poor planning," Moore said, with a grin, "but it's true. I need just a little more space for the east wing." He pointed. "There. It's to have a veranda overlooking the river. The veranda isn't necessary, true, and it can be put somewhere else, and I agree with the hands-off policy for Beauty's vegetation, of course, but I'm also a picky old architect who hates to change a plan once I've come to love it. In short, I goofed and I need to cut down one tree."

Teddy had seen the tree-lined river from the air several times. It extended through the plain for hundreds of miles, and to her admittedly uneducated eye the trees all seemed to be of one variety. Several of the trees were in bloom right now. Perfect, sweet smelling, purple flowers, tiny and vibrant, lined the outer edges of every plate-sized leaf. The tree Moore wanted to cut down was not in bloom, and that made Teddy's decision easier. After all, what was one tree among so many?

"Well," she said, "I guess we can humor the picky old architect just once."

"I've got the form all filled out, up in the office."

Moore said. "We can go up and get it signed and then it'll be time for lunch."

In the office Teddy signed the variant form. Moore picked up a communicator and gave orders for the tree to be cut down and the stump excavated, then he led the way to the dining hall. The construction gang was already at table, men with hair slicked back, wet with their perspiration, women in work blue with hair tied up neatly but also damp with the sweat of honest toil after a morning at the wheel of an earth mover or mixer. There was a buzz of conversation, greetings as the three of them took a table. The food was standard Beauty fare, foods frozen on Earth, but the Buffalo House cook, Matt noted, knew how to add a little zing to a plate of hash.

"Where did your cook get fresh hot peppers?" Matt asked, after one bite.

Moore grinned. "Our resident plant picker found them," he said. Teddy stopped chewing. "Oh, don't worry. They're not poison. Tested every way. Gives the hash a fine flavor."

"Well, slowly but surely we're all becoming acclimated," Teddy said. "We're eating a few jungle fruits over on Africa. And they're making some test plantings of a few vegetables. Soon we'll be growing a lot of our own food in carefully sealed greenhouses designed to prevent the release of any Earth seed that might like the conditions so well it would try to take over."

"I've wondered about that," Moore said. "How do the animal boys keep the brutes from carrying over some undigested weed seed in their stomachs? Do they give them all enemas before they let them off the ship?"

Matt laughed.

"Don't have to," Teddy said. "They're fed processed foods for days before they're loaded and during the trip. Any stray seed has been passed through their systems before they board the *Ark*."

"I'm relieved," Moore said. "I'd sure hate to have the job of giving an elephant an enema."

"What a pleasant topic for table talk," Matt said, but he didn't stop eating.

"You'll have your buffalo in about thirty days," Teddy said. "Will you be ready?"

"Sure," Moore said. "We're right on schedule, except for that veranda, and we'll have it caught up—" He paused as an outside door burst open and a workman stuck his head in.

"Boss," the workman yelled, "you'd better get out here fast."

Matt and Teddy followed Moore out, Teddy bumping her thigh painfully on the corner of a table. The workman who had called Moore ran ahead toward the bank of the river. Matt arrived just after Moore, who had moved surprisingly fast for a man of his age. Teddy, breathing hard and rubbing her thigh, came to stand beside him.

A cut had been started in the tree that was in the way of Moore's veranda. The long blade of an impulse cutter was still caught in the shallow cut, the weight of the power head causing it to vibrate slightly as the electric motor hummed, the blade jammed. At the foot of the tree lay a mass of yellowish white over which two men were working frantically, colored to the elbows by the yellowish-white powder. With a gasp, Teddy realized that the mound of yellowish white was a man. She could tell mainly by the fact that the mound was heaving. The two workmen were frantically trying to brush away the yellowish-white dust from the man's face.

A medic came rushing up, carrying a kit. He pushed a workman aside and rammed his fingers into the man's mouth, digging out sticky, dampened powder. "My God," the medic said, "he's crammed full of the stuff.'' He ran his fingers down the man's throat and dug out more of the gummy mass that clogged mouth and nostrils.

"What the hell is it?" Moore asked.

"I dunno, boss," a workman said. "We didn't see anything, just heard the cutter going and then Eddie coughing and gasping and he was like this, all covered with this dust."

The medic was fitting a mask to Eddie's face and there was a hiss as the respirator began to try to force oxygen into the man's lungs. Eddie's body jerked, chest pumping, and then he was still.

"Got to get him to the clinic on the ship," the medic said. Two workmen leaped to help carry the man, who was no longer gasping for air. "Get a move on," the medic yelled.

Matt bent, touched the yellowish-white powder that lay in piles on the ground. "Very fine," he said. "Where did it come from?"

"Out of the tree?" Moore asked, bending to look closely. He saw only a dampness of juices seeping out around the stuck blade of the cutter, wrestled the cutter out of the tree, looked at the cut again. "Nope, there was too much of it to be sawdust from this small cut. Wet sap seeping out."

Matt sniffed at the powder. It had the fragrance of the small flowers that bloomed all around the large leaves of some of the trees. He walked upstream a bit to a point where he could reach a low limb whose leaves were in bloom and touched the flowers. His finger came away with a film of yellowish-white dust. "It's pollen," he said. "Pollen from the flowers." He shook the limb and a dusting of pollen fell. "But the tree that fellow was cutting wasn't in bloom, so he didn't just shake down pollen from the vibration of the cutter."

"He was covered from head to toe," Teddy said. "So much of it. It was inches thick all over him."

Teddy looked around and saw the graceful, huge, obviously old trees in a new light. She'd been on Beauty so long that she'd started taking things for granted. The planet had been so benign, so kind. She'd started seeing the trees, the grasses, the various vegetation much as if she had been looking at the vegetation of Earth, as something commonplace, ever-present, harmless. But these trees, with their huge, round leaves and their masses of tiny, fragrant flowers were not on Earth, but on an alien planet about which they really knew so little.

"Get some samples of that stuff and take it to the lab on the ship," Sandy Moore told a workman. He ran his hands through his sun-bleached hair. "I don't like losing a man."

"Maybe they revived him," Teddy said.

"I hope so," Moore said, but his hopes were dashed as a workman came running from the direction of the ship.

"Boss," the man said, "Eddie's dead. His lungs are all gummed up with that stuff, the doc says."

Teddy turned away. Where Eddie had lain there was a crude drawing of his body outlined by the yellowish-white pollen. The river gurgled quietly. The wind sighed in the leaves of the trees and the flowers perfumed the air. From far off came the muffled boom of a sonic blast as one of the survey ships made a run. The sound seemed an incongruous contrast to the quietness of the river, the sigh of the wind and, somehow, very, very lonely.

Chapter 12

Genna Darden dried herself in a soothing rush of arid, heated air. She fluffed her short, ash-blonde hair, glanced at herself in a full-length mirror, pinched her flesh at the waist between thumb and forefinger and nodded in satisfaction. She could not even pinch half an inch. She stepped from the sanitary area of her apartment in the nude, slim and lithe, rounded, Venus emerging from her bath. When she noted the gaze of the man propped up on her bed, she posed for him, smiling naturally, the pose seeming not at all affected. She was Genna, and she was Icelandic, and icy blonde, and her skin looked as if it had never seen the African sun. It had, but never without a protective coating.

''Genna, Genna,'' the man on the bed said softly. He showed wear, not age, although his hair was grizzled, cut short and stiff. His upper torso showed the results of regular workouts on handball courts and in swimming pools, his hands were blunt-fingered, but the nails were carefully kept. He had a nose once broken and never repaired. That nose made a statement to the effect that this man didn't give a damn what others thought. His steel-colored eyes were warmed, at the moment, by the glow of Genna's skin, but it was evident that they could be as hard as the metal whose color they imitated. His name was Shardan. A few, Genna among them, knew his first name, but, knowing it, forgot it. He was Shardan. To close friends, such as Genna, Shard.

"Come live with me and be my love," he whispered, as Genna moved to the bed, sat on the edge.

"All right," Genna said.

"I'm serious," Shardan said, putting one of his strong hands on a shapely knee.

"I have to go to work," Genna said. "Unfortunately, I am but a poor, working, Icelandic girl who does not have the freedom, as some do, to loll in bed and report to my office by communicator."

"Live with me," Shardan said, "and set your own hours."

"Ah, Shard," she whispered.

Shardan laughed. "Not quite ready to give up the excitement of being ambitious?"

"I do like my work. I think it is important."

"Damned important," Shardan said. "It can be done, if not as well, by others."

Genna rose and went to a chest, pulled out filmy, silken things and, facing Shardan, began to dress. "You have made no comment on what I told you last night," she said.

"I have thought about it," Shardan said, sighing as he sat up.

"And?"

"Everything is as you said. The planet is to be devoted exclusively to animals. Some African herd animals are already there. Reznor has built and is continuing to build facilities to conduct animal research, to oversee the implantation of Earth animals in various locations. A second ground facility is underway, and an exceptionally good alert system has been put into place around the planet. Reznor has converted a colonizer to carry animals and the ship

is making round trips from Earth to the planet as
soon as it can safely be turned around.''

Genna was not at all surprised that Shardan knew
the current status of Reznor's project. ''And is there
nothing that can be done?''

Shardan spread his hands. ''I'm not sure anything
should be done.'' He thought he knew why Genna
was so interested, so incensed by Reznor's skillful
tactics which had resulted in the prevention of human settlement on a fine planet. He knew many
things about her, some things, perhaps, that she did
not know he knew.

Genna's resentment about giving an entire planet
over to animals had deep roots, going back to her
childhood and the Icelandic mentality that was a
product of being hard working and high-achieving,
yet confined to a tiny, inhospitable island whose
meager natural resources and lack of expansion room
limited both an Icelander's world and his imagination. While the majority of people in the world bred
like flies, Icelandic girls had implants at puberty and
had to have government permits to remove the birth
control implants and could never have more than two
children. This fact alone influenced the women of
the island. Deprived of the natural satisfaction of
choosing their own time for children, they generally
expressed nature's most powerful urge, the urge to
procreate, in enticing, heart-pounding ways. In the
new age of morality, Icelandic women were not
amoral, they were just natural, and it was natural for
a girl like Genna to have a man if she wanted him.

Oddly enough, very few Icelanders had migrated
out to the new worlds. Many of the young ones left
the island and, more often than not, achieved success in whatever field they chose. They were not, in
general, anti-colonization. If others wanted to leave
the Earth, that was well and good. As for them, the
great world outside Iceland was so beautiful and so

varied that they could do all the expansion they cared to right on Earth. In Genna's case, this meant coming to Africa to work as interagency coordinator for the Bureau of Colonization. But even though Genna had no desire to settle elsewhere, the waste of good living space on animals was upsetting.

Shardan knew that he was not the only man who had ever seen Genna slip into something clinging and flimsy and then cover that perfect, slim, rounded body with a modified Bureau uniform skirt and blouse and jacket, and that didn't bother him. He was sincere in his often repeated offer to take her permanently, and would have done so gladly, but he knew, too, that she was one of the world's great natural assets, uninhibited, natural, sensuous. Those qualities made her a very good interagency coordinator. He, himself, although he was one of the most self-contained men in the world, a man who was not only entrusted with secrets but with their protection, often lowered his defenses just a bit and told Genna more than he would have told anyone else in her position. That quality, the ability to make men want to please her, would make her, he knew, a valuable employee. So when he was turned down, not unkindly, on his offer to have her come with him and be his love, his counter offer was a position at Intel, and that, too, was always refused, though not ungratefully.

"Something should be done," Genna said. "Shall I have breakfast sent up?"

"No. I'll grab something on the way to the office," Shardan said. "I don't think it would be worth the hassle. Legally, that planet is a possession of the United States by act of Congress under provisions of the Pax Five treaties."

"But something could be done?" she persisted.

"Not right away, I'd think," Shardan said. "Later on, if the governmental and free-lance explorers fail

to find good planets for, oh, a period of four or five
years, then some gentle pressure might be brought
to bear on the United States."

"By whom?" Genna asked.

"It would have to come from the Pax Five Council, first. A few screams of outrage from the maggot
countries would help." Shardan had little regard for
those large, differently hued areas of exploding population. "A few bleeding heart media people could
amplify the screams from the deprived poor." He
mused for a moment, scratching his chest. "It would
have to be orchestrated carefully for the public opinion you'd be seeking would have to come from the
haves, from the bleeding heart sectors of the advanced nations, and you'll find in those same sectors
of the population a strong sentiment for, quote, ecology, unquote. The whole thing would backfire on
you if Reznor began a counter campaign pointing out
the plight of some obscure species whose last habitat
was being destroyed by development. If there's anything the liberals of this world love more than the
downtrodden poor, it's the downtrodden, obscure
species of animal, or bug, or plant. Now they'll allow the grizzly bear to become a zoo animal because
the grizzly is on *their* lands, and they'll allow low-
cost housing to be built in the habitat of the Venus's-
flytrap in North Carolina, the only place it can grow
outside a greenhouse, because it's their downtrodden
poor who need new apartments to dirty and destroy.
But if it's someone else's land, say in Africa, or
Asia, or on a distant planet that has nothing to do
with them, they might sympathize with the poor animals instead of the poor people."

"If you were going to try to do something about
it, before it was too late, where would you start?"
Genna asked.

Shardan gave it some thought. "Well, I'd want
your boss on my side."

Genna smiled.

"No problem, huh?" Shardan stood, stretched. He was a well-built man, in very good condition for his age. "And I'd start cultivating some molder of public opinion, some media giant with an international audience. I'd move very slowly. There's time. It's a big, empty planet. There are a half dozen continental land masses, and some nice islands. It'll take decades for Reznor to even really begin his work there, and there'll be empty, wasted, habitable land areas for fifty or a hundred years. I'd aim for just a chink in the armor, a concession on Reznor's part to allow one continent, or one large island to be opened up to human settlement. After that? Well, all you have to do is look at the history of Earth. In a hundred years or so some follower of Reznor would have to begin to move animals off *that* planet to make room for the huddled masses."

"To put pressure on the United States from the Pax Five," Genna said. "You could engineer this."

"So can you." He had a sudden inspiration. "But you could do it better from an Intel base. You'd have more information, more possible points of entrée to influential individuals at the Pax Five level, more resources."

"And your cooperation?" she asked, coming to kiss him lightly.

"I'm shameless. Yes, I would buy you with that promise, if that is what it would take."

"Then that is a possibility for the future," Genna said. "I must go now."

"I'll be in Paris tonight," Shardan said.

"And I will be busy," Genna said. "Call me when you return, dear Shard."

Chapter 13

The body of Eddie Jones, the first man to die on Beauty, was flown back to the medical labs at Africa House. Matt was invited to watch the autopsy by the medical people, but with the first slash of sharp scalpel into dead, white, human flesh, he bolted and waited for the results in his office. He was there now, stomach still a bit queasy, booted feet on the edge of his desk, reading the doctor's initial report. When Teddy came in, dressed in cute little tan shorts and a loose blouse, he looked up and made a face.

"I told Sandy Moore to hold off cutting down that tree," Teddy said.

Matt nodded. "The man drowned," he said.

Teddy waited.

"On pollen. It filled his lungs and became pasty and allowed no oxygen to get through."

"Terrible," Teddy said, placing herself carefully on the edge of Matt's desk where he couldn't reach her. But Matt's mind was, for once, not on Teddy's nice legs.

"Kerry Hertz wants to fly over to America and take a look at the flowering trees," Teddy said.

"Fine. Tell her to requisition any equipment or material she needs, and draft anyone she wants to help her." He tossed the autopsy report onto the desk. "Damn it, Teddy, those pollen grains are minute. How did so much of it get on and in that man?"

"That's what Kerry hopes to find out," Teddy said.

"I think I'd better go over there myself," Matt said.

"Me, too. I feel sort of responsible since I was the one who signed the variant slip."

They flew over in the same exploration ship with Kerry Hertz. She had taken surprisingly little equipment, and had not asked anyone to go with her. When they landed, work was going on normally, except on the river side near the tree that still oozed sap from the shallow cut in its bole. Kerry Hertz examined the cut, touched her finger to the oozing sap. Then she strolled up and down the river for a few minutes, returned to her little pile of equipment and selected an instrument, asked for a ladder, and used the ladder to climb high enough to suck pollen from the tiny flowers that ringed one big leaf. She repeated the operation, pausing to make notes after each sampling, until she had moved about a hundred yards away from the tree that grew where Moore wanted to put his veranda.

Kerry's hair and nose were dusted with pollen when she came back to where Matt, Teddy, and Sandy Moore waited, seated on the grass beside the river and having a cool one.

"There's hardly any pollen left on the flowers nearest the tree," Kerry said. "The farther you get away from the tree the more pollen there is left on the flowers."

"So?" Matt asked.

"Making a rough estimate of the amount of pollen that fell on—for a lack of a better description—that poor man, it took the total pollen load of approximately thirty or forty trees."

"And how did it get on him?" Matt asked.

"You tell me," Kerry said. "On Valhalla there's a weed that can spit its pollen about ten yards with the proper wind. The pollen has acidity and can irritate the skin. But on Valhalla we found out things like that before we started building and bringing in people."

"Well, I'm so damned glad you people were so intelligent on Valhalla," Matt said. "I'd appreciate it, Dr. Hertz, if you'd quit comparing us to the Germanic perfection of Valhalla and just concentrate on telling me how a man got enough pollen into his lungs, in a very brief period of time, to die of asphyxiation."

"Our fearless leader is testy today," Kerry said, smiling at Teddy. She turned her smile to Matt. "I'd suggest, since we seem to be determined to rush forward single-mindedly on this planet, that you continue the cut on that tree and see if anything happens."

"No," Teddy said quickly. One dead man was enough for her. She didn't have the faintest idea how it had happened, but it had happened when, for the first time, man attacked a major plant form.

"I'll do it," Sandy said. "I'll wear a breather."

"It makes sense, Teddy," Matt said.

Teddy chewed on her lower lip. "All right," she said, "but a full suit, not just a breather."

"All right," Moore said, springing to her feet. He was back within minutes, driving a material transporter with a sealed cab and its own life support system. He parked the transporter where its windscreen would give a good view of the tree, but far enough away so that if and when the tree fell it would not hit the vehicle. The he came waddling toward them with an impulse cutter in his hands.

"I think it would be a good idea for you three to sit in the transporter, sealed up." he said.

From the vehicle, with Teddy squeezed tightly

against Matt and Kerry on the outside, they watched as Moore started the electric motor of the cutter. Matt was operating the transporter's visual recorders. The radio was set to the local talk frequency.

"Are you ready?" Moore asked.

"Ready," Matt said, starting the cameras.

Moore took a wide-legged stance and, with the impulse cutter humming, inserted the blade into the cut made by the dead man. The blade began to sink quickly.

Matt and Teddy were watching Moore. Kerry was looking downriver. "Hey," she said, her voice tense, as she tapped Teddy on the shoulder.

Motion whipped through the thick, meaty leaves of those nearby trees that were in bloom. Erratic puffs of wind seemed to be moving the leaves. Kerry looked upriver, and saw the same motions among the leaves and then, as she tensed, she saw miniature yellow-white clouds rushing toward the tree where Moore's cutter was sinking into the bole. Within second the clouds were raining down on Moore and his suit was covered with pollen. The little clouds continued to speed toward him until, as the pollen accumulated, he was standing in over an inch of the yellow-white grains, and his movement, as he raised a gloved hand to wipe pollen from his faceplate, stirred new clouds.

"Stop, Sandy," Teddy cried.

"I'm almost through," Sandy said.

"So," Kerry said, "trees with a community watch system."

"Sandy, please stop," Terry said. "The trees are trying to protect one of their own."

"They killed one of my men," Sandy said, as the bole of the tree began to make snapping noises and the top began to lean. Then the cutter was within inches of the far side of the bole and the tree began its slow, heavy fall. Sandy stepped back, stopped the cutter, and watched through a faceplate smeared with pollen as the tree crashed down. Limbs shook and then were still.

"It's over," Kerry said. "No more pollen clouds."

The air was clear. There was no motion among the leaves, save for that engendered by a gentle westerly breeze.

"They have consciousness," Teddy said in awe. "They know when one of them is being hurt, and now they know it's dead, or dying."

"You sound like Cassie, giving human attributes and intelligence to animals," Kerry said.

"You saw and yet you doubt that it was a community effort, an intelligent effort?" Teddy asked.

"It can be nothing more than reflexive," Kerry said. "Like the Earthside cactus that throws its spines when something brushes it, like the Venusfly-trap or other insect eating plants that respond reflexively to a stimulus."

"And how is that stimulus transmitted to trees over a hundred yards away?" Matt asked.

"Perhaps by interconnected root systems." Teddy said. "I remind you that we are on an alien planet. And while it may appear on the surface that things are very much as they are on Earth, appearances can be deceiving."

However, the knowledge of one tree's being cut was not transmitted by interconnecting root systems. Sandy Moore, still dressed in his isolation suit, rooted the stump and roots of the tree out with a big earth mover. There were no pollen attacks during the operation. The tree had a large, shallow root system, but close examination and some hand digging showed conclusively that the roots were not connected to nearby trees.

Kerry Hertz asked for and got permission from Teddy to take a crew to an area a good distance from the construction site and run further tests. A suited workman approached a tree with a humming cutter. The cutter had barely touched the bark of the tree when he was covered with pollen. On the second try, the pollen clouds began to blow forcefully against the protective suit even before the cutter touched the tree's bark.

"Trees with a capacity to learn when a new threat comes at one of their members?" Teddy asked, having been an interested spectator. "Let's not damage any more trees, Kerry, at least not until we know more."

"We are not giving pain with our current tests." Kerry said. "I don't think it will be necessary to do any more damage."

"Any ideas about what's happening?" Matt asked.

"Ideas, that's all," Kerry said. "There's something tickling at my mind, but it won't come clear. Let's leave the trees in peace for a while.'

There was no objection to that suggestion, since, from the beginning, the policy had been to do as little damage to Beauty's surface and plant growth as possible. Kerry disappeared into her laboratory-office. Matt and Teddy had other work. The job of making Beauty's seas fruitful was beginning. To prepare the icy waters near the planet's pole for the insertion of life, a newly completed tanker ship arrived, its hull consisting largely of a huge, saltwater tank, that tank teeming with antarctic krill. On its next trip, the tanker ship brought a cargo that seemed to mark a milestone. With planktonic life already naturally plentiful in Beauty's oceans, the next step was to build the food chain of the ocean with plankton eaters, and the variety of life dumped into the seas had been chosen carefully for their prolific breeding habits.

Teddy had quickly discovered that she was out of

her depth. Life had to build on life. Whales could not be introduced until, in the case of the baleen whales, the krill population had reached productive levels, until small fish such as herring, sardines, and capelin were plentiful. It was like trying to build a skyscraper of playing cards. One slip and the whole edifice came down. One species introduced at the wrong time, breeding freely in the absence of natural enemies, could sweep the seas. And the oceans were large, of course. For example, what had appeared to be a massive number of krill dispersed quickly in the cold polar waters and seemed to disappear. The staff of experts at the main facility grew, as Teddy called for help. She began to think that Kerry was right, that there had been insufficient planning for the development of Beauty into an ecosystem that mirrored that of Earth. Staff meetings often became loud debates as the partisans of particular species clashed. And still the great ships lowered thunderously to the surface and disgorged their living cargo.

One of the most successful of the early programs made Cassie Frost a happy woman. Hundreds of monkeys were thriving and breeding, having found the fruit and vegetation of Beauty's jungles to be perfect for them.

Meanwhile, the herds of grass eaters were in the process of doubling. The staff of veterinarians and animal handlers had to be expanded. There was no longer time to supervise the birthing of every young one, and there were the inevitable casualties of birth, requiring the importation of scavengers. Vultures. For the first time in its history, Beauty's skies knew the beat of living wings, and human eyes turned upward to see the great, dark birds lazing along on the thermals rising from the ever more populated plain.

Birds and bugs occupied Teddy's time. The first birds to be approved were fruit eaters released in the jungles. Gallinaceous birds were introduced to the plains, where members of the quail family seemed to adapt most quickly, finding plenty of food among the seeding grasses. Vegetarian waterfowl were released onto the lakes of America. Since most common songbirds were insect eaters, there was still no early morning twittering on Beauty, but her population was growing as, two by two, groups of different animal and bird and marine species made the journey from Earth.

The most frustrated people on Beauty were the staff entomologists. One could only spend so much time studying the spread of the termite colonies in the jungles of Africa. Aside from the termite project, the only other victory scored by the entomologists had been to be allowed to bring in a few thousand earthworms, but their earthworm colony was rigidly contained, with metal barriers below and at the sides of the chosen plot of land, and with a greenhouse atop. It would take time to prove that earthworms did not have some unbalancing effect on soil bacteria and vegetation. Then the entomologists began to campaign for bees. They could do no harm, the bug men said.

"They are not needed," Kerry Hertz said. "Beauty's plants have been pollinating themselves for millions of years."

"We can have no bee-eating birds, then" the entomologists said, "What would it matter if bees assisted the natural pollination?"

"Who knows?" Kerry said, with a shrug. "Conceivably, forced cross-pollination could be harmful to some species."

Kerry knew that she had become known as Beauty's Cassandra, in spite of Cassie's name and reputation. "Give me some time," she told the bug people. "I have been working on a method to study the pollination process."

"How long?" the bug people asked.

"As long as it takes," Kerry said, and Teddy, the arbitrator, upon whose pretty shoulders would fall the blame for any misstep in the terraforming of Beauty, had to take the path of caution and go along with Kerry.

The tickling in her mind that had come to her during the testing of the defense mechanism of the trees along the American river had led Kerry back to her books. She secluded herself in her office and drew on the main computer, scanning hundreds of books over a period of several days. She knew, of course, that the phenomenon of the pollen attacks could not be matched by anything on Earth, so she scanned the botanical literature from the newly colonized planets first. Then, not expecting to get any clue, she went back to basics and reviewed the standard literature from Earth.

Almost by accident, she found some food for thought. A footnote she had at first passed over referring to some odd work done in the middle twentieth century by a non-botanist. The second time she ran across a footnote referring her to the work of one Clive Baxter, however, she checked it out and snorted in derision. Baxter had used an instrument that measured minute electrical currents to "prove" that plants could read human minds, that a plant threatened with fire or with mutilation "fainted." Baxter's fanciful conclusions were something to the effect—she'd lost interest by that time—that plants communicated, or sensed, by some unknown process that could, Baxter maintained, possibly lead to faster-than-light, instantaneous communications using plants as something like a medium.

It was mumbo jumbo and totally unscientific, Kerry thought, but she couldn't get it out of her head. Somehow, someway, the trees along a clear, lovely river on the continent they called America knew when a fellow tree, as far as two hundred yards away, was being damaged or—after a period of learning—threatened. She didn't discuss this plant magic with anyone. Instead, she went ahead with plans already made.

With the help of technicians, she rigged a sensitive electronic screen across the aerial pathway between two flowering shrubs in the highlands inland from the Africa House. She chose shrubs that were just coming into bloom, and that were still rather small, so that the electronic screen could be of a reasonable size. The screen was in place when the flowers first began to open. The screen recorded the passage of objects down to microbe size and, when coupled with a computer to enhance images, would allow identification of all particles that had passed through the screen in a given time.

The botanists had not been idle. Not all of them were as preoccupied as Kerry with the problem of just how pollination was accomplished on an insect-free planet, but enough work had been done to discover that the majority of flowering plants tested were unisexual, thus requiring cross-pollination. A few hermaphrodites had been discovered in the jungle areas, and, of course, cataloging was nowhere near complete. The shrub Kerry was working with proved to be one of those plants that guards against self-pollination by separation in time of the sexes. The stamen of the flowers burst and shed their pollen before the stigma became receptive to fertilization.

Kerry and the technicians spent several days in the highlands, where it was comfortably warm during the day and cool enough for a sleeping bag at night. The flowering shrubs did not shed vast amounts of pollen, like the trees along the American river. Nothing was visible to the naked eye, but the electronic screen recorded minute particles in movement. Vertical and horizontal wind movements were recorded, as well, so that pollen or other particle movement could be matched against air movement.

It seemed illogical to Kerry, and to the other botanists, to think that such a rich and varied plant community could rely on pollination by wind movement only, and yet there was no other visible method. Kerry's tests were to be a first step toward measuring the efficiency of wind pollination.

When Kerry had asked for technicians to operate the electronic equipment, she'd been surprised and pleased when Earl Fabre, the man in charge of the technical section, a big man, six-four, well-built, blond, blunt, and smiling, said he'd like to go along. She'd worked with Earl before, since he'd been the one in charge when the electronic equipment had been installed in Kerry's lab and office, and she liked him as well as she liked any man. She had had her fill of men early on, having experimented, as most young women did, while in college, with the mating dance of the juveniles. As a young girl she had tended to be overweight through self-indulgence and had been on a perpetual dosage of a pill known as ''the fat eater'' since it cut down on the digestive system's ability to utilize caloric intake and caused the body to burn its own fat cells. Potential side effects of the fat eaters made constant usage undesirable, so that at times Kerry ballooned up to twenty pounds overweight and became, in an age of almost universal slimness, what some men thought was cuddly. At such times, with her self-image eroded by the knowledge that she was merely being self-indulgent by overpartaking of rich foods, she was flattered by male attention. So, plump and cuddly, she surrendered her virginity to a medical student when she was a sophomore in college and found the experience to be so interesting that she had an implant and did some more experimentation. Men were fun animals, with such intense urges. When she was slim and rather attractive, a different type of man was drawn to her. One such man convinced her that they should be married. That was when she was in grad school, earning an advanced degree in botany. It only took one year for her to discover that that cute little urge built into most men could be a distraction from her work and the age-old myth of male superiority was not dead, at least not in the mind of her husband. (She rarely thought of him anymore, and when she did it was not by name.)

She had ended the marriage when she went to Valhalla as a very junior member of the botanical survey team. After a couple of tries at the man-woman thing on Valhalla, one with a man who was different, kind, loving, and full of respect for her growing knowledge of things vegetable, she gave it up. The kind, loving, respectful man's wife arrived with the first wave of colonists. In hurt and anger Kerry had her implant removed, vowing to be celibate for the rest of her life. Earl Fabre was to change that status on a sleeping bag in the highlands of Beauty on a clear, starry but moonless night.

Kerry had once laughingly told a female friend on Valhalla that she had revirginated. "The hymen," she said, "is regenerative, don't you know? It's not an unpleasant state of mind. I'm thinking of franchising hymen transplant clinics on all civilized plants. The donors can be young girls about to get married, or those who consciously decide to rid themselves of the maidenly membrane."

Actually, the revirgination of Kerry was mental and not physical. After a few years of abstention she found herself to be perfectly content, and when specialized nerve ending twitched in her dreams she accepted that release as being nature's own and was grateful for it.

Kerry liked Earl Fabre, had liked him from the beginning. She liked smiling men who were married,

as Earl was, and apparently happily, since he was
always seen off duty in the company of Nan Fabre,
a computer specialist. From the beginning of the
highlands expedition, the relationship between Kerry
and Earl was easy and friendly but quite business-
like. She explained to Earl what she wanted to accomplish and Earl did the things necessary to allow
that accomplishment.

During the day, when the screen required one man
to watch it, electronic gadgets being what they were,
and always fallible, Earl alternated with the technician he'd chosen for the trip. Kerry wandered, never
far from camp, collecting species and enjoying
Beauty's highland summer. On occasion, Earl
walked with her; at other times, the technician did.
Earl had a curious mind and he listened and asked
intelligent questions in Kerry's field.

As darkness came, the men lit a fire. The fire made
things quite cozy and was pleasant as the night grew
cooler. Food smelled and tasted great. It was prepared in the cooking facilities of the transporter that
had brought them into the highlands. Earl had dug
out an old-fashioned coffeepot on the first night, ex-
plaining that coffee boiled over an open campfire beat
hell out of prepared coffee, and Kerry had quickly
decided he was right.

Bedtime was early. They were awake with the sun.
The routine was unvaried until, on the morning of
the sixth day, the small electrical generator began to
hiccup. To Kerry's ears the conclusion seemed to be
that the flammus was bytuperating and that, by
Gawd, some idiot had not loaded a spare flammus
and that, damn it, there was nothing to do but order
out a new flammus. The call was made. There was
no ship available at Africa House, but an explorer
was due to pass near their site on a survey run and
could, perhaps, return the part sometime the next
day. That wouldn't do. It was a six hour drive by

transporter. Perhaps the generator would hold until the technician could drive to the facility and return, getting back before midnight. The transporter lumbered away and was soon lost to sight among the scrubby hills.

Kerry went wandering with her specimen bag, returned late in the evening, let Earl, who had been nursing the hiccuping generator, know that she was back, went to the stream near the campsite and bathed. She pulled a camp stool over to where Earl was now seated beside the fire. The generator jerked and sputtered but managed to keep the juice flowing so that the screen was operational. Pollination, surprisingly, did not decrease with the coming of first twilight and then darkness under a sky filled with stars.

"Lots of activity," Earl said. On the monitors blinking dots of light indicated impacting particles.

"It's odd how activity seems to come in clumps," Kerry said, as the monitor lit with a large number of particles passing through the screen.

"A regular orgy," Earl said. "Flowers in a breeding frenzy."

Kerry made no comment.

"Shameful. Such goings on in mixed company." Earl said lazily. "It can never be said that God didn't have a sense of humor."

Kerry, sipping some of Earl's good coffee, feeling tired and a bit lazy, questioned the apparent change of subject. "Ummmm?"

"Birds do it, bees do it." Earl sang.

The late twenty-first century was mired in a sea of nostalgia. Social scientists explained the preoccupation with the minutia of the past as being a subconscious search for stability in a time of immense change, when millions of people were leaving the familiar, if crowded, four corners of old Earth for the unknown. It was as if everyone, especially those who knew of the vast reaches of interstellar space, wanted something of the old, the familiar, to savor. There had been various spin-offs of the nostalgia fad. Schools were producing an oversupply of historians. Specialty manufacturers ran round-the-clock shifts producing reproductions of antique musical instruments such as the saxophone. Male and female fashion styles had been copied from a time before the exploding population of Earth, then with no release available other than famine or war, had reached five billion. Sight and sound laboratories on several planets catered to this preoccupation with the past by searching for musical sounds going back to the beginning of recording technology. Odd, scarcely understood half hour and one hour productions from the television age were processed into a semblance of modern dimensions. Ancient movies were dimensionalized after being resurrected from their historical vaults and were watched avidly in all their flatness and faded color. The music of the past, and particularly one brief era prior to 1950, was the vogue. The publications of Evert's *Slang and Speech Patterns of the Twentieth Century* a decade past had injected Amenglish with what Evert said was the argot of Americans of over one hundred years ago. Novelists studied Evert and the works of mid-twentieth century popular writers and tried to imitate the style.

The song Earl was humming commented on the fact that most living things *did it*.

"The animal with two backs," Earl said.

"The beast with two backs," Kerry said.

"Whatever. Odd, isn't it? And damned ingenious. Sex, a tool of natural selection, gene diversifier, assurance of eonic change. And here we are using some pretty complicated electronic gadgets to spy on the bedroom habits of flowers."

Kerry laughed. "Not all living things make the

beast with two backs. Fish don't couple. Mainly mammals. And birds.''

"Imagine the poor whale," Earl said.

"Umm," Kerry said. It was only idle talk. There was absolutely no sexual innuendo on her part, nor she felt, on Earl's.

"I guess one of the most amazing things is. that sex is present in plants. Wonder how much kick a flower gets when the stamen bursts and expels pollen.''

"It quivers with deep excitement," Kerry said, eyes closed, thinking seriously about taking a nap.

"Really?"

"No, I suppose not."

"But as I understand it, it is a sexual act, the cross-pollination business." Earl said.

"Well, I guess. Maybe a lot of it is the result of our own sexuality, the terms applied, I mean. We call the pollen grain male. It has half the chromosome number found in the parent plant. The moist stigma of the pistil—

"Doctor, you're talking dirty." Earl grinned.

"—is the female reproductive structure. The pollen grain travels down through the pistil into the ovules, within the ovary. See how we've applied human sexual terms? Some plants, such as the primrose, have flowers of both sexes, of different structure, on the same plant."

"Incest," Earl said lazily.

"The plant world gives us the most dramatic proof of the importance of gene diversity. Two distinct results can be shown quite readily from cross-pollination. Cross-pollinated plants produce more vital seeds. In the long run, experiments have shown that the process of natural selection chooses from the pool of mutations created by cross-pollination and selects out the stronger ones."

Earl opened one eye and looked at the screen

monitor. "Well, our subjects are either taking a nap or having an after coital cigarette."

There were only a scattered few impacts of minute particles registered on the screen.

"Lecture over," Kerry said. She leaned back and closed her eyes and suddenly knew the strongest surge of pure physical desire she'd ever experienced. Her eyes flew open. Earl lunged forward in his chair, his eyes wide and startled, but when he turned his head to meet Kerry's eyes they hooded themselves, and become sultry, knowing. Kerry stood. She removed her shorts first, then the rest of her clothing. By the time she had turned and walked away from the fire Earl was also nude. She walked unhurriedly to the pile of sleeping bags and quickly arranged them into a soft, padded mass. She lay down, opened her legs. He came to her and, to her surprise, she was ready. For one wild moment she remembered that she had no implant, but that inhibiting thought warmed into an eerie knowledge of her own reproductive system and she could feel, or sense, or see an egg lodged safely in her left ovary. No impulsive egg cantered down her tubes to rush headlong into union with the sperm which, quite quickly, became hers. That overwhelming desire, a fire she'd never know, exploded.

"My God," Earl yelped, jerking himself away. "What the hell happened?" He wiped his face, seemed to be near weeping. "Kerry, please believe me. I had no intention—no thought—"He was at a loss for words.

Kerry's mind was aswim. She'd done some pretty impulsive things in her life, but never anything so totally consuming, so swift, so unexpected. And then, into her puzzlement, came a thought, and she spoke it aloud. "It's all right. They just wanted to know how it felt."

"What?" Earl asked.

She couldn't say it again, because the knowledge, the surety, was gone. "It's all right," she said. "It won't happen again."

"Kerry, I'm so sorry. I don't know what came over me." Earl said.

"It's not your fault," she said, quite sharply.

Nor could she blame herself, and she certainly couldn't tell him that she thought they'd been influenced by the plants of Beauty. She rose, gathered her scattered clothing, and went to the stream for another bath. Earl followed her and bathed himself around a bend in the stream. When Kerry came back to the camp he was rebuilding the evening fire.

"I think we need to talk about what happened," he said. "I can't explain it, but I wasn't really myself. I'm not trying to come across as a prude or the perfect husband, but I've been married to Nan for twenty years and that's the first time—"

"I don't think either of us were ourselves," Kerry said. "You weren't being untrue to Nan."

"Kerry, we both started peeling off our clothes at the same time. Until that moment I had nothing like that on my mind."

"Neither did I."

"So?"

"You won't laugh at me if I voice a wild theory?" she asked.

"Not a chance."

"It just might be possible that we've encountered our first extraterrestrial intelligence," she said.

Earl looked around. He looked at the low growing bushes, weedlike things, grasses, and some low growing succulents.

"I have not felt desire for a man in years," she said. "And I wasn't feeling desire for you, no offense, but it wasn't for you. It was for all, and none, for something facelesss, for *maleness*. And for a moment I was fully aware of the inner workings of my reproductive system.''

''The plants?'' Earl whispered. ''You said *they* wanted to know how it felt. You think that they have some kind of intelligence?''

''I can't think of any other explanation.'' she said. And in her guess she was both right and wrong.

They were asleep when the technician returned, the sound of the approaching transporter waking them. Earl brewed coffee as the vehicle came nearer. The technician had coffee while Earl changed the flammus on the generator. The machine purred. Two more days of observations gave Kerry enough data. They drove home. It was as if nothing had happened between Kerry and Earl. Indeed, she felt as if the event had not involved her at all. She fed the data from the screen into the computer and began enhancing images and getting a count on pollen grains. The computer eliminated dust grains and motes and gave a count of the three different kinds of pollen grains that had crossed through the screen. The majority of impacts had been the pollen of the flowering bushes that had been the targets of the pollen count. The puzzling thing was that the grains of pollen moved compactly in masses, surges, the invisible grains spreading over an area roughly one foot across and roughly circular. There seemed to be no pattern of timing. Sometimes two surges would pass almost simultaneously. At other times an hour or more would pass before a mass of pollen passed through the screen.

Chapter 14

"I hope that you're not put off by my forwardness," Genna Darden said, as Davis Conroy held her chair and she arranged the sleek, long skirt of her favorite red cocktail gown and took a seat.

"I'd like to be flattered," Conroy said, "but I think I'm mostly curious." He sat across the small table from her and there was only small talk until the wine steward had done his thing, and Conroy had performed the ancient charade of tasting and approval.

Genna had suggested a restaurant away from the Bureau complex. It was a place frequented by the international community, so the only black faces were those of the waiters. Genna selected Australian prawns as her entrée. Conroy shrugged and followed suit. Over salad, Genna began.

"Shardan wants me to come to work for Intel," she said.

Conroy's first thoughts were purely selfish. He would miss the small things, like simply catching sight of Genna now and then in the building. He would miss, most of all, the occasional evenings with her. And he would be sorely tested to find another as capable as she to fill her not unimportant position.

"I think, then," he said, "that your decision is

117

made, else you wouldn't have brought me to neutral ground to tell me."

"I haven't decided," she said.

"Shall I ask you not to go?" he asked.

"It isn't as simple as that, Davis," she said, with a smile. "There would be a small increment in my salary, but that isn't important."

"And I suspect that your reasons for considering Shard's offer are not strictly personal."

"Not at all," she said.

"My chief rival, then, is still a world called Beauty."

She frowned. "With Intel I would have certain advantages. I would have access to influential men whom I cannot reach as an interagency coordinator."

Conroy had hoped that Genna's preoccupation with Reznor's world would fade with the passage of time, that she would recognize that Reznor's coup was complete, and that it did not matter in the long run.

"How long has it been since the exploration ships discovered a habitable planet?" Genna asked. Then, answering her own question, "Over a year. At one time, Davis, you intimated that you would help me, that you would put me into contact with the right people."

"Well, press of business and all," he said.

"With Intelpax I could make my own contacts."

"You're exerting some gentle blackmail, aren't you?"

She smiled. "Is that what it will take?"

The entrées replaced the salads. The prawns were delicious.

"In my opinion, the time is not right," he said. "However, we are to have a visitor, a high-level one. General Igor Milyukov is arriving this week. He will inspect the space facilities, and he will want a tour of at least a part of Africa, I'm sure. I think that such a tour could be conducted by the inter-agency coordinator.''

"Who said blackmail doesn't work?'' Genna said, with a wide smile.

General Igor Milyukov was the archetypal Russian. He had a shock of wiry, dense hair, heavy eyebrows, small, dark eyes. He was a short, burly, hasty man who moved with nervous energy. With a very attractive ice blonde as his guide, he made a whirlwind tour of the Bureau's embarkation facilities, made a speech to a group of African colonists about to board a colonization ship, and invited Genna to dinner. She accepted. At dinner he made two wishes apparent. He wanted to see something of African wildlife and he wanted to create some wild life on his own, preferably with Genna as his partner. She parried the second wish and explained that African wildlife was confined to the game parks behind high fences. The next morning found them aboard a yacht leaping on a ballistic trajectory for South Africa, where the largest concentration of African animals lived behind fences and were fed like zoo inmates, since the small area under fence could not possibly provide natural provender for so many animals.

During the short flight Genna learned why Milyukov was interested in seeing African animals.

"I am an anachronism, my dear,'' the general explained. "I am a man out of my time, a savage at heart, lost in a world where the natural instincts of the human animal have to be suppressed. I should have lived in the time of early man, when a person faced the elements and the more powerful and cunning creatures of nature with nothing more than a crude, stone-tipped spear. At worst, I would have been an African explorer, antique firearm cradled in the crook of my arm, on guard for the rogue elephant, the man-eating lion.''

"You do not find the man-eating politicians to be enough challenge?" Genna asked.

Milyukov roared with laughter. "You have engendered vivid pictures in my mind," he gasped through his laughter. "At the next meeting of the Pax Five Council I can see myself appearing with a rifle in hand, and when, let us say, the delegate from the United States makes one of his speeches I will give him a running start and blast him." He sobered. "No, that would not be sporting, for the chief delegate from the United States is old, and he would not be able to run fast. Nor is he large enough to be potentially dangerous, as, say, a polar bear can be dangerous when encountered in his own icy range."

A delegation of South African officials met the Bureau yacht. Milyukov impatiently endured a state level luncheon, speeches of welcome and solidarity, and kept looking at his watch. A South African general and a representative of the government accompanied the Russian and the interagency coordinator to the state game preserve, a mere few hundred acres packed with animals. The animals were so tame that they tried to approach the vehicle carrying Milyukov and his party to beg for handouts. Well-fed lions, born in captivity and thoroughly acclimated to humans, watched their passage lazily. The park's small herd of elephants were congregated in the sparse shade of some bedraggled trees whose foliage had been denuded to the height that could be reached by elephant and giraffe. The big beasts switched tails and trunks slowly, although there were no insects in the park to bedevil them.

Thinking, perhaps, that it would be a special treat for the distinguished visitor, the park curator, who was driving the vehicle, halted it, handed Milyukov a bag of peanuts, and the second most powerful man in the Soviet Union held out small nuts and spoke Russian coaxingly, and then fed a cow elephant and

her calf from his hand. To her surprise, Genna saw
the Russian reach up surreptitiously to wipe tears
from his eyes. She thought, at the time, that Milyukov was merely displaying a Russian characteris-
tic, an emotional appreciation for beauty, for there
was majesty about those great, gray beasts. Or, perhaps, she felt, he was mourning the passage of such
majestic animals in the wild.

It was not until Milyukov had managed to shed
the South African delegation and had rather easily
convinced Genna that an overnight stop at the five
star hotel at Victoria Falls would be interesting and
restful, not until Genna, with some interest—she'd
never bedded a Russian general—had granted Milyukov's second wish for his African stay, that she
was told the real reason why Milyukov's eyes had
misted while feeding peanuts to a mama elephant
and her calf.

Russian generals, she had found, were not at all
different from other men—if a bit more appreciative
and demonstrative. Milyukov, the man, was different.

"Do you know why I decided to come here with
you?" she asked, as they enjoyed a cigarette.

"I would be interested to know," Milyukov said.

"Because you shed tears over the elephants," she
said. "That showed me a warmth, and I like a man
with warmth, a man who, in spite of his position,
and his evident manliness, can become emotional
over beauty, or an idea."

Milyukov looked at her, his bushy eyebrows
raised. "It was not beauty. It was not the plight of
the elephant. I am sorry to disillusion you, my dear,
but my tears were tears of pure frustration and self-
ishness."

"Oh?"

"I was mourning the fact that I, Igor Alisandro-
vitch Milyukov, would never see an elephant as some

men have seen him, sighting down the barrel of an elephant gun.''

''Really?'' she asked.

''Alas,'' he said, spreading his hands and grinning wryly. ''I told you previously that I am a throwback. My tears were because I will never know the gut-wrenching fear, the thrill of standing with my feet planted carefully, with my rifle raised, and with a trumpeting bull elephant charging down upon me. I will never know the test that was met by the first white men in Africa, when they faced a charging lion with nothing more than their courage and a primitive rifle, knowing that their lives depended upon their aim and their reflexes and their courage to stand fast.''

''I'm not sure I understand,'' Genna said.

''Most women didn't. Oh, a few did. There were female big game hunters in the golden age, who bagged all the trophy heads, elephant, lion, buffalo, rhino.'' He put out his cigarette and squeezed his eyes closed. ''How glorious! How wonderful it was.'' He looked at her again. ''I know, you see, for I have faced an animal in the wild, an animal capable, quite capable, of killing me if I missed him. I was able to do it because of my position. I went to the frozen wastes of the Russian arctic. I stalked and was stalked by a great polar bear. I faced him, with the wind howling, with flying snow causing my eyes to tear, with the cold biting through my clothing and with ice freezing on my eyelashes.'' He seemed to be more intensely alive than before. ''Some would say that I had the advantage, that I had in my hands a weapon that could kill from a distance. But, you see, I went to the bear's own ground, and I stalked him on foot, alone. He circled back on me and came at me from the rear, having lain in ambush for me, invisible among the snow hummocks. He was almost upon me, moving at speed, when I turned. The vulnerable target areas of his body were not accessible in his head-on charge. I was not using a modern rifle, with a high-impact projectile that kills from striking force alone. I was using a gun from my collection, a very old one, such as was used by those men of the golden age when they had no choice but to face the animals of Africa and carve out a place for themselves. I shot first when the bear was no more than fifty feet away, and I hit him, but not in a vital spot. He only became more dangerous. My second shot, for his heart, was fired from a distance of no more than thirty feet and he went down, but with a bullet in his heart he came at me again and when he died, at last, his great claws were no more than five feet from my toes.''

Genna felt a bit sick. "I thought polar bears were protected.''

The general laughed. "So they are, but they are wild things, perhaps the very last of the wild things, and if facilities in the far north are threatened, if a bear attacks a man—''

"I have hunted grouse,'' Milyukov said, "and that is a rewarding pastime. The grouse makes good eating, he is swift of wing and a difficult target, but I have lived, truly lived, only once, and that was when I was alone on ice and it was just Milyukov against the bear.''

The only thing Genna had ever seen killed violently had been a dog which had wandered onto a high-speed expressway. She was trying to understand Milyukov's obsession with killing living things, and then she realized that she did not have to understand. Suddenly, a glimmering of an idea began to come to her.

"So, my dear general, you can imagine yourself facing the charge of a lion or an elephant?''

"With intense longing,'' he said.

"And what would it mean to you to be able to

live your dream?'' she asked, running her fingers through the thick, graying hair of his chest.

"Any price,'' he said. He laughed. "Even my honor would not be safe in the face of such an opportunity. But we talk the impossible, for there is no place left on Earth where the large game animals roam freely in their natural state.''

No, Genna was thinking, *no place on Earth.*

So it was an odd personality quirk of a Russian general that was the final ingredient to Genna's decision to leave the Bureau of Colonization and move into a small, highly secure office at the home base of Intelpax in Paris. Intel was one of the very few Pax Five agencies that had not been dispersed into an undeveloped area. Shardan, pleased with her decision, told her to take as much time as possible to acclimate herself and to gradually learn the workings of the agency.

"Our interagency coordinator will be due for retirement in two years,'' Shardan told her over lunch on her first day in Paris. "Would that position interest you?''

Genna considered it. In the coordinator's job she would be working, essentially, with the same people with whom she'd come into contact in her job at the Bureau.

"That would seem to be nothing more than a horizontal move,'' she said.

"Well, a decision is not necessary now,'' Shardan said. "Take some time.''

"Shard,'' she said, "I would like to work in the off-Earth intelligence branch.''

"Ah, the lady thinks that we are still glamorous spies here at Intel,'' Shard said, smiling.

"I am not accustomed to being a butt of amusement,'' Genna said icily.

"A pleasantry,'' Shard said smilingly, but her tone had raised his hackles, making him wonder if he'd been wise in placing personal considerations, his weakness for the silk-smooth body of this Icelandic woman, above the usual policy for acquiring additional personnel.

"I'm very serious," Genna said soothingly, wise enough to know that she'd been unwise in using that tone of voice with Shardan. "Humor me?"

"I would guess," Shardan said, "that the intelligence you seek most concerns a certain planet far from the zone of settlement?"

Genna smiled and lifted her glass.

Within a few weeks, Shardan no longer had doubts. In his bed, Genna was Genna, and spectacular. At work she had proven to be an organizer of extraordinary talent. In a few short weeks she had spotted areas of inefficiency in the gathering and compilation of off-world intelligence and had devised a computerized system of interrelating items from different worlds to, often, present a picture of commercial or political activity that would not have been apparent for months, or perhaps years, under the old system.

Shardan made it a policy not to talk shop during his nights with Genna, and that seemed to suit her. Her office was not in the same building as Shardan's, so she did not see the agency head too often. When her secretary announced that the chief was waiting in the reception area she leaped to her feet and threw open the door and said, "Please come in, Mr. Shardan."

He paced toward her, a tigerish man, his face expressionless until the door closed behind them and he winked at her. "Miss Darden, I happened to be in the building and decided to stop in and congratulate you on the system which you've devised for the correlation of off-world intelligence." His formal tone was belied by his proximity to her and his lips touching her smooth neck. Then he stepped away and took a chair.

"Thank you, sir," Genna said. "In fact, I'm pleased that you have come, for I was preparing to ask for an appointment with you."

"I have a few minutes," Shardan said. His expression did not change when Genna pushed buttons that activated a privacy screen that was the state of the art. With the screen active, no known intelligence gathering method could penetrate it.

"You once put a ship past Beauty's eyes and ears," Genna said. "The pilot's name was Jake Jordan, a mercenary. He transed into atmosphere without being detected."

Shardan's eyes narrowed. "You realize that you've just turned Intel upside down, don't you? That information was for my eyes only. I will have to ask you how you came by it."

"Oh, not from Intel," she said. "Your personal files are inviolate. If you're interested, I can show you how I know that, for I did try to penetrate them."

"Then where did you get your information?" Shard asked.

"From a diamond smuggler out past Valhalla," she said. "Remember that my field is off-planet intelligence."

"I remember," he said grimly. "Then it was Jordan who talked?"

"Of course. He's a pilot. He performed a feat that isn't often done. How could he not brag about it?"

"The son of a bitch will never have another assignment from Intel, or any government agency," Shard said.

"Shard," she said softly, "please don't make that a hard and fast decision just yet."

Her use of his familiar name told him that she was finally going to call in his obligation to her. Whatever she had in mind was so important to her that she was going to claim the marker he'd extended to her in his eagerness to have her more accessible.

"There is a small herd of elephants in the wild on Beauty," Genna said. "They have adapted quite readily. They are under observation, of course, but they are not in daily contact with man, as are, for example, the elephants in Earth's game parks. They have already begun to revert, and now they flee when they are approached. There is one very interesting record of a female with calf making threatening movements against a survey party. Such movements have not been seen in an elephant since the last wild herds were gathered into the game parks."

"Elephants?" Shardan asked. *And bedamned Beauty.*

"I would like to have Jake Jordan put a man on Beauty's surface," Genna said. She was smiling, but she tensed, waiting for Shardan's reply.

"That's a big order."

"I know, but it's important."

"To whom?" Shardan asked.

"To me, and to millions of people who could lead a rich and rewarding life on a planet that is now being wasted on a few animals," she said.

"I see." He didn't, really. He knew more about this blonde woman than about most other human beings, but he still could not quite understand her preoccupation with Reznor's zoo world. But then, in his study of history, he had never been able to understand several things: why well educated Jews helped establish communism in Russia only to fall among its first victims; why wealthy men in America had almost reduced that nation to socialism, when under true socialism they would have been deprived of the most; why, at various stages in history, otherwise intelligent people had given their lives in various causes that had made so little difference in the big picture.

Shardan sometimes felt there was a fatal flaw in the human animal, a defect he thought of as the "god complex." Throughout history there had been men and women who wept over the plight of the "pee-pul," the masses. Their sincere concern made it possible for the purely power hungry to continually reverse the order of things, to replace one minority, a power elite, with another minority, a new and of-ten temporary power elite. Nothing else was changed, except for those who buried their dead as a result of falling under the sway of those seeking to upset the power basket once more. To see the flaw so powerfully at work in this thoroughly delectable woman made Shardan just a bit uneasy.

"Who appointed you as the protector of the peo-ple?" he asked.

"What?" She looked puzzled.

"Never mind," he said, but he could not resist one more statement. "Genna, the most cruel and damaging thing you can do to a man is to do for him permanently that which he is perfectly capable of doing for himself."

She looked at him as if he were drunk. She would, he knew, never understand the meaning of his state-ment. He had made a trade with her, and he could not back out of their deal. He, himself, had no great stake in it, for although he didn't mind Reznor's an-imals having a place of their own, he wasn't the sort to bleed over the extinction of a species of animals when, in Earth's history, millions of species had be-come extinct. If man chose to exterminate the mos-quito and, as a result, mosquito-eating birds and insects disappeared as well, what single human be-ing suffered or was deprived of anything more than freedom from the itch and potential infection of a mosquito bite?

"Can it be done?" Genna asked. "Can Jordan put a man on Beauty's surface, leave him there for, oh, perhaps an hour or two, and then get him off and away?"

"You must know more about the situation on Beauty than I," Shardan said, "since you've compiled quite a file on the planet."

"I know the methods of surface patrol," she said. "I know that the space alert system is quite good."

"Then you can answer that question better than I," he said. "Can a man be landed without detection if a ship transes past the space eyes?"

"Yes," she said.

He shrugged.

"Perhaps it would be best," she said, "if the file on this operation is not released from your personal files."

"I'm beginning to think that I don't even want it there," he said.

"Oh, no," she said quickly. "I will have your permission. I will not be left hanging out in the cold to be chopped off in the event something goes wrong."

Shardan leaned forward. There was more to this than just putting a man, any man, on Beauty's surface. "Who?" he asked.

"A member of the Presidium of the Soviet Union," she said.

"Damn," Shardan said.

"He will, of course, indemnify us," she said.

"Igor Milyukov," Shardan said. "That mad son of a bitch. You're going to put Milyukov on the surface and let him shoot an elephant."

"You impress me, as always," Genna said sincerely, wondering if he knew about the night she'd spent with Milyukov in Africa.

"And then you'll have the second most powerful

man in the Soviet Union tucked into your lacy bra,''
Shardan said. "One down and four to go.''

"Three," she said, "for if I have four of the Pax
Five insisting that Beauty be opened for colonization
the United States will have to agree.'' She leaned
across the desk, handed him a folder. "Here is the
authorization and specifics.''

Shardan read quickly and closed the folder. "Jordan is the weak link. He has already proven that he
can't keep his mouth shut.''

"The payments to Jordan will be extended for a
period of ten years," she said. "If, during that time,
he talks about his second flight to Beauty the payments will be stopped. With a man like Jordan that
is a more potent incentive to be silent than force,
threats, or his honor.''

"Ummmm," Shardan said. "But would the good
general keep his pledge to neglect to mention you or
Intel if he is caught?''

"If you would care to read my file on General
Milyukov I think you will understand that he is what
he, himself, considers himself to be, a magnificent
throwback to simpler times, when a man's manhood
was measured in different ways. He would have been
in his element as a knight in armor, protecting his
honor fiercely, or dying to protect the honor of a
lady.''

"He is known as a man who keeps his word, and,
because of him, the word of his country is kept, in
spite of quite a different tendency in the Premier,''
Shardan said. He sighed "My beauty, I wish you
would forget Beauty with a capital B.'' He raised his
hand when she started to protest. "But since I know
you won't, consider this—'' he signed the authorization ''—a very large down payment on my bargain
with you.''

"Thank you," she said.

"Seems a shame," Shardan said, pausing on the

way to the door. "Have you ever seen any of the
old documentaries where elephants, when one of
their members is shot, try to lift the stricken beast
to its feet?"

"It is only one animal," Genna said. "I am thinking of millions of human beings."

"For the maximum benefit of the most people,"
Shardan said, closing the door behind him as he left,
wishing, but not too passionately, that he could have
been around to throttle the man who had first conceived that thought.

He couldn't get the old pictures out of his mind,
however, as he walked down the corridor to the lift.
Big, gray beasts minding their own business. The
sharp bark of a rifle, and that chilling moment when
something as big and vital as an elephant went suddenly limp and dropped so heavily that dust puffed
up around the thing that had lived but was now nothing more than a useless heap of flesh, skin, and
bones. He imagined the small herd that had been
released on Beauty, and for a few moments as the
lift dropped quickly, regretted giving in to Genna.
But, hell, it was only one animal. How many billions of animals had man killed? Trillions? How
many trillions had he eaten—fat, stupid cows, swine
whose original DNA had been altered over the centuries to produce bacon with just a smidgen of fat,
hams that baked deliciously. Living animals. Living
men. In the cosmic scheme of things what was the
importance of a living man or a dead animal? Animals weren't the only thing man had killed. How
many billions of men, women, and children had
died, slain by others of their kind?

Elephants. Ugly beasts. A dead end of evolution.
Creatures of the past as surely as their ancestors, the
mammoths, were creatures of an even more distant
past. Had man lost anything by the extinction of the
mammoth? What if man were still ass-deep in saber-

toothed tigers? Things changed, and whether for the better or worse only God knew.

But still, it was a pretty picture to imagine an Africanlike landscape, elephant country, and to see the great, gray beasts lumbering slowly through a land not plowed or coveted for the plow by men.

In his office he called up the images that had been released to American broadcasters just recently by Reznor Enterprises. He saw green plains dotted with grazing animals, a picture from Africa's past. He saw a half-dozen odd looking monkeys leaping from branch to branch in a virgin jungle. He saw a cow elephant make a stand, charge forward a few steps, trunk raised and trumpeting a warning, and listened as an eager narrator rhapsodized over this first instance of the return of natural elephant behavior in the wild, a mother protecting her young, a formerly tame elephant relearning the natural ways of her kind.

What he did not see, for people like Kerry Hertz were still puzzling over it on Beauty, were the pictures taken not long after the release of the herd of a dozen elephants, nine females, a virile bull, and two juveniles. Those pictures would have interested him, although he would not have shared Kerry's absorption in them, for he would not have had Kerry's knowledge of events along a certain river and another event in the highlands.

He would first have seen an elephant tearing at tender foliage. Elephants are messy eaters and not at all concerned about the damage they can do to smaller trees as they uproot them in order to get at the leaves. Since he had trained himself to be a good observer, he would have noted that something seemed to be in bloom in every picture from Beauty. He would have seen a small, dusty cloud form around the head of an elephant tearing at low growing foliage, the annoyance of the elephant, the shaking of head and the flapping of ears, the small clouds of dust expelled forcefully from the elephant's trunk, and he would have wondered where the cloud of dust came from. He would have wondered, too, why after several individual incidents in which dust clouds seemed to form spontaneously around feeding elephants the phenomenon had ceased, and, surprisingly, the feeding habits of the elephants had changed drastically.

Chapter 15

On the second anniversary of the discovery of Beauty
Andrew Reznor threw a party to honor those intrepid
explorers, Matt and Teddy Tinker. There were other
distinguished guests. Andy and Denise Reznor had
flown in from Earth, bringing with them the distinguished Senator from Massachusetts, the honorable
Gravner Smith, known to most as Gravel Smith.
Smith was the most powerful and, therefore, the most
expensive jewel in the Reznor collection of gems
from the two Houses of Congress.

Teddy didn't mind playing hostess to Reznor's son
and his wife, or even to the senator—after she very
quickly let the distinguished gentleman know that
her hospitality did not extend to having her anatomy
pawed. Teddy's doubts, from the time the excursion
from Earth was approved, had been centered on another person, a man with a face that was familiar to
anyone who ever watched the transed news programs
from distant Earth.

"Sir," Teddy had told Andrew Reznor, when
Reznor had called her to his office to get her opinion
on a request from his son, Andy, to be allowed to
bring the newsman to Beauty for an in-depth look at
the project, "I don't think we're quite ready for this.
If we could limit the cameras to point only at the
plains where you can see the wildlife because the

herds stick together, it wouldn't be so bad. But what the cameras are going to see, mostly, is empty country, fertile, often beautiful country, with no animals in evidence.''

''You're thinking of a few malcontents who say that we're depriving humanity of a fine world,'' Reznor said. ''Wouldn't this be a good way to counter that talk? I think most people are fair, Teddy. I think we can present a good case for our world of animals.''

So, in spite of Teddy's misgivings, Peter Golding, with a camera and his writing crew, landed on Beauty with Andy Reznor's party. The small but complex cameras that could capture sound at great distances and images in three dimensions were unobtrusively present at the party and Golding interviewed both of the explorers. Other than that, it was like most other formal dinners, with Reznor making a short speech, praising his son as the man who would be around to see Beauty reach the goal of being as much like pre-man Earth as possible.

It fell to Teddy to be the guide and hostess for Peter Golding and his crew. On the morning after the party she drafted Matt to assist her and together they loaded the news crew into a transporter and headed for the plains. The cameramen took some shots of the Africanlike landscape and Golding winged it, describing the scenes as the transporter approached the herds. The voice tracks for any material used could be, if necessary, redubbed with carefully written material.

Golding was a small, elegant man with a handsome, regular face that shouted friendship. His pieces, usually gathered in the field, were the featured bits on one of Earth's most watched evening news programs. The program originated in the United States and was broadcast worldwide. Every English speaking person in the world had seen Peter

Golding's face at one time or another, and many non-English speakers had as well, for Golding's better pieces were picked up, with the proper dubbing in the proper language, by broadcasters in countries ranging in development from advanced Japan to struggling, tiny nations in the nonindustrial areas. Only recently Golding had discovered that one of his most interesting fans had a private office in the Intel complex in Paris.

"What's going on over there?" Golding asked Matt, as the transporter approached the herd.

Matt recognized the vehicle used by Jack Frost. "The animal scientists are always running tests," he said.

"You might be interested in talking with our number one animal man," Teddy said.

"Sure, why not," Golding said.

Golding was impressed. He had had no idea that this new world already contained such a variety of grass eating animals, and their sheer numbers gave him hope that, after all, he might go home with some usable footage. He had begun to think that he'd allowed himself to be talked into a pointless trip. He had explained to that pretty little fan of his in Intel that he could not manufacture villains if no villains existed. The days when the so-called media functioned as a sort of fourth arm of government through their power to slant the news and influence the always fickle masses had ended with the constitutional crisis at the end of the millennium when newspapers and broadcasters had faced the unthinkable—government control—and had escaped that fate by the narrowest of margins. The masses were still fickle, but if a newsman got carried away with his own voice and his handsome face on the screen and began to insert what the review board, a panel appointed by the media, itself, felt to be editorial comments, he'd find himself before the board and in danger of a rather hefty fine.

He'd told Genna Darden that he had no objections to saving what was left of the world's animals, that he felt there would be ample space for those people who wanted to leave Earth. He still was of the same opinion, for he'd found no villains, only a few idealists. It did rankle him a bit, in all honesty, to realize that he, whose face was known everywhere, whose voice reached a couple of billion people each weeknight, would never own a private space yacht like the one he'd traveled on to Beauty. Even if he lived to be four hundred, and that was not likely, he'd never have a fraction of the wealth which had been accumulated by the old man. Most of the time he was realistic enough to understand that there was a financial difference between himself and men like Andrew Reznor because he had not done what men like Reznor had done to relieve himself of dependence on his salary and his sometimes unwise investments.

One thing had never changed in the broadcast industry, the fact that it attracted people with bloated egos and low self-image, the difference between ego and self-image also being a measure of the success of men like Andrew Reznor. Golding had his ego. He had his lack of self-image, although it would have taken years of consultation with the right sort of behaviorist to get him to admit that he operated from ego and not from self-worth.

So, although Golding would not have set out to deliberately give a slanted picture of what was happening on Beauty, lest he be called before the board, be sued by the powerful Reznor interests, or just present a boring segment, he was subconsciously searching. People like people who like them, and if the person who is liked happens to think the liker is probably the most sensuous woman he's ever known, he's going to be searching for a way to please that sensuous woman.

Golding's conscious mind recognized that the Reznors were doing something worthwhile, quite admirable, in fact. He'd had long talks with Andy Reznor on the way out and although Junior didn't jump up and down with joy at the mention of his father's pet project, he could present a logical explanation of his father's aims. The old man was something else, healthy and active as he aged past the century mark, willing to spend billions of his well earned assets on a project that would never return even a fraction of what he'd spent. And a man who would spend billions to give a home and a new chance at life to something as large as an elephant and something as cute and appealing as a chipmunk—some of the latter had taken up residence near Africa House and were quite tame and frisky—could not be all bad.

Golding liked Matt Tinker and his dynamic wife, too. Tinker made sense when he explained, in an obvious attempt to counter a few scattered criticisms back on Earth, that it would not be economically feasible to develop Beauty as a colonial world. After all, she was too far off the beaten track, too far outside of that fan-shaped area of interstellar space that included the colony worlds.

Golding remembered three nights in Paris, and he could see Genna Darden's face, and other physical aspects of that Icelandic wonder, as if looking at a big screen. Because of his vivid memories, he tried a few lead-ins for size, voicing them in his mind.

"This is Beauty, a world ideal for human colonization, a world that is to be devoted exclusively to animals."

And the board would say, "What is your source for the statement that the planet is ideally suited for humans?"

"The source is me, through my observations."

"You are not a source. You are a newsman. You do not originate news, you report news," the board would say.

The fine would be large. He'd receive a little note from the Board saying, "Provisions have been made for authorized persons representing the major news media to voice opinions in editorial form. The body of a news program is not the proper forum for editorial opinion of any kind."

"Just the facts, ma'am," Golding said, as Teddy Tinker steered the transporter toward another vehicle. There was activity around the vehicle and as the distance narrowed, Golding saw a lion.

"Get that," he said to his number one cameraman. "What the hell?" he asked Teddy. "I didn't think you were bringing in the big cats for a while?"

Teddy laughed. She, too, had been startled at first. "Take another look," she said, as the lion stood on its hind legs and turned to face them as the transporter came to a stop near Jack Frost's rolling veterinary lab. Jack's face, glasses askew, emerged from under a lion's skin.

"Hey, just in time," he said, as Peter Golding dismounted and moved aside so that his cameramen could record pictures of a man with a lion's skin draped over him. "We're just about to begin to educate the herds to some facts they'll have to face in the near future."

Teddy made introductions. Cassie Frost looked at Golding and his busy crew with disapproval. To her husband she whispered, "Jack, maybe we'd better postpone for now."

He winked at her. "It'll make a good story for Peter."

Cassie's simian eyes went blank. True, Jack had met Peter Golding at the party, had said hello and exchanged a handshake. That didn't make Jack familiar enough with the famous newsman to blithely call him by his first name as if he were an old friend.

Golding listened with interest as Frost explained. "Pretty soon now we'll be bringing out the lesser carnivores. Then the big cats. These animals have never seen a carnivore. They've never been hunted, with the object being to invite them to dinner as the main course for a lion, for example. They'll have no fear. So it's up to us to teach them that something big and toothy coming toward them is the occasion for getting the hell out of there."

"So you're about ready to introduce the serpent into Eden?" Golding asked.

For once, Jack didn't interrupt Cassie. "A one-dimensional biosphere would not be worth the effort, Mr. Golding. It is the nature of life to change, and without challenge there is no change."

"I imagine those little antelope out there would question the desirability of challenge in the form of something with teeth that was intent on eating them," Golding said.

Jack was intent on getting a good fit with the lion skin.

"Mr. Golding, we're not here just to make a zoo display," Cassie said. "There is a serious purpose underlying our efforts. If you divided the millions of years during which animal life has been in existence on Earth and distributed the eons proportionately on the face of a clock, the time of man on Earth would be indicated in red, for danger—at least to all the other life forms—in the last minute of the clock face. We're the first species ever to be plentiful enough or powerful enough to upset the natural order. Here on Beauty we're going to restore the natural order, minus man, and in the thousands of years ahead those who come after us will be able to see what would have happened on Earth without man's meddling."

"That's truly a long-term view," Golding said.

He was thinking that what would happen to a bunch
of animals a few thousand years down the road
wouldn't have much impact on a subsistence farmer
in India who dreamed of having his own fertile farm
on a new planet.

"I think I've about got the hang of this thing,"
Jack said, down on all fours, the lion skin covering
him. "I'm going to give it a try."

A cameraman looked questioningly at Golding,
who shrugged and nodded. Frost went slinking away
from the vehicles, looking very leonine. A browsing
group of zebras ignored him until he activated an
amplifier placed in the head cavity of the lion skin
and the grunting, chilling roar of a lion reverberated
over the plain. That got the zebra's attention. A little
stallion flicked his ears at the lion and snorted. Females lifted their heads and poised themselves for
flight. A new mother zebra nuzzled her colt and ran
a few steps, but the colt stood fast, eyeing the approaching shape with interest. The roar came again
and the little colt trembled, but he'd been chosen for
blood tests just a couple of days before and had been
fed a couple of sugar cubes by Jack Frost to ease his
tension about being pricked with a needle. He
scented the source of those sugar cubes, along with
a dry, stale odor coming from the lion skin. He trotted, a bit unsteadily, toward the familiar scent.

"I don't think it's working," Golding said with a
chuckle as the tiny colt trotted happily toward something that was, in nature, a deadly threat.

The chilling sound of an adult lion's roar came
again. The colt halted, snorted back at the sound,
but the memory of sugar was still strong, he'd never
faced danger, and he trotted once again toward Jack,
now crouched under the lion skin as if ready to
charge.

"Well, back to the old drawing board," Cassie
said, just as, with an amplified roar, Jack the lion

charged, leaped upon the zebra colt and bore it, bleating with panic, to the ground.

"Isn't he being a little too realistic?" Golding asked, noting that now two cameras were running.

Lion skin clad man and snorting, squealing zebra colt rolled on the ground.

"What the hell is he doing?" Matt asked. Teddy spread her hands. Matt ran toward the animated tangle of skin and legs, both human and animal. Jack had pinned the colt under him and, as Matt arrived on the run he was making growling sounds in his throat, not nearly as impressive as the recorded lion's roar but more chilling, because, as he made that growling sound he was trying to bite through the colt's exposed neck with short, human teeth not designed for such a purpose.

"Jack, damnit," Matt said, skipping among the flying little zebra hooves to grab Jack. He got a handful of lion skin and the skin came away and the zebra was still squalling in panic as Jack gnawed, a thickness of tough, loose skin in his mouth. Matt got a zebra hoof on his knee as he tossed the lion skin aside and went for Jack again. This time he seized Jack's arm and pulled. He heard Jack's growling turn into something like male sobs and Jack, pulled free of the zebra, whirled. Matt looked into staring, piercing eyes and a face of animal frenzy. The zebra colt, freed and unhurt, leaped to its wobbly legs and stilted after its mother.

"Jack?" Matt asked. "Stop it, Jack."

Jack had been crawling toward him as he backed away. Suddenly the fierceness faded from Jack's eyes and he looked around, puzzled, then he turned back to Matt.

"We had to know," Jack said.

"Damnit, Jack, what kind of stunt is this, and in front of that bastard's cameras?"

"We had to know why," Jack said, and then he

looked around again. ''Matt, did I do what I think I just did?''

''I don't know what you thought you just did, but you damned sure did something stupid,'' Matt said.

''I don't—'' Jack paused. ''Something's going on here.''

''Yes, I know. Peter Golding's cameras have just recorded a respected scientist trying to eat a baby zebra alive.''

''I'll cover that with Golding,'' Jack said, dusting his clothing. ''Then we've got to talk. We've got to get everyone together and have a talk.''

Matt didn't know exactly how Jack planned to ''cover'' his actions with the newsman, but he didn't have any ideas so he let Jack do the talking. ''The little rascal had to be taught a lesson,'' Jack said to Golding, grinning, straightening his glasses. ''He had no conception of danger, no idea of what a lion could do to him. He's the new generation. He's also weak, and if there were real lions around he'd be a natural target, and not only for lions but for lesser animals like hyenas or jackals. A pack of Cape hunting dogs would have him for a meal very quickly.''

''So you were trying to bite his neck for his own good?'' Golding asked.

''Exactly,'' Frost said. He wanted to put his finger into his mouth because he was afraid he'd broken a tooth. And he wanted to be alone with Cassie, to tell her what had happened.

''Okay, folks,'' Teddy said brightly. ''It's elephant time.''

It took a few minutes to pull Golding away from Jack Frost, and the more Jack talked the less logical his attack on the zebra colt seemed. Teddy didn't like the amount of interest the incident had aroused in Golding, and she could imagine the evening news going out to a couple of billion people showing a man who was supposed to be an animal lover trying to kill a baby zebra with his bare teeth.

Jack watched the transporter leave. Cassie was off in that peculiar little world of hers, eyes glazed. He brought her back with his hand on her arm. "Cassie, I was watching that little beggar and laughing at him because he was so damned cute, and so curious. I had no intention of jumping on him. It just came over me. Suddenly I *was* a lion. I could smell that little animal, his warm, red blood, his tender flesh. I could taste the red, juicy meat. And I felt that I was not alone."

"I don't understand," Cassie said.

"I was multiple. I was *we*. And *we* had to know why the I of me, the lion, wanted to sink teeth into that little zebra's neck."

Jack opened his mouth and fished around in it with a thumb and forefinger. "And I broke a damned tooth."

"I'm afraid, dear," Cassie said, "that you're pretty much of a bust as a lion."

"Not too impressive, huh?" Jack asked, with a grin.

"With a small animal, you should go for the top of the neck," Cassie said, "not the throat. You break the animal's neck, you see."

"Cassie—"

She looked at him, her warm, huge eyes concerned. "Put it all on tape while it's fresh on your mind, how you felt, everything you've told me and more."

Meanwhile, Teddy and Matt had transferred Golding and his crew to Andy Reznor's yacht. It would have taken hours to reach the margin of the plains, where rolling foothills began to show ever more densely packed trees, shrubs, and bamboolike thickets along the watercourses. They spotted the elephant herd easily, having followed the progress of their feeding by uprooted small trees and broken limbs. The herd was in dense cover, using their trunks to pull down a variety of spindly, tall trees in order to strip succulent leaves. The yacht was brought to hover. At first, Teddy was watching Golding's reaction. He didn't seem too interested.

"Can we approach them on the ground?" Golding asked.

"Yes," Teddy said.

The yacht landed beside a nice stream. Elephant tracks and droppings showed that the stream was being used as a watering place by the herd.

"Are we in any danger?" Golding's number one cameraman asked.

"Not really," Matt said. "Not unless we get too close. There's a female with a calf and she's quite protective of it. She's accustomed to men, but I wouldn't want to get too near the calf."

They looked down on the herd from a little rise, their view partially blocked by growth. The sound of snapping limbs came as the elephants continued to feed. Messy eaters, Teddy thought, and quite destructive. At first the plants of Beauty had tried to defend against the elephants' stripping of foliage, but they had, apparently, given up. The elephants were definitely feeding. As always, there were blooms about to provide pollen for the defense mechanism, whatever it was, but no clouds of pollen gathered around the feeding beasts' heads.

But something was different. She'd seen the devastation of which an elephant was capable. Their progress through dense country could be traced by the broken limbs, the uprooted small trees, the stripped foliage. The area where they were feeding now didn't look devastated at all. She picked out an individual, the female with calf, and watched as she looped her trunk around a small sapling and began to strip tender bark. She took only a few bites and released the sapling. The bark had been stripped away on only one side of the sapling. Then the elephant moved to another small tree and repeated the process. The other animals seemed to be eating with equal care. When a plant or a small tree got in the way, they did not simply trample it or uproot it. They moved around it to get to the tasty ones.

"Well, you've seen one elephant you've seen them all," Golding said, motioning to his cameramen to cut it off.

The next day, Golding's crew recorded the antics of some of Cassie's monkeys, a growing termite colony in the jungle, a few brightly colored, fruit-eating birds, an anteater gorged with termites, and the friendly chipmunks near Africa House. Toward evening, Andy Reznor's yacht lifted off and Beauty belonged, once again, to those who loved her. The *Ark* landed with a new load, with new species of small animals to be distributed on two continents. Jack Frost, as Director, called a conference of specific people. Kerry Hertz made a quick trip to the foothills to confirm Teddy's impression that something had changed the feeding habits of the elephants.

Chapter 16

"I want you all to hear a tape I made the other day, immediately after the lion incident," Jack Frost said. He waited for the expected chuckles and got a couple. He pushed a button and his amplified voice filled the conference room, which was not very full of people, those present being Matt and Teddy Tinker, Cassie, Kerry Hertz, Sandy Moore and Earl Fabre. They were the department heads. Jack and Cassie had decided, in view of the odd contents of the tape that Jack was playing, to get an opinion from a few responsible people.

Jack's voice droned on, but everyone listened with interest. When Jack described his feelings, his awareness of not being alone, Kerry looked quickly toward Earl Fabre to see him looking at Jack attentively.

"Okay," Jack said, turning off the player. "The quick and easy answer is that I went a little nuts, and—" he laughed "—that is not entirely possible. If it weren't for some of the reports Dr. Hertz has made, I might just dismiss it as maybe a temporary dose of sun or something."

"Cassie, does he eat his meat raw at home?" Sandy Moore asked, with a chuckle.

"The only things he eats raw are carrots and me," Cassie said, with a sweet little smile. She had a way of using shock, at times, to show that some things were serious and not subject to jokes.

"What I want is a discussion," Jack said. "Let's consider a few things. One, the incident on the river on America. Two, Dr. Hertz's tests that showed that the trees along the river were capable of learning and could distinguish a real danger from a simulated threat. First you have apparently intelligent behavior from trees. Then we have Dr. Hertz's tests on the method of pollination in the shrubs of the foothills. Are you all familiar with that information?"

"I'm not," Sandy Moore said.

"Kerry?" Jack said.

Kerry cleared her throat and cast a quick glance at Earl. "Dr. Fabre set up an electronic screen to my specifications," she said. "I wanted to measure wind-borne pollination. We got some very interesting readings. Even when the wind was blowing the wrong way, or not at all, pollen passed from plant to plant over a distance of some feet, even yards in some cases. The most intriguing point was that it seemed to move in clumps. Not in great concentrations, as at the river where it totally covered a man and was taken into his lungs, but with hundreds of grains in a small area, not concentrated enough to be visible."

"The question being," Jack said, "what is the motive force that moves grains of pollen without wind, or against the wind?"

Kerry looked again at Earl. She had, of course, left out in her reports any mention of that odd occurrence between them. That bothered her. Jack's experience on the plain, his feeling of not being alone in his own body and mind, concerned her, for she had had the same feeling. She remembered all too well how she'd said, "They wanted to know how it felt."

Now Jack had said, "We wanted to know why."

"There's something else, too," Teddy said. "I'm sure Kerry hasn't had the time to study it or draw any conclusions, but the elephants seem to have become conservationists. You know how they normally tear up things? Well, now they don't damage any plant they're not going to eat, and they don't kill the trees they eat. They leave enough leaves on the trees to allow them to survive. They don't strip away enough bark from a single tree to kill it."

Kerry nodded. "Admittedly, we've only observed this for a couple of hours. It may be a temporary condition. It could have something to do with the way the plants taste. We can't draw any conclusions as yet."

"Except that there's something damned eerie going on," Sandy said.

"Kerry has a theory," Cassie said.

"Not a theory," Kerry said quickly. "Nothing even as positive as a theory. Just a thought."

"You stated it pretty strongly to me," Earl Fabre said, he, too, feeling a bit guilty for not telling the group about his peculiar experience. He had his wife to think of, however. "You said, Kerry, that we just might have encountered our first intelligent alien species."

"Intelligent plants?" Sandy asked.

"They communicate," Jack said.

"They seem to communicate," Kerry corrected.

"Whatever they do, they get the job done," Jack said. "One tree is damaged and trees two hundred miles away know and recognize the same danger when they're approached by a man with a cutter in his hand."

"Is someone trying to tell me that plants are talking to elephants, saying, 'Hey, big boy, I don't mind giving you a little, but don't eat enough of me to kill me'?"

"I don't know," Jack said. "I'm open to opinion." He spread his hands. "I'm open to a theory of divine intervention if someone will give me a bit of documentation."

"I think we should put the entire project on hold until we have some answers," Kerry said.

There was a silence. Cassie broke it. "I don't think you'd get approval on that from the old man, and I don't think it's necessary, not yet."

"I think we're hinting at an assumption that the vegetation on Beauty is more advanced than we might think," Earl said. "Since there's not much to study on Beauty but vegetation, we've got a bunch of botanists running around all over the place cataloging plants. Is there anything in their reports to make us think that there might be thinking plants?"

"In form and in individual adaptations the flora here is different, but the same life processes go on here as on Earth. My people aren't even close to observing all the varieties of plant life on the planet, not even in the near vicinity of the houses, but nothing has turned up yet to indicate anything in any plant that might function as a brain or as an originator of anything resembling thought."

"Here's something else that's been bothering me," Earl said. "When a man tried to cut down a tree, things happened. When the elephants first started ripping and tearing at trees, they were attacked by clouds of pollen. But there are a few thousand hoofed animals continually eating grass and there's never been any reaction."

"Unless grass is overgrazed," Jack said, "grazing doesn't really harm it. In fact, the grass is improved. Cropping encourages deeper and thicker root systems. Animal manure enriches the soil."

"So the grass eaters are left alone because the grass is intelligent enough to know that it's being cropped for its own good?" Earl asked.

"There's an alternative explanation," Cassie said.

"For example, Earl, you pushed up some rough vegetation when you cleared the sites for the houses here and on America and nothing happened. Perhaps there are lower and higher forms of life in Beauty's vegetable biosphere."

. "Or, if you're a science fiction reader," Matt said, "you might add the possibility of the hive mind concept."

"Meaning?" Kerry, who was not a science fiction reader, asked.

"Each plant, or at least every individual of some, or many species, is one cell of awareness in a community brain. That would account for the apparent communication."

"Well, I don't think we should reject any idea, however wild," Jack said, with a wink at Matt.

"I think we need to get to work," Kerry said.

"I agree," Earl said.

"And where do we start?" Teddy asked.

"With the plants," Kerry said. "Dr. Fabre, if you agree, I'd like to borrow a few of your technicians and equipment."

"Sure," Earl said.

"Do you have an idea?" Jack asked Kerry.

"For the moment I'd like to keep it to myself," Kerry said. She frowned. "I hate being laughed at."

"No one's laughing," Teddy said.

The rains had come to the African plains in earnest. New green changed the tone of the landscape. A ground blizzard of flowers covered all. There was good, sweet, new green for every herbivore. The elephant herd moved down from the wooded foothills into the fringe of the plain to feast on new growth among a variety of low bush that seemed to especially please them and often they were seen mixing with the smaller grass eaters.

Kerry was in the process of turning everyone into amateur botanists. Any field team that went out brought back samples. Kerry, herself, roamed the countryside far and wide with a team of technicians—Earl Fabre was not among them. The rains hampered the work, but some tests were possible between showers. They were measuring the minute electrical currents generated within plants. Kerry dissected smaller plants, studied various trees with x-ray scanners. Digging machines bored far into the earth to search for anything unusual in the root systems of various plants. The only positive result of the digging was the discovery of a fungus that, after testing, proved edible and tasted much like a truffle.

There were no incidents, no pollen attacks, even when core samples were taken from larger trees with a pulse auger.

The communications sector recorded a transed relay of Peter Golding's featured piece on Beauty. There was no editorializing. The assembled audience clapped and whistled when Teddy's face appeared on the screen and, in about ten seconds, she told how she and Matt had discovered Beauty. There were excellent scenes of the herds, a brief look at the elephants and a frisky chipmunk, and the piece closed with Jack's attack on the zebra colt, with only one statement from the narrator, Golding.

"Dr. Frost said that the purpose of his experiment was to reinstill the zebra colt that which has been lost by animals bred only in captivity, the natural fear of the predator."

Definitely not an editorial opinion, just the facts, ma'am. But one cameraman, using one of those marvelous long lenses, had managed to shoot directly down into Jack's face while he was fruitlessly worrying the little zebra's neck skin. In silence, the camera moved even closer, and the screen was filled with the eyes of a madman, nose buried in zebra skin, saliva showing white at the corners of Jack's lips as he chewed wildly. Then there was a freeze

frame with those wild, madman's eyes left on the
screen for a full ten seconds to fade out.

"Damnit," Teddy yelled, leaping to her feet.

"Overall it was very positive," Matt said.

"Oh?" Teddy demanded. "Tell me one thing you
remember better than that last freeze frame."

Jack had sunk down in his seat, looking glum. "I
see what you mean," he said. "When anyone who
saw that program hears about Beauty, they're going
to see a mad scientist, eyes flaming, trying to chew
on a defenseless little animal."

For the next two weeks, Peter Golding ran pieces
on the colonized planets. He showed peaceful scenes
of fruitful agriculture and growing cities. He showed
scenes where prospectors, or simply loners, had penetrated into hostile environs in search of precious
metals or jewels or just solitude. On the last program
of the series he featured the planet Coldernhell. That
frozen world, locked in an ice age that left only a
small band of brief summer at the equator, was not—
and Golding carefully said so—an official colonization planet. It was inhabited—and Golding carefully
said so—by a few thousand miners and their fami-
lies. Golding's cameras followed one mining team,
showing how surface deposits of heavy metals,
gouged from the crust by glacial action, were located
by electronic means through the dense ice. Sun generators were used to melt the glacial overburden
and the process seemed hellish on screen, with fur-
bundled men hidden by clouds of steam. A thin,
scruffy woman, wife of one of the miners, spoke
sadly about the hardships of living on Coldernhell.
Golding carefully pointed out that the miners were
on the planet by their own choice, that the purpose
was profit, and that Coldernhell received no settlers
under Bureau auspices. However, to end the week-
long series, the cameras did a slow flyover of para-
disaical islands in the balmy south seas of Beauty,

empty and inviting, of the lush, green plains devoid of life, of tree-green, temperate zones.

"These views of the planet so aptly named Beauty conclude our look at the populated planets," Golding said. Period. No editorializing. No reprimand from the Board. No fines. Just, in the minds of billions of people on Earth and the other populated planets, the stark contrast between the hardscrabble minors on Coldernhell and the vast, empty, fertile expanses of Beauty, which were peopled only by animals and their keepers.

Teddy sat through a second showing of the compiled features by Golding in Andrew Reznor's quarters. When the last scene had faded, she said, "I think it was quite deliberate, sir, to save Beauty for last, to contrast her with that ice planet."

"Quite skillfully done," Reznor admitted. "But, I think, with no malice. That young man seemed to be very nice when he was here. What does he have to gain by turning public opinion against the project?"

"Audience. Ratings."

"Well," Reznor said, "let's not worry about it at the moment." But when Teddy was gone, he sat down in front of his communicator and had himself patched through to a scrambled trans line to Reznor headquarters on Earth. Andy Reznor had just arrived at work to start a new day when the call came through.

"Good morning, Junior," the old man said. "You're looking bright and chipper."

In fact, Andy did not look bright and chipper. He looked even more glum than usual.

"What do our public opinion polls show regarding Peter Golding's series on populated planets?" Reznor asked.

"We have only the preliminary data," Andy said. "Ratings were high. Media reviewers praised the series. In our questionnaires we didn't single out Beauty directly, but a great deal of sympathy was shown not only for the miners on Coldernhell but for the people of other planets still undergoing the terraforming process. Still, I don't see any ground swell of popular opinion against the project. At least, not yet.''

"I think you'd better give the good senator a call," the old man said. "Tell him to be on the alert for any change of mood in Congress. We're too far along to have to fight now."

"Yes, I'd made myself a note to do that," Andy said. "I think I'd better sign off now, Dad. I'm due to leave for Rome in half an hour. General Igor Milyukov is going to address the Pax Five Council this afternoon."

"Bit unusual for him, isn't it?"

"Quite," Andy said. "That's why I want to be there. As you well know, Milyukov is the Kremlin's hatchet man. He's the one who breaks the news of any new Soviet policy."

"All right, my boy," the old man said. "Keep your eyes and ears open."

"By the way," Andy said, with a wry smile, "the *rest* of Reznor Enterprises is thriving."

Reznor laughed. He was used to getting a little bit of needling from his son about his project. "With you in charge I expected nothing less," he said, reaching for the switch.

Reznor was preparing for bed when the trans call came from Earth and for the second time in a day he was looking at the face of his son. "Back from Rome so soon?" he asked.

"General Milyukov showed the last segment of the Golding series to the council," Andy said, his face grim. He was eloquent regarding the hardships of the miners on Coldernhell. He didn't go quite so far as to call for Pax Five reconsideration of the treaty provisions that allowed us to have Beauty, but he did ask if it were sound policy to devote such a splendid world to animals when humanity was suffering so on other, much less desirable planets.''

''I would hope that our people countered by saying that the miners on Coldernhell, if they work at all, can retire in some luxury in two or three years,'' Reznor said.

''We pointed out that Coldernhell is not an official colony planet, that those who go there do so of their own free choice. We didn't make a lengthy rebuttal because it was felt that to do so would place too much importance on Milyukov's speech.''

''I suppose that was wise,'' Reznor said.

''I had a chat with Gravel just before I called you,'' Andy said. ''He was a little upset. There's been a series of incidents. The home of the congressman from California was broken into last week. Some hacker managed to tap into the computer in the office of the senator from Georgia. And Gravel's personal accounts and computer records have been subpoenaed by the Gestapo.''

Reznor frowned for two reasons, because of the news, and because he did not approve of his son applying the popular name to the Internal Revenue Service.

''A series of coincidences?'' he asked.

''Probably,'' Andy said. ''Nothing to worry about. Gravel's records are perfect and clean.''

But Andrew Reznor had food for thought. First there'd been Peter Golding's skillful attack on the project, then Milyukov's attack at the Pax Five. Now three of his pet politicians had been victims of the incidents. Perhaps, he thought, the break-in, the computer tampering, the IRS audit of Gravel's books were coincidental. Perhaps Gravel's records were perfect and clean. But he'd learned long ago never, never to underestimate the greed and stupidity of a politician. It was time to make a countermove. He placed a call.

Within days, on a dozen planets, all Reznor Enterprise commercials were replaced by sincere, heart-warming scenes involving animals, most of them young animals, since any young thing is appealing. The theme was, "We're giving them a chance." Public opinion polls showed that within two weeks there was no public memory of the Golding series, and that Beauty, as a haven for the mistreated, dying, disappearing animal life of Earth was a very popular ideal.

Chapter 17

There were bees on Beauty now. And beetles that rolled up small, round pellets of animal dung. Hummingbirds thrived and had a population explosion during their first breeding season. Food was everywhere for the large assortment of hummers placed in every suitable habitat. The first hummingbirds had been released into a large, flower-filled enclosure of fine nettings and the pollen phenomenon had been observed again, with the little birds' first efforts at nectar gathering greeted by small clouds of pollen. The hummers' swiftly beating wings dispersed the clouds and, accustomed as they were to pollen, they went happily about their business and quickly the pollen clouds ceased to appear.

There were hares and foxes. There was a family of hyenas on the plains, content, for the moment, to scavenge those animals who died of old age—for the zoos of Earth were taking advantage of the opportunity to decrease their animal populations to more economical levels, with assurances from Reznor that specimens would always be available for Earth zoos when needed—and many animals were old or past their prime, but none were turned away. All were given their chance to die in a habitat like that of their lost heritage on Earth.

The krill population had exploded and now supported other life in the cold seas. Random samplings in plankton rich waters showed a pleasing increase in the population of plankton-eating fish and other marine animals. New marine species were introduced with each arrival of *Ark II*, the salt water tanker ship. On America, it had taken only two winters for ducks and geese to establish a pattern of migration. Prairie dog cities were growing. Slowly, a species at a time, the lower end of the food chain was being established on land and in the seas. But not even Andrew Reznor had fully appreciated the gargantuan task he had set for Beauty's keepers. They were trying to accomplish in that last few years of one man's life what had taken millennia on Earth, and they had to keep in mind the horrible examples to be gleaned from earth's history, when man tampered with nature's scheme: the rabbit in Australia, the Mediterranean fruit fly.

Continuous research kept turning up odd little niches into which some Earth species would fit nicely, but there was always the possibility that a species that had become mortally endangered on Earth might find Beauty to its liking and explode into pestdom within a few years.

The bug men continued to be frustrated. Their only breakthrough had been the implantation of certain moth and butterfly species in the jungle areas, and the ornithologists were looking forward to introducing the first insectivorous birds to feed on the larvae and adult forms.

Only the computers could, after three years of the steady flow of life through space, remember the number and the names of all the different species introduced, and things were going quite well. Peter Golding's attempt—if, indeed, it had been that—to muster public opinion for the human colonization of Beauty had been forgotten. Igor Milyukov had appeared, once more, before the Pax Five Council,

backed by delegates from individual nations, India
the most notable among them, to call for the opening
of designated areas of Beauty to humans. The China-
Southeast Asia bloc sided with the Russians. The
United States, the Anglo-European unit, and the
Brazilian Commonwealth voted for the animals.

The political front had been quiet for a year. On
Beauty, although measurements, tests, questioning,
wondering, frustrated stabs into nothing continued,
the secret of Beauty's vegetation was still a mystery.
There had been no further incidents. Even a colony
of beavers in America went about that work that
beavers do so well unmolested, cutting trees for
building and for food without so much as one pollen
attack. For lack of progress, and in total frustration,
Kerry Hertz had a tree cut down on the American
river. Nothing. She cut others, from the jungles to
the high mountains. Nothing.

Sandy Moore returned to his building. Now there
were facilities in several spots on the globe. Matt
Tinker's job held no further challenges. The whole
world was peaceful. There had not been an unauthorized ship near Beauty since that one memorable occasion when the intruder had shouted his success and
skill as a pilot by burning a fireball path across the
skies over Africa House. As the animal population
grew, new scientists came. Having new faces helped,
but a sameness was developing. For the botanists,
there was a surplus of plenty, thousands of unknown
species to catalog and study. For the technicians assigned to Kerry Hertz, there was more of the same
as Kerry continued in her efforts to solve Beauty's
secret. Others might have put the early incidents out
of their minds, but Kerry remembered only too well
and sometimes with a sort of inner excitement that
scene with Earl Fabre when they were alone in Beauty's wilderness.

Matt Tinker was ready to think about change.

Three years, he told himself, was enough. All the challenge was gone. Visits by the cattle boats, as he'd begun to think of the animal transporters, were routine. Not even Jack's and Cassie's plans to introduce the first large cats on the plains could hold his interest. The wife of one of the botanists had given birth to a fine, eight-pound boy, and he was reminded of his desire to have a son of his own, but Teddy, ever involved in building a complex of animal life, still had her implant.

Matt traveled to the south polar regions with a team of marine zoologists and biologists to release the first colony of penguins and to dive in the frigid water to witness the first penguins feeding. The penguins found the same food they'd eaten on Earth and seemed to be perfectly happy and content. It was a stimulating trip, in good company, but it was flawed by an observation from the marine team of scientists. "It would be nice to be able to live to see the job done," one young man said, as they watched penguins with full bellies shoot up out of the frigid water and land on the ice.

The remark brought home to Matt the fact that only a tiny fraction of the target species had been brought to Beauty, and that the spread of marine species into waters suitable for them would take, at best, decades and, some said, hundreds of years. The oceans were big. The numbers of individual species that could be planted were so discouragingly small.

Matt did not need an excuse to board *Tinker's Belle* and lift her into atmosphere and then into the cold black of near space. Beauty rolled beneath him, the minute changes wrought by man invisible from space. At his back was the bigness, the emptiness, the lure of the unknown. He remembered with great fondness the time he and Teddy had spent together on *Belle*, when it was just the two of them; and he remembered how they'd spent hours dreaming and planning what they'd do with the bonus money when, not if, they discovered a planet suitable for Reznor's purposes. Now that rather sizable chunk of money was on Earth, invested by one of the Reznor banks, growing daily, enough money to give the ship a total overhaul, enough to live on while *Belle* pointed her pretty nose outward, or inward, in search.

He sent *Belle* downward. When he landed, he went to the kitchens, had a picnic box prepared, put it aboard and, with serious intent, drove a goat to the office building, bursting into Teddy's office without knocking. She was with Cassie Frost. A projection of two adult cheetahs was on the walls.

"Hi," Teddy said brightly. "Take a look at this. This one—" she pointed, "—is Ramses. This is Nefertiti."

"I'm thrilled," Matt said, making a mock bow toward the projected pictures.

"Jack and Cassie had decided against lions as the first of the big cats, " Teddy said. "These beauties will be out on the next run of the *Ark*."

"Has Jack started training the herds with a cheetah skin?" Matt asked.

Cassie laughed. "No. The hyenas have done the job for us. They haven't killed yet, but they have done some practice chasing. I think every animal on the plains has seen them, and they're leery of them, won't let them get close."

"Ugly brutes," Matt mused, looking at the hulking knot of muscles at the base of the cheetahs' necks.

"Beautiful," Cassie said. "Poetry in motion."

"Tell that to the animals who'll be their meals," Matt said.

"Nefertiti is pregnant. We're bringing a pair, instead of just females, because Ramses is the only cheetah in captivity who has successfully impregnated a female. We won't get quite the gene diversity we'd like, but natural breeding, of course, is going to become necessary sooner or later. We can't go around artificially inseminating every animal forever.'' Cassie, in the absence of Jack, was often quite coherent.

"Bully for Ramses," Matt said. He turned to Teddy. "I'd like for you to close up shop and come with me."

"Oh, Matt, I have a million things to do," she protested.

"This is an emergency," he said, looking grim. "It calls for top level consultation."

"Well," she said.

"I was just going," Cassie said.

Matt put off Teddy's questions as he drove her to the ship. She perched behind him, arms around his waist. They were airborne before she questioned him again, her face showing a bit of worry.

"You'll see, soon," Matt said, checking the route both by computer and visual observation. He flew toward the mountains, lowered *Belle*, saw the glint of the little river below, and settled neatly onto a carpet of lush grass beside a crystal clear stream. They were high enough for the heat of the plains to be behind them. The mountain air was deliciously cool, crisp. The little stream gurgled and laughed as it made its sparkling way over shining, smoothed rocks.

"Now just what the hell is the emergency?" Teddy demanded, looking around as Matt escorted her off ship, carrying the picnic basket.

"The emergency is that if I don't have some time with you I'm going to start looking more closely at Kerry, or some other unattached female," Matt said, with a suggestive grin.

"You pulled me away from my work—" She

didn't continue, for his face darkened. "Really?" she asked sweetly. "Do you miss me that much?"

Matt spread a blanket, put the picnic basket down, opened it. Teddy discovered that she was hungry.

They lay side by side, basking in the sun. The nearest pair of eyes, animal or human, was hundreds of miles away. The lovemaking had been, as usual for them, sweet and lasting. Teddy dozed. Matt leaned on one elbow and studied her face. In sleep, she looked so young. She was young, as he was. Thanks to advances in medical science, and to the fact that they were definitely not poor—with their nest egg growing all the time since there was no place to spend money on Beauty—they could expect to live well past Andrew Reznor's hundred years. But nature was still operating on her own schedule. At some point between forty and fifty the age-old changes would occur in Teddy's body and her childbearing years would be past.

Teddy's eyes opened and she stretched languorously, the movement making her stomach concave, her breasts upthrust. She made an ummming sound and saw the look in Matt's eyes. "See something you like, sailor?" she asked in a sultry voice.

"Glutton," Matt said.

Teddy sat up, reached for the last of a packet of shamefully rich sweets containing a lot of honey. "It's time to get back."

"Not yet," Matt said. "I think it's time we had a little talk."

"I think I know the subject," she said, looking away.

"I had lunch with Reznor yesterday," Matt said. "He was asking me if I knew of a couple of good free-lance exploration teams."

"Matt—"

"Let me finish," Matt said. "He has ships of his

own out, of course. It's been two years now since anyone has filed a good planet.''

"Things are quiet on Earth," Teddy said. "There's no pressure on Beauty anymore."

"Not at the moment," Matt agreed. "But Reznor thinks it would be a good political move to find a sweet planet, like Beauty, and turn her over to the Bureau of Colonization."

"Matt, we're just getting started here."

"Yes," he said, somewhat heatedly, "and fifty years from now we'll still just be getting started. Honey, Beauty is Reznor's dream."

She was silent for a moment. "And your dream?"

"It hasn't changed much," he said. "A few kids while we're still young, a lot of transing—taking them with us for a while until they're school age. Another discovery and take the bonus in the form of land and settle down to build something for the kids and their kids."

She nibbled at the sweet and did not speak.

"It was your dream, too," he reminded her.

"I know, and it still is, but—"

"But?"

"Matt, I have an opportunity here that is unprecedented. We're building a whole biosphere, starting from scratch. The terraformer who does the job will have her name in the textbooks, in the history books. But it isn't just that. I'm no bleeding heart, but I feel that I'm part of every animal that's born on this planet. When I look up and see a vulture soaring on a thermal, I can imagine the skies teeming with graceful water birds, hawks, magnificent eagles. I've come to think that the giving of life is the most rewarding thing I can do. I know that the project could go on very well without me, but I *want* to be a part of it. I *want* to see this planet filled, gorged with life, with life taking up every available little nook and cranny, as it once did on Earth. I never fully appreciated the amazing, the astounding variety of life. I'm learning things about life that thrill me. And the complexity of the incredible interrelationships of life on Earth is a continuing miracle.''

The depth of her emotion silenced Matt. He gazed up at the still distant snows of the mountaintops.

"But I'll go with you if you feel we must leave," Teddy said softly. "There's one life that matters more to me than all the others put together."

He grinned at her, touched. "Anyone I know?"

Teddy had known for months that such a conversation would take place, and she had dreaded it. She had also known for years that she could manipulate her man, as women had been manipulating men for millennia. She felt a bit guilty. She took Matt's hand and put it on her waist.

"None of that," Matt said. "We're having an important discussion."

She moved his hand toward the rear, to that area just above her hip, pressed his fingers into the softness there. "Feel anything?"

He looked at her thoughtfully, his fingers probing for the tiny hardness of the implant under the skin. He let his fingers cover a wider area, came back to the spot.

"I had it taken out over three months ago," she said, smiling.

The statement impacted in Matt's mind and he felt a flush of warmth. It took three to four months, after the removal of an implant, for the residual effects of the fertilization inhibitor to be cleared completely from a woman's body.

"Can you think of a better place to raise a kid?" she asked, with a little smile. "No disease. No insects. Dozens of fond, self-styled uncles and aunts who dote on the few kids we have here. Wide open spaces. Sun."

"I think I've just been had," Matt said wryly. But

he was feeling better. Beauty was a great place for kids. He could picture a little girl, looking like Teddy's baby pictures, playing with her dolls in the sun on the beautiful lawns around Africa House. "All right," he said.

"If you say we go, we go," she said, and held her breath, waiting for his reaction.

He mused for a moment or two. "Two years," he said. "We'll give it two more years. That'll give us a couple of years in space to find another planet before she's ready for initial school training."

"She?" Teddy asked.

"Don't you want a girl?"

Teddy smiled and reached for him. "I don't want to choose," she said. "I want God to decide. That's why I didn't tell you I'd removed the implant, so that you wouldn't be tempted to choose the sex of our baby."

"Well, that's fair enough, I guess," Matt said.

"A little boy who looks like you wouldn't be bad."

"Think so?"

"Ummmm." She pulled herself to him. "Listen, fellow, making a baby isn't all fun and games. You have to apply yourself to it, and you're neglecting your work."

For a while, he worked diligently. They were packing up the picnic dishes when both heard the sound at the same time, the low, distant, lonely-sounding rumble of a ship on G.D. At first, the sound was not directional, then, as it came nearer, Matt spotted it, coming from the far mountains, a mere speck that was initially visible as a minute darkness against the background of snowy peak.

"Survey ship," Teddy said.

"Guess so," Matt replied, gathering the blanket and basket. "Wanta take a dip in the stream before we go?"

Teddy was already dressed, as was he. "The water is too cold," she said.

They walked toward *Belle*, hand in hand. The low thunder of the approaching ship came from slightly to the north now, and the speck of her bulk was larger. She was going to pass them to the north, a few miles away, flying low and slow. They boarded the ship and Matt closed her, hit the buttons to warm up the G.D., flipped on the visuals idly and set them to automatic scan. *Belle's* computer gave him a ship sighted warning light and the visuals zeroed in on the passing ship and clicked as the screen was put on magnification.

"Matt," Teddy said, an oddness in her voice. "Look."

He looked up at the screen and shot forward in his seat. The ship that was passing by a few miles to the north, flying low and slow, was not a Reznor ship. It was a ship he'd seen before, a sleek, handsome, converted space yacht painted black with silver trim.

He reached for the communicator, lifted it, then put it back. If he called the base in the open, the call could easily be monitored by the intruder, thus alerting him. Teddy saw him put the communicator back in place and understood his thinking.

"We'll let him get below the horizon," Matt said.

"Who is he and why is he here?"

"I don't know who he is, but he's been here before."

Teddy chewed on her lower lip. "The same one you chased off into space?"

"Unless there are two or more black ships with silver trim and no markings," he said. He could still remember the startled look on the face of the pilot of the black ship when he had eased *Belle* so close that they had stared at each other from a distance of less than ten feet. And he remembered, too, the outlines of weapon ports on the prow of the black ship.

He would not take any chances, not with Teddy aboard.

When he'd given the black ship time to get beyond visual detector distance, he lifted *Belle* hard and fast and, beyond the last scattered molecules of atmosphere, started his search. *Belle's* instruments spotted the black ship far below. The ship was moving toward the edge of the plains, toward the ever-growing herds.

Chapter 18

Igor Milyukov knew an inner excitement that he had felt only once before, when he was alone, moving across the ice packs knowing that somewhere near was an animal fully capable of smashing, rending, and eating his relatively frail human flesh. During the interminable months since he had made the bargain with Genna Darden, he had relived his conquest of the polar bear countless times. He had told the story to a man who had been a surprisingly good traveling companion on a convoluted journey designed to confuse any observers. Milyukov knew the boundless curiosity of the various intelligence agencies, and he would not have put it past Intel to have him followed, filmed, and later gently blackmailed.

Now the long wait had ended.

He wore hunting clothing tailored in London. He sat tensely beside the pilot as the ship flew westward. Her screens showed teeming life ahead on plains very much like those that were so familiar to Milyukov from his collection of antique films taken in Africa before the advance of civilization had pushed the vast herds and their predators into the oblivion of history and the game farms.

"There they are," the pilot said. He fiddled with controls and the magnified images of great, gray beasts appeared. There was a group of five adults feeding near a small stream. Milyukov studied the terrain and was pleased. His approach would be through broken thickets. He had discussed the procedure several times with the pilot. His luck was holding because the elephants were feeding in a transition zone between the plains and the rising, wooded foothills. Unless some scientist from Africa House just happened to be in the field, the nearest guardian of Beauty's animal life would be at least fifty miles away. If they had installed a surface warning system the ship might be detected, but the latest intelligence—garnered through Intel's checks on shipments of equipment and material to Beauty—indicated that such a system had not been put into place. He would have time to fulfill a dream, time to stalk, time to observe, and then—

"I'm going to put down on that little rise," Jake Jordan said.

The rise, Milyukov estimated, was half a mile from the stream and the elephants. That was good. The animals seemed to be accustomed to the low thunder of a ship on G.D. and had not been disturbed, as yet. He would earn his moment by a half-mile stalk through broken growth and then, at last, he'd be face to face with the largest land animal still in existence.

He gave his weapon one last check as the ship lowered. It was a valuable antique in perfect condition, chosen from his extensive collection. It was an odd-looking rifle by modern standards, with two barrels, each charged with a .600 Weatherby Magnum load that would deliver, at relatively close range, bullet energy equal to five thousand foot-pounds, a blow of enormous power.

Yet even with that potential for destruction, the first shot would have to be accurately placed for a quick kill. The antique double-barreled Weatherby gave him a safety factor, the second shot. He knew from his reading, from the old films, that a wounded bull elephant can move at daunting speed and become an engine of destruction.

He chose his prey. There was one adult bull with the part of the herd that was lazing alongside the river now, swaying on their huge, padded feet, seemingly just enjoying the sun.

"Be courageous," he thought, directing the words toward the well ivoried bull.

He checked a side pocket of his hunting garb to be sure the small impulse cutter was in place. He intended to take at least one tusk with him, perhaps both, if Jordan did not signal danger of discovery after he had made his kill.

The ship touched down.

"Cameras ready?" Milyukov asked.

"I'll be shooting so close you'll be able to see your anus pucker when one of those things tries to stomp you," Jordan said.

Jordan didn't care much one way or the other about the death of an elephant. His concern was to get it over with fast and get the hell out. The Reznor exploration ships being used for surveying and transport on the planet carried the usual weapons permitted to spacegoers by Pax Five, and although his black ship, with its illegal armament, could outgun one ship, he didn't want to take chances with more than one. He wanted to avoid having to use his weapons, although he'd been assured by his contact at Intel—the icy woman who had refused to conclude the deal by taking a quick and intimate little side trip aboard ship—and by the Russian, that if push came to shove and he had to shoot his way out he'd be covered. He'd been on the shady side of the law a few times, but he'd never gone to war and he intended to do everything possible to prevent that from happening.

The Russian, Jordan felt, was a sick man. Jordan had killed only two living things, two diamond smugglers out beyond Valhalla who had gotten cute and tried to hijack back a load of gems that had been properly paid for, and he hadn't taken any joy in that. It was something that had had to be done to protect his investment and his own life, because it was a certainty that the smugglers would have killed him. There was, after all, honor even among thieves in the gem belts. The two killings were not reported because the robbing of a man who was useful in transporting their illegal jewels to market would have been frowned upon by the other miners.

Why a man would want to blast some animal with an old blunderbuss that looked more deadly than a modern pulse rifle was beyond Jordan's imagination, but he was being paid well, damned well. He'd refused to take the job for less than enough to replace the ship, buy the finest lawyers in the civilized galaxy, and have enough left over to retire in luxury to one of the frontier planets where a man could buy anything he needed, up to and including a bodyguard of gunslingers and pretty little girls.

Whatever happened, this was going to be Jordan's final job. As the Russian checked his equipment one last time Jordan mused about that new planet off toward the periphery from Earth, raw and fertile, with vast lands that could be purchased quite cheaply and colony ships arriving on set schedules with their human cargo that included—in a trade that was whispered about but not generally known—surplus girl children from the overpopulated sinkholes of Earth. If a family approved for emigration cared to take along a couple of orphaned girls of say eleven to thirteen—and it didn't matter if the girls were pretty and deliciously mature beyond their age—it was fine with the Bureau of Colonization. The object was, after all, to reduce Earth's population, to give its crowded billions a new chance. And if a few girl children simply faded from sight on a new world there was no one to protest. On a new world, if there was a government, everyone was against it. Freedom was a heady thing, and the sudden freedom from control by Pax Five law, international law, national law, state law, county law, and city law was a contagion. Of course, even on the rawest planet, murder was punished, robbery was cause for deportation to a grim facility on Sahara, a desert planet, and rape still carried the death penalty under the eye-for-an-eye code that had come into effect again on Earth as she was poxed by her billions before the age of space.

A bit of genteel slavery, however, if one were suitably set up with an estate protected by the privacy laws in effect on the new planets, was a risk worth taking.

"You know the withdrawal signal," Jordan said, as Milyukov stepped out of the hatch onto arid, sparsely vegetated soil.

"Red burst," Milyukov said.

Jordan started the cameras as Milyukov strode into the bush, the big Weatherby carried at port arms. He would have to raise ship and hover to follow the Russian to the river and that was both good and bad, bad in that there'd be the sound of the G.D., good because if several of Reznor's ships came in shooting he could trans directly into space with the settings for the trans already entered into his computer. He'd be in trouble with both Intel and the Russians in that event, but he'd be alive.

Milyukov had walked a hundred yards when a sound in the bush froze him. He clicked the safety on the big rifle and faced the source of the sound. A small, dun-colored antelope snorted at him and hopped away as if he had springs for legs and Milyukov smiled, for the unknown sound had sent a thrill of adrenal alarm though him. He felt alive for the first time since his splendid adventure on the ice.

He breathed deeply and walked on.

He heard the trumpeting of an elephant after he'd walked for about ten minutes. He fancied that he could smell the beasts. His heart was pounding in anticipation. He had begun sweating in Beauty's heat, and he liked the feeling. A man should have to pay a price for achievement.

He caught a glimpse of the river through the bush that grew to a height over his head and slowed his pace, creeping now, imagining himself to have been, somehow, taken back into time when the wild herds owned the African plains. He rounded a clump of brush and froze in his tracks. There they were. The herd bull was facing him, and for a moment he feared that the beasts would be alarmed and run before he could get a decent shot. He was two hundred yards away. The wind was in his face. The herd bull turned and munched leaves. He had not been detected. He wanted to be nearer, to clearly see the small, intense eyes, to be near enough to hear the smack of the bullet into flesh.

He crawled the last fifty yards, his well-tailored pants and jacket picking up a burden of dust. He was close enough now. And yet he wanted to be nearer. He wanted, as much as anything, to extend this precious moment in time, for when the rifle spoke it would be over, and he would never have such a chance again.

He crawled. Certainly the elephants had spotted him now. He prepared himself to leap to his feet and take a shot into the elephant's heart from the side if the bull grew alarmed and started to flee, and he crawled still closer. The bull was huge, intimidating. Milyukov's sweat had taken on a sharp, acrid odor. The danger was delicious, a drug in his blood.

He was no more than one hundred feet away, hidden from the elephants—or perhaps they were simply so accustomed to being observed by man that they didn't care—by low brush. He took a deep breath, rose slowly to his feet.

The female with calf raised her trunk and blared a challenge. The bull trumpeted a second later, stomped clouds of dust, faced Milyukov and flapped his huge ears forward.

"Be brave," Milyukov whispered, as he sighted.

The bull made a mock charge, that reversion to instinctive behavior that had so delighted the scientists of Beauty.

The shot was perfect. The nitro-express charge pushed death into the bull elephant's brain with a mighty force and an impact sound that cracked like doom. Just as he'd seen it happen in films, the life went out of the animal instantly and tons of flesh sagged and collapsed with the pillarlike legs suddenly gone limp. The body raised a cloud of dust as it hit the ground with a whump. A torment of trumpeting filled the air as the females milled about. The elephant calf, confused and frightened, ran a few steps toward Milyukov and then scurried back to its mother. Two of the older cows approached the fallen bull and tried to lift his motionless body by using their tusks. It was, Milyukov felt, quite touching.

He had to get the cows away so that he could claim his trophies. He walked slowly toward them, yelling, brandishing the rifle. The cow with calf was the first to flee, the calf hard put to keep up with her. Then the others began to withdraw. Milyukov started to move forward and something hit him in the back with enough force to send him sprawling. The rifle flew from his hands in his surprise. On hands and knees he felt another impact, directly in the seat of his well-tailored pants. He yelped in surprise and turned to see a small, dun-colored antelope with cute little horns preparing to make another attack.

He laughed and started to rise, but the antelope

butted him again, catching him on the thigh. "Enough," he said, kicking the animal which only came to his waist. He dodged the next attack and scurried to pick up his rifle. He heard the trumpeting of the cow elephants and the pounding of feet as the little antelope came at him again and he sneaked a look over his shoulder. The elephants were lumbering toward him, trunks outthrust, and their cries were bone-chilling, the thumping sounds of their running feet booming with genuine threat. Milyukov exulted as the knowledge of *real* danger made him alert enough to kick the charging antelope on the nose and set the animal painfully back on its haunches. He lifted the rifle, prepared to take his second shot, the life-saving shot for which the double barreled Weatherby had been designed. He would drop the lead cow and the others would flee.

As he pulled the trigger, he was hit on the backside by the antelope. The shot went over the head of the charging cow elephant and then she was on him, trunk seizing him like a muscular snake. He did not scream as he was lifted high and slammed to the hard, dusty soil. He landed on his head and shoulder and the impact broke his neck so that he was only dimly and fleetingly aware as huge, padded feet stomped with tons of force and very quickly pounded the last, straining bit of awareness from his brain.

Jake Jordan, hovering on the low thunder of the G.D., watched the events with avid interest. He was moving the ship forward quickly as the elephants charged, but he was not in time. The Russian was a ragged, red, dusty, tattered flatness which was still being pounded by elephant feet.

"Well, General," he said, "I *did* get it all on recorder."

Chapter 19

Teddy could not believe what *Belle's* screens were showing her. Matt shared her incredulity. He blamed himself, for he'd seen a figure in some sort of unusual dress emerge from the black ship and had delayed action. In his own defense, he had made some logical assumptions. He had assumed that the black ship was merely spying, even if that didn't make a lot of sense. Beauty had nothing to hide. Since the visit by the world famous Mr. Golding and his camera crews, other media people had visited the planet, many of them at the instigation of the old man. The coverage had been, on the whole, very favorable, so favorable that Beauty's administrators would not have refused a visit to anyone with a legitimate purpose. Matt could only guess that the black ship was from one of the sly spy outfits. Only governmental entities would use such a roundabout method to take a look at the elephant herd, the obvious purpose for that solitary figure's walk down on the surface. As the old man said, never underestimate the stupidity of a bureaucrat.

That ship down there had weapons. There was, in Matt's mind, no logical reason why he should face an armed ship with his wife aboard, and, if they'd been lucky, the minute beginnings of his first daughter inside her beautiful little stomach.

He was high enough to send a tight directional beam to the communications room at Africa House without splashing it all over the airwaves to be picked up by the black ship. He chatted with the communications tech on duty, describing the ship and the actions of the man on the surface. He broke off in mid-sentence, for things were happening down there. The eyes of *Belle* were clear enough and strong enough to make it seem that they were looking down on the walking man from the height of a four-story building. The man was creeping, then crawling.

"What is he doing?" Teddy asked.

Matt turned power into *Belle's* biggest eye. The resulting magnification lost some quality of definition but seemed to leave them sitting a few feet above the head of the rather blurred figure. Matt concentrated on the thing the man was carrying.

"That's a weapon," Teddy gasped.

Matt did things that sent *Belle* falling, boosted a bit past the second-per-second acceleration rate of a freely falling object, kicked in a bit more speed. He didn't want to fireball and thus warn the black ship because a call had gone out for the exploration ships to burn toward the site, and this time he wanted to have a personal chat with the pilot of that ship. They were near enough, still falling in silence, to see through *Belle's* eyes the sudden, sad collapse of the one bull elephant on Beauty and to witness the odd happenings that followed.

Belle's armament consisted of a half-dozen H.E. missiles and a hydrogen laser that had been used only to zap a couple of drifting pieces of space rock in target practice. Matt had had no intention of using either weapon on a manned ship, but somewhat to his surprise, there was a fury in him. He had not realized how closely bound he had become to the project, to the animals of Beauty. To see the bull uselessly slaughtered was a tragedy that made him see red.

"Arm the missiles," he ordered Teddy, as he kicked power into *Belle's* G.D. and sent a low roll of thunder ahead.

Jake Jordan had been moving his ship toward the scene of the elephant's orgy of Russian stomping, trying to figure out if he could use his cargo loader to somehow remove a blob of incriminating evidence. If he left what remained of Milyukov's body on the planet, it would be identified by teeth or fingerprints and someone, somewhere, might be able to link Jordan with the Russian. He had deemed to use the soil sampling attachment of the cargo loader to scoop up the Russian a bit at a time, complete with the bloody soil underneath and around him. He was near the body, and the animals had begun to move away, when his ship pinged alert and the detectors pointed up, toward a ship coming down fast.

Belle was trailing a sonic boom behind her. Two missiles were armed and ready and lodged in the launch tubes. "Let's get him," Teddy hissed bloodthirstily, but she would not fire without Matt's order. He hesitated. He had never killed a man. He did not know if there was one man or more on the black ship, which was such an easy target. And as he hesitated, a civilized man naturally reluctant to kill in spite of his anger over the elephant's death, Jordan acted. He punched a fire button and two lances of smoke rose vertically from the black ship.

"He's fired," Matt yelled. "Missiles to defense."

Teddy's fingers flew, even as Matt began to deflect *Belle* from her downward plunge. He had only a few seconds.

"Missiles away," Teddy yelped, as the ship jumped with the firing of missile rockets.

"Fire three and four on target," Matt said, as he

felt the pull of g forces. *Belle* was struggling to vector away from her vertical drop and twin streamers of sure death were curving to follow.

"Trans, trans," Matt was thinking, even as he tried to alter course on G.D. power. With his left hand, he punched in a trans and was about to push the button when the first defensive missile impacted an attacker and the sky burst yellow and red so near *Belle* that she jumped like a frightened filly. Then the second missile made good its intercept and there was another burst of brilliant color and smoke and worlds collided with a metallic crash. Matt jerked his finger away from the trans button. *Belle* was hurt. The scream of atmosphere at supersonic speed was in his ears. *Belle* was holed. To trans into space would be instant death as she underwent explosive decompression. He took a quick look at the screens. The black ship had disappeared. There were no missile tracks visible. If more missiles came, *Belle* would be a sitting duck.

"Remaining missiles to defense," he snapped. He turned his head away from the controls for a split second to see that Teddy was not in her chair and his heart began to pound with fear, for there was blood on the seat. "Hey?" he yelled, even as he manhandled *Belle* down from her supersonic speed, the danger of missiles forgotten now.

He kicked in the automatics and *Belle* started doing a hula dance. Her tail was shaking. She had been struck amidships and apparently some of her structural integrity was gone. He had to take her off automatic. He stood in a cramped position and saw that Teddy was crumpled and jammed into the space between her chair and the side of the control compartment. Her auburn hair was matted with the brighter red of fresh blood.

"Tedra," he bellowed, loosing his grip on the controls, and *Belle* bucked and tried to do a somer-

sault. He had to get the ship down. He took quick
bearings. He could make Africa House almost as
quickly as he could put *Belle* directly down, and
there'd be medical help there. He tried his communicator, but it was dead. He cursed, something he
did only rarely, tried to reach Teddy but couldn't
without taking both hands off the manual controls,
and when he lifted his hand *Belle* tried to roll in six
directions all at once. There was nothing to do but
pray and steer and center on the lawn directly in
front of Africa House where he'd pictured his kid
playing with her dolls and, *oh, Tedra, don't be dead.
Don't be dead, or seriously hurt. Damnit, Tedra.*

Belle bottomed out with a crunch of ripped hull,
dug little holes in the new lawn with tattered metallic
sheathing and Matt was bending over Teddy's seat
to feel the pulse beating—pretty strongly, he felt—
in her throat. People were streaming out toward the
ship, *Belle's* G.D. had been giving off unmuffled
thunder, the silencers having been blasted by the explosion of two missiles closed inboard and no one
on the grounds or in the buildings was unaware that
a ship in trouble had landed on the front lawn.

Matt was cradling Teddy's head. He'd tried to lift
her, but he couldn't get the proper leverage. His hand
had encountered blood at her waist as well, so he
was afraid to manhandle her out of her jammed position between seat and bulkhead.

Jack Frost was the first to reach the ship. He
pounded on the hatch and Matt moved quickly to
open it.

"Get an M.D.," Matt yelled.

"I'm a doctor," Jack said, climbing in.

"This is not a hurt zebra, it's Teddy," Matt said,
"get a goddamned M.D."

"Take it easy, boy," Jack said, pushing past Matt,
taking in the situation at a glance, feeling Teddy's
pulse and then spreading her matted hair to look at

the wound to her head. "Shallow cut," he said. "Nothing more serious than a mild concussion at worst."

"There's blood around her waist." Matt said.

Jack ran his hand down Teddy's body. There was a lot of blood coming from below her waist. He inserted his hand into the waistband of her shorts, under her tights, and his fingers slid on blood and smooth skin to feel a ragged, rather frightening hole. It took two fingers held together to fill the hole at the surface of her skin.

"All right," he said, "let's get her out of here, and quickly."

It took some doing. *Belle's* control area was tight. Matt lay across the console and Jack leaned over the back of the chair. Matt lifted under Teddy's knees while Jack had her under the arms and as she came out, Matt saw a new welling of blood that rapidly soaked her shorts and ran down her thigh. Then she was out and they were handing her to men outside, one of them Dr. Wells Smith, the Africa House M.D., who hadn't had much work to do on Beauty since the humans were healthier than many of the animals.

Within minutes, Teddy was lying on an operating table in the infirmary and Smith had removed her lower clothing and was gingerly probing the gaping wound in her stomach, lower than and left of her navel. Matt had pushed his way into the room over Smith's objections and stood, wanting to scream, yell, hit something, looking at the frightening hole in Teddy.

"Scanner," Smith snapped, and two nurses immediately rolled a portable scanner to point its nozzle at Teddy's stomach. Smith turned his head slightly to see the scanner's screen and ummmed. Matt's heart raced, because, although he could make nothing of the shadows and dark blotches, he did see what could only be jagged pieces of metal lodged deep within Teddy's stomach.

Smith turned to face Matt. "All right," he said, "we have to go in, and go in quick. She's bleeding internally, and, among other things, her colon is ruptured."

The all-important question was on Matt's lips, but he couldn't ask it.

"I think she'll live," Smith said, answering the dreaded question, "but I've got to move fast and I can't work with you hanging over my shoulder."

"She has a head wound, too," Matt said.

Smith fingered her head, parted her hair, nodded. "Scalp wound. No problem. Now scat."

Matt left. The nurses were building an edifice of gadgetry around Teddy, stripping away her upper clothing, beginning to clean the blood away. The last Matt saw was the lowering of the electronic helmet that would control Teddy's brain activity, acting as the safest method of anesthesia yet devised by medical science.

A good portion of Africa House's inmates were in the waiting area. Cassie Frost handed Matt a cup of coffee. Kerry came and kissed him on the cheek.

Jack Frost was using a portable communicator. "Matt," he said, as Matt sank weakly into a chair, too numb yet to know how frightened he was, "there's a dead man out there."

"I know," Matt said. "What about the ship?"

"No sign of it," Frost said. "He must have transed out. What the hell happened?"

"I don't know," Matt said, not wanting to remember, thinking only of Teddy with a hole in her stomach. Then he remembered something. Leaping quickly across the room, he jerked the communicator out of Jack's hand.

"Put me on intercom into the operating room," he told the communications man.

"Doc's got his red light on," the man said. "No can do."

"Put me on or I'll come there and shove this thing down your throat," Matt said coldly.

Jack leaned over Matt's shoulder and said, "Put him on to the operating room."

"Dr. Smith," Matt said, "this is Matt Tinker." He repeated his call twice and then, snarling, Smith's voice came back.

"Tinker, I'm doing some pretty damned delicate work in here."

"She had her implant removed over three months ago," Matt said, "I thought you should know."

"I know it, damnit, I was the one who took it out," Smith answered. "Now leave me alone."

Kerry patted Matt's shoulder. "She's going to be fine," she said.

"I know it," Matt said, because he could believe nothing else.

Jack was in a corner again, using the communicator, speaking in a low voice. He came to stand before the little group around Matt. "They've picked up a badly bent and damaged antique percussion rifle," he said. "The dead son of a bitch used it to kill Jumbo."

"I don't understand any of this," Cassie said.

Matt understood one thing. He was going to have to find the pilot of that black ship, and when he did, he was going to kill him.

Cassie and Kerry stayed with him for the entire three hours. It seemed more like three years. When Wells Smith came out of the operating room, still suited up in his sanitary gear, Matt jumped to his feet.

"She's fine," Smith said. "I need to talk with you in private, Matt.

Smith lead the way into the operating room. Teddy was still surrounded by gadgets. There was a relatively small pressure bandage on her head. Only a patch of hair had been shaved. Her lower body was under a tent of white, sanitary material.

"I had to do some rebuilding," Smith said. He picked up a jagged chunk of metal, almost an inch across at its widest axis. "This thing went in spinning and pieces shattered off. She has a new section of colon and her small intestine is about a foot shorter. I gave her the kidney of an eighteen-year-old boy. There was a rent in her stomach lining and a piece of the metal evidently broke off and destroyed her left ovary."

"Good God," Matt breathed.

"It was bad enough, Matt," Smith said, "but I've seen worse results from a ground vehicle accident. She'll be as good as new in a couple of weeks. What I wanted to talk to you about is this. She's carrying a fertilized egg."

"Uh," Matt said, as if he'd been hit in the stomach.

"I'd say it's no more than four or five days fertile."

So she had conceived, Matt thought, and not on that sunny, grassy spot where they'd picnicked in the mountains, but sometime within the last week. Ah, he had it. A quickie before sleep. Not nearly as satisfying as if she'd conceived there in the mountains.

But what the hell was he thinking about. He knew what was coming next.

"Now it looks like a very good egg, Matt, but—" He paused. "She's young and healthy, but she's had quite a bit of reconstruction inside. It takes time for a transplanted kidney to integrate properly, time for patching on the gut to be strong."

"You're saying you should take the egg?" Matt asked.

"I'm highly advising it."

Matt was glumly silent. How glad he was that they had not chosen to select the sex of their first child, for if he'd known that it was *his* little girl there inside Teddy in the form of a tiny little blob of life—

"A pregnancy could be harmful to her?" Matt asked, stalling for time.

"Within three months the embryo will have mass," Smith said. "Her entire body will be changing. I'd say that we'd have a fifty-fifty chance of having to take the baby."

After it had formed, after it had human fingers and toes and the beginning of a brain. Knowing Teddy, she would never, even at the threat of losing her own life, agree to that.

"Do what you think is best," Matt said.

"Oh, no, you don't," Smith said. "I'm going to keep her under for a week with accelerated healing, so I can't wait and ask her. It's your call, Matt."

"Take the egg," Matt said, his voice choking off at the end.

It was a very simple procedure.

Teddy rested, only the necessary activities allowed by the electronic helmet she wore. The incision and the impact hole, new skin grafted, healed as if by magic so that she soon looked normal, looked as if she was simply having a nap.

Smith removed the helmet and administered a stimulant one week to the day from the operation. Teddy opened her eyes, looked around, saw Matt and let her eyes linger for a moment before she zeroed in on the tubes in her arms, glanced up at the intravenous bottle.

"I hope it's not chocolate flavored," she said. "You know how I hate chocolate."

"It's strawberry," Matt said, wiping tears with the back of his hand.

She sighed. "I'm all in one piece?"

"With some new additions," he said.

"What?"

"A kidney, a length of colon, some skin." He

took her hand and she squeezed, hard. "The kidney is from a young boy, but don't you go trying to be bisexual on me."

"Hmm," she said.

"You won't be able to eat as much. He had to take out about a foot of your intestine."

"Pooh," she said. "That's no more than two bites worth. I'll take advantage of my condition and force you to supply me with all sorts of disgustingly sweet and rich foods and get gloriously fat."

He laughed, leaned to kiss her.

"I feel good, but restless. When can I get up?"

"Right now," Smith said. "Soon as we take the plumbing out of you."

They walked down a corridor outside the room, Teddy wrapped in a silken robe that showed her body shape. It looked to Matt like the same old Teddy. He had decided, and Smith had agreed, that she need never know that she'd been carrying the miracle of merged egg and sperm.

"Trouble is," Matt said, "that we're going to work twice as hard, when you're ready, to make that little girl baby."

"Sounds like good duty," she said, hugging his arm and beaming up at him.

"We'll have to wait a few months."

She was examining his face. "There's something else."

"Well, you are now a one ovary woman. The left one is gone, But the right one is very healthy, and will do the job nicely. We'll just have to make sure we hit the launch window."

"Oh," she said, and looked down at the floor as they walked. "Oh, well," she said, and then, "Did we get that son of a bitch?"

"No," he said, and for the first time in his life he felt the bitterness of complete failure.

Chapter 20

There was no identification on the thoroughly smashed body of the man who had killed Jumbo the bull elephant, but in the modern age that offered little challenge. It was not even necessary to use the D.N.A. identification method. There were fingers intact. Images of the fingerprints were soon transed to Reznor's home office on Earth, and it was child's play for Andy Reznor to have a check run through the massive computers that linked the world's law enforcement agencies. He whistled when he saw the dead man's identity and put in a call to Senator Gravel Smith even before sending a scrambled and coded report to Beauty. He didn't like broadcasting such potential dynamite, but the private Reznor code had just been changed and even if, as was highly likely, Intel or some national intelligence service had cracked the previous code, it would take a while to decode the new one.

Andy's bookkeeper's mind operated on point to point logic. The second most powerful man in the Soviet Union dead on Beauty, after committing a senseless act of slaughter, fit nowhere into a logical pattern, and he was unhappy about it. Senator Gravel Smith arrived in his office within two hours. Andy clicked in the max security electronics and gave the senator the facts.

Gravel's face screwed up into an expression of intense concentration. "Why?" he asked simply.

"I just don't know," Andy said.

Gravel was feeling decidedly uncomfortable. He was in his fourth term in the Senate and there was a sweet little behind-the-scenes campaign going on his behalf among leaders of his party to test the presidential waters in advance of declarations for the next election. For the first time, he wished that he'd never taken a Reznor dollar, not out of guilt, but out of fear, for this was a situation laden with political poison. Of course, Pax Five didn't elect American presidents, but that wavering, easily swayed beast out there, the American people, seemed to count the moments between interesting bits of scandal in Washington. The media, still smarting after nearly a century, carried a memory of the grand old days when a mere innuendo could result in huge, black headlines and serious-faced, doom-voiced shock on billions of screens. Give that hungry animal a real chance to tear into a senator without fear of reprimand from the board and a man's career was finished.

"Andy, I'm afraid I can have nothing to do with this," Gravel said.

Andy laughed. It was not a laugh of humor. It was a cold, deadly sound to the senator's ears. "The first thing I want you to do, Gravel, is get me a personality profile, in fact, the entire file on Milyukov."

"Andy," Smith said, "I just can't do it."

The eldest Reznor son leaned back, staring at the senator with cold, gray eyes. "Once, a long time ago, Gravel, you ran a business. Now I'm quite sure you haven't forgotten that a good businessman does not make an investment without certainty of return. If you'd care to know just how much we've invested in you over the years I can have the figures for you in a few seconds."

"I am not ungrateful," Smith said, "but—"

"Being, I think, a good businessman, I have ways of protecting my investment. I get rather nasty when I am cheated."

"Now see here," Gravel blustered.

Andy leaned forward and punched a button. A screen came to life, on still frame, showing the face of a well-known anchorman. The image grew in three dimensions and began to speak. After a few seconds, Gravel Smith sank back into his chair, his face ashen. Andy let the picture run for another minute and then turned it off. The brief exposé had detailed the financial arrangements between Senator Smith and a certain medium-sized aerospace firm.

"Needless to say," Andy said, "that was a recording, and the only copy is safe in our computer vaults."

"How'd you—" Smith could not complete the question.

"As I said, Gravel, we protect our investments. We were a little worried about this deal, and I came very close to talking with you about it at the time."

"But that media son of a bitch *knows*," Gravel protested.

"He knows much more than that," Andy said. "In our computer vaults are several hundred of those juicy little tidbits, one or more for every member of Congress, plus many others of our sterling members of government."

Smith jerked to his feet and paced in nervous silence. He turned. "You're bluffing. If you released that, I'd implicate Reznor Enterprises. I wouldn't go down without a fight."

"Here at Reznor, we're a bit more careful," Andy smiled. "Only by your word could anything be traced to us. And it would be your word against Reznor and the Washington world."

"Blackmail," Smith said.

"Survival," Reznor said. "Don't be naive, Gravel. How do you think the slide toward socialism was stopped? Through the wisdom of the American electorate? How do you think the business world prevented, first, the usurpation of all profits and then nationalization by people like you who, in the name of humanity, wanted to divide all wealth equally among billions?"

"But you're saying that you are the government," Smith said.

"In the absence of honest and capable men who want to serve," Andy said. "Of necessity. Do you think, Gravel, that I could be elected president?"

Smith hesitated before answering. "It might take eight years, a lot of money, but, yes."

"Why don't I want to be president?"

Smith, who wanted to be president more than anything, could not answer.

"Because I can contribute more here," Andy said. "Reznor creates more new jobs each year than the Federal government. And to create a new job we spend about one-fourth of what it costs the taxpayers for you to create a job. I like that favorite speech of yours, Gravel, the one you deliver for a fee of fifty thousand dollars every chance you get, where you praise freedom. In practice, however, your definition of freedom is the freedom for a majority of our population to be unproductive, to live on the productivity of the minority. A long time ago my father and a few others decided that it was too late to change that on Earth, but we're going back to basics on the new worlds. And when the population of Earth is reduced sufficiently, we'll see what can be done here."

"You're talking treason," Smith said. "One worldism."

"Not at all. My counterparts elsewhere in the world are just as deeply rooted in their own cultures as I am in mine. We share two things in common—good business sense, and, at the bottom, a sincere belief in the ability of mankind to achieve. The resources of the new planets, the new wealth available, give every man a chance. We've been severely crippled by the limit of Earth's natural resources. Since the early 1900s there just has not been enough to go around. You know that, but perhaps you don't admit it. Gravel, the worst thing you can do to a man is to permanently provide for him that which he is perfectly capable of providing for himself. We'll always have our genuinely weak and helpless. We can provide for them, but only if we return to the basics of personal responsibility, to the work ethic.''

Smith had returned to his chair. ''I don't see what all this has to do with Milyukov's death.''

''Perhaps nothing directly. I don't know. I have no idea what led Milyukov to go to Beauty and shoot an elephant. But you have recognized the potential problems. It could be something as unexplainable as Milyukov, for some reason, simply wanting to kill a large animal. Men used to go to great expense and risk some pretty serious tropical diseases to do that in Africa. But it could be part of something more complicated, part of the beginning of a new campaign to annex Beauty for colonization. It could be an attack on Reznor Enterprises through a weak point—Beauty. I'll admit that I was not in favor of giving over the finest planet yet discovered to animals, but my father wanted it, and if it were not for my father there would be no Reznor Enterprises. He's earned his dream, and he's going to have it.''

Andy put his elbows on his desk. ''As a member of the Senate Intelligence Committee, you can extract all available information about General Milyukov. I want it, and within two hours. I've opened up to you to make it a bit more palatable to you. If I've insulted you by my lack of regard for public servants in general, I'm sorry. I've always liked you, Gravel, and I think that if you'd stayed in the private sector you'd most probably be on my side.''

"Since I have no choice—"

"Since you have no choice, please expedite my request," Andy said.

Two hours later he had software containing more about General Igor Milyukov than he wanted to know. He skimmed quickly past Milyukov's background but sighed when he came to a listing of the general's private book and film library. There was an obvious preponderance of material relating to big game hunting in the past. He clicked his teeth with a fingernail as he read of the man's slaying of a polar bear, and made notes about his association with one Genna Darden, who had begun her public service career with the Bureau of Colonization and now worked for Intel.

If it had not been for the Intel connection, he might have decided that the otherwise stable Russian was just a bit off-balance in his desire to kill animals.

Reznor's department of intelligence had never made any attempt to penetrate Intel. Under the direction of the man with one name, Shardan, Intel was the most highly professional intelligence agency in history, and each time others had tried penetration they had failed, sometimes fatally or, at best, embarrassingly.

Andy discussed the situation at length with his chief of intelligence. His decision had already been made, but he was relieved when the chief came to the same conclusion without being led. For the moment, nothing would be done. What was left of Igor Milyukov's body would be preserved on Beauty. More information would be gained if the next move came from those others who knew that Milyukov had traveled to Beauty. There had to be at least one who knew, the pilot of the ship that had attacked

Matt Tinker's ship before transing away. Andy suspected that others knew, as well. The disappearance of a man of Milyukov's importance would flush them out quickly.

ntal Takeover amp before fleering away. Nady experienced the others knew as well. The divergence o
oba itam of M Pinkhew's intransacs should flush them
no quasi.

Chapter 21

The two cheetahs, Ramses and Nefertiti, looking like
something out of an ancient Egyptian wall painting,
stood a few paces away from a release cage on the
plain near Africa House and examined their new sur-
roundings. They were of a size—sleek, deadly-beau-
tiful animals, the state of the evolutionary art in a
biological speed machine. Satisfied at last, perhaps
pleased by the smell of Beauty's unsullied air, head
jerking with each movement of grass in the wind,
Nefertiti began a careful exploration, looking back
now and then to see if Ramses was following.

Ramses, who had just come into his adult prime
and was younger than Nefertiti, suddenly leaped into
action, racing the wind that blew across the rich
grasses, turning with great lashings of his balancing
tail to topple his mate playfully. The two sleek animals rolled in the grass for a moment, then Nefertiti,
also feeling the new freedom, raced away and
Ramses was soon neck and neck with her as they ran
for the joy of running without having to watch for
the confining fences.

During training on Earth, Nefertiti had shown
more interest in simulated hunts than Ramses. With
that blazing, brief speed of which she was capable,
she'd chased simulated animals dragged behind a ve-

hicle to be rewarded with fresh, red meat from which the blood dripped tantalizingly.

The newly released cheetahs had been well fed. It would be an interesting vigil, Jack Frost thought, waiting until hunger rumbled in their bellies to discover whether Nefertiti's training would transfer to a living animal as prey.

One milestone had already been passed. The hyena pack had pulled down a yearling wildebeest with a broken leg only two days before the release of the cheetahs. A few hours after release, their playful energies having been dissipated, Ramses and Nefertiti found the hyena kill, chased away the pack, and gnawed on already well-chewed bones.

Jack and Cassie were hoping that the cheetahs would not make their first kill in darkness. They had packed field rations and would stay on the plains to observe until Ramses and Nefertiti were definitely integrated into their new life. There were encouraging signs on the second day. The cheetahs discovered that the grass eating animals ran from them, and there were several chases that seemed to be not much more than an extension of play, an expression of the cheetahs' joy in having a wide, unfenced range. They were not yet hungry enough to get serious.

That night Jack asked Matt if he'd like to observe the cheetah's first kill, guessing that hunger would force action either during the night or the next day. Matt didn't have much else to do, except stay so close to an apparently normal Teddy that she had trouble getting her work done. Matt told her that she was taking some time off, that they'd share a picnic basket with Jack and Cassie next day. Teddy had not recovered her former level of energy. She felt great, had no pain, her surface wounds were healed nicely, but she tired easily. Her work was fairly well caught up, so she made no protest.

It was a great morning, the sun brilliant, the sky

cloudless, with a little breeze that would be welcome as the day warmed. Jack set a slow pace, leading the way on a goat. Matt had wanted Teddy to ride with him, but she'd insisted on a goat of her own.

The cheetahs were lying in the place they'd chosen, in the shade of a tree beside a water hole in the bed of a stream that ceased to run during the dry season. Jack picked an observation point on a knoll. Each of them had a set of powered binoculars.

"I think Nefertiti is restless," Cassie said, soon after they had arrived on the knoll.

"There she goes," Jack said, as the female cheetah left the shade of the tree and stalked smoothly off into the grass. Ramses followed. Ahead of the cheetahs a herd of wildebeests grazed. There were calves among the herd.

"Look, look," Cassie said excitedly. They were all looking. Nefertiti had seen and smelled the wildebeests. She melted into the grass to become almost invisible and, as Ramses came to her side and followed suit, began a careful stalk.

"The instincts are still there," Jack said.

A nervous wildebeest must have caught a scent. He swished his tail, jerked his head. At that moment Nefertiti burst from the cover of the grass, Ramses behind her, and the herd bolted. The cheetahs seemed to make a graceful blur as they ran, but Nefertiti had chosen an adult male to single out and the wildebeest held his own for fifty yards or so and then began to pull away. The rest of the herd had scattered in other directions. Nefertiti slowed and halted, tongue lolling.

"You'll have to pick a young one, baby," Jack said.

Teddy jerked her head toward Jack. That thought had not occurred to her. It seemed unfair.

Twice more Nefertiti made bad choices, once with

zebra and once with a pair of young kudu antelope who saw the charge early and easily outdistanced it.

It was clear now that Nefertiti was frustrated. She led the way back to water and then eastward. The four observers had to leave the knoll and follow. The cheetahs seemed to think that covering ground was desirable, and they loped along, Nefertiti leading, as usual. The goats kept pace, at a distance.

The climax of the day came among the scattered brush and grass within a few miles of the precipitous cliffs which climbed to a higher level of the plain leading toward the mountains. At first, when Nefertiti began to stalk, her intended prey was hidden. However, as she charged, Teddy saw a flurry of motion and a family of beautiful little gazelles bolted from a clump of brush, a male, a female, and a calf only a few months old.

"Ah, you're learning," Jack said, as Nefertiti slung her tail for balance and changed directions to follow the little gazelle calf. The distance closed quickly and with one raised paw Nefertiti smashed the small calf to tumble in the dust. Teddy gasped. Quickly, Nefertiti closed her jaws on the little animal's spine and there came, even over the sound of the goats' idling engines, the calf's agonized death scream.

A flood of compassion flushed Teddy's face. The calf was fighting, struggling for its life, and through her binoculars she could see the open, drooling mouth, the wide, staring, panicked eyes. With a shake of her powerful neck, Nefertiti put the gazelle out of its pain.

Unreasoning anger, pity, questioning. Why was the life of that ugly-beautiful cheetah more important than the life of a little gazelle? Horrible. The victim so helpless, so terrified, feeling the death grip of those huge, sharp teeth.

For a moment she felt her emotions amplified, as if shared, saw spots before her eyes through the glasses, saw glowing white globes dancing around Ramses and Nefertiti as they tore into the still warm flesh of the gazelle. She lowered her glasses and wiped perspiration from her forehead.

"Matt," she said, "I'm a little tired."

She reconciled it all as they rode slowly back toward Africa House. He who had created life had fashioned both cheetah and gazelle. For the gazelle that was hollow comfort, perhaps, but so had it been for all the eons of the history of life in an ecosystem that was based on eating and being eaten. Matt had agreed to stay on Beauty for two more years. As she went to her room and lay down to rest she wondered, as she fell asleep, if it wouldn't be advisable to relieve him of that promise, tell him that she was ready to go, to renew their love aboard *Belle,* after the ship was repaired. But a decision never should be made after dark or when one is tired or ill, so she thought, instead, of the pretty little stream where she and Matt had picnicked and made love. She could almost hear the gurgling of the clear, cold waters and soon she was asleep.

Chapter 22

Genna Darden was a bit worried. Igor Milyukov was weeks overdue. As evidence that she was not the only one who realized that something was wrong, Shardan had not shown up at her apartment since Milyukov had left Earth, and he had not invited her to lunch or dinner. She felt that Shardan was telling her something by his absence, saying, "I have discharged my debt to you, and I will incur no more obligations."

Although it was not her nature to consider bestowing the charms of her body as strictly a business activity, she was realist enough to know that others might feel she'd prostituted herself in pursuit of her goals. She felt that, since it was her nature and her inclination, giving herself to a man was her pleasure, and if a man was influenced to give something in return there was no shame in taking it. To think that Shardan was measuring their relationship on a value for value trade basis angered her, but he was, after all, Shardan, one of the world's most powerful men. To seek him out would be admitting that he was right in thinking that she'd welcomed him into her body only for the advancement of her own goals.

However, when the media reported, without editorial comment, that General Igor Milyukov had been absent from the latest Soviet state occasion, she knew a crisis was near. When the Soviets announced that Milyukov was merely on an extended vacation she became even more concerned, for such an announcement was, she knew, a delaying tactic that would buy only a small amount of time. She expected to be accosted at any time by faceless, dark men with Russian accents, although Milyukov had assured her that no one in Russia knew of his relationship with her and that in the event of unforeseen trouble during his quest to Beauty there would be absolutely no way of implicating her.

But Shardan knew, and Shardan would put international relations ahead of personal relations. She actually breathed a sigh of relief when she was summoned to the chief's office. He did not rise when she entered. He was in formal uniform, his steely eyes boring into hers from the moment she entered. She sat down without being asked.

"I have been officially asked, by the Soviet Premier, to look into the disappearance of General Igor Milyukov, Miss Darden."

She noted the formal form of address and felt a chill.

"The Soviet intelligence agencies have traced the general to an out-of-service yacht port in the mountains of Yugoslavia. He was seen to board a private craft without markings. I have decided to assign only two of my best operatives to the case for the moment."

Genna waited, hardly breathing.

"It is not necessary that you know who will be handling the investigation here on Earth," he said. "You will cooperate with agencies on the colonial worlds. This will require considerable travel, and you'll be assigned a pilot and an Intel cruiser. Your assignment is to determine if General Milyukov landed on any of the out-planets. Do you understand?"

"I do," Genna said. She opened her mouth to say more, but Shardan interrupted. "If all is clear, Miss Darden, that is all."

Her mouth was open. She started to protest, and then with a flick of his hand he touched switches and she realized that everything, to that moment, had been recorded. He hit another button and she knew, from previous experience, when their meetings in his office had been of a more personal nature, that he had isolated them by raising a security screen.

"Christ, Genna, have you been sitting on your ass waiting for a miracle?" he demanded. "Don't you realize the seriousness of this?"

"While sitting on my ass," she said icily, "I have been trying to locate the pilot. He has disappeared."

"That's logical, since Milyukov has also disappeared," Shardan said. "What measures have you taken?"

"Routine inquiry through the agency. A check of Jordan's known associates, including the illegal miners in the asteroids. He has not been seen in the past few weeks."

"Reznor Enterprises changed their code two days before Milyukov was supposed to land on Beauty," Shardan said.

"Do you think there's a connection?" she asked, leaning forward. "But how would they have known he planned to land on Beauty?"

"They change codes now and then," he said. "It could be coincidental, but we've been unable to break the new one. The brains say it might take another month. And we don't have a month."

"There is no way we can be linked with Milyukov," she said.

"There's Jordan," Shardan said. "And your association with Milyukov."

She shrugged. "Yes, I knew the general. A charming man. We were social friends, not close.

We had dinner together, let's see, it's so difficult to remember—''

"One touch, anywhere on your body, by a Russian's hand containing a small, almost invisible needle and you'd describe your nights in bed with Milyukov in erotic detail and sing out everything you know about Jake Jordan and Milyukov's desire to go to Beauty and kill some damned animal. We've got to see that it doesn't come to that. We're going to make a sincere effort to find Milyukov.''

"Beauty,'' Genna said.

"Not immediately,'' Shardan warned. "Hit half a dozen other planets first. Meanwhile, I'll be laying the groundwork for you to visit Beauty. We can't have you dashing in there yelling. 'What have you done with the man who will one day be the next Russian Premier?' I think Intel is going to request a complete workup on that planet, for future reference. I think you'll be in charge of an Intel inspection team that will be invited to Beauty in the spirit of Pax Five cooperation.''

"I've wondered about an accident in space,'' Genna said. "It doesn't make sense to think that Milyukov actually got to Beauty. If he did and achieved his purpose, there'd have been a great cry of protest from the Reznor people there. If he got there and was caught, they wouldn't dare hold so important a man.''

"You'll be working with Jeff Soutine. He's a fine pilot, among other things. You'll have time to learn a few things from Jeff during your early travels so that you'll be ready when you arrive on Beauty. Incidentally, Jeff, not you, and mark this well, is the senior man. You're to do as he tells you and consult him before you make any move.''

"Thank you very much,'' Genna said sarcastically. Shardan did not smile. He rose and that was a signal for her to go.

With a swiftness that dazed her, she found herself aboard a sleek Intel cruiser, well armed, powerful, luxurious. She met Jeff Soutine there for the first time, shook hands, was told to buckle up, and within an hour they were in deep space.

She had had a chance during the takeoff and the first trans to examine Soutine. He seemed an ordinary looking man at first, not too handsome but definitely not ugly, just a man with brownish-black hair, a face that could be forgotten easily—rounded, calm, brown-eyed, with a nondescript nose. He moved well, however, making her realize that his relaxed pose hid the quick reflexes of an athlete. He did not speak until the ship was deep into space.

"You'll find a set of small books marked SECRET-SECRET in your cabin. Study the manual of field operations first, then, when you've memorized that, start on METHODS OF INDIRECT INTERROGATION."

"Yes, *sir*," she said.

Soutine's eyes narrowed as she inflected the "sir." She felt a slight chill of apprehension.

"Just do it," he said.

She went to her cabin and began to read. The material was absorbing. She soon realized that she had been kept at the Intel home office as a pet, that she had no conception of covert operations, and she determined to remedy that. She would prove to that cold-eyed bastard Soutine that she was not some bit of fluff.

After three hours of concentrated reading, she was tired. She showered, dried and stood nude in front of a mirror to dry her hair. When the door opened, she whirled. Soutine's eyes measured her from face to knee.

"I would appreciate it if you'd knock before entering in the future," she said coldly.

"We're orbiting Ingleside," he said. "Our destination is on the nightside. We'll sleep here until local morning."

"Thank you," Genna said.

Soutine walked to the bed and began to remove his clothing.

"What do you think you're doing?" Genna demanded.

"Following orders." There was a faint smile on his lips, the first hint of expression she'd seen. "The chief told me to spend as much time with you as possible, teaching you."

"Get out of my cabin," Genna said.

Soutine kicked off his slip-ons. Nude, his body showed that he was well conditioned. "Come," he said, crooking a finger at her.

"You arrogant bastard," she hissed, picking up the nearest object, her hair dryer, and throwing it. He dodged it easily and in a series of quick, fluid motions he seized her arm with one hand as she tried to hit him in the face, and pressed the fingers of the other hand into a secret place at the front of her neck. She cried out, for the pain was quick and severe.

"Come," he said. "Although I doubt I'll be able to teach *you* much about the subject of study for tonight."

The pain was so intense that she could not scream. Then he was pushing her forcefully down onto the bed and the pain was gone. After one repetition, as she struggled, she decided that she wanted no more pain. Incredulously, she allowed him to take her. Her retribution could come later. She was a citizen of a sovereign and civilized nation, a member of the Pax Five Community of Independent Nations. There were still laws, and Earth's laws applied to her citizens, no matter where they were in space.

"You can go now," she said, when he'd finished.

"I like it here," he said. He dozed with his hand

clasped around her wrist and when she tried to remove her hand he awakened just enough to squeeze
her wrist painfully. When he took her again, it was
with as much dispassion and straightforward pur-
posefulness as it had been the first time. To her
shame, she responded and, at her movements and
obvious interest, Soutine laughed sardonically. The
contempt in his laughter drove all passion from her,
leaving only hate.

When, at last, she was allowed to sleep, she
seemed to die a small death. She awoke to Soutine's
voice, but it was coming from the communicator.
"Get it out here, sweet pants. Now."

The ship was in motion. She dressed quickly and
joined Soutine in the control area. Soutine was in
communication with a ground controller. Ingleside
was a planet of vast oceans and scant land area, blue
and beautiful.

"We'll be down at Armstrong Space Port in half
an hour," Soutine said. "I want to use about two
minutes of that time to tell you just a little about
me."

"I don't care about you," Genna said. Ingleside
was a civilized, English-speaking world, the second
world to be settled. The society was based on the
early American Republic, but with the weaknesses
inherent in the original American Constitution
strengthened. The mostly white, Anglo-American
populations of Ingleside's scattered land areas were
known for their respect for law and order, personal
freedom, individual rights.

"I have a wife and three kids at home," Soutine
said. "I'm quite fond of them. My wife is the
daughter of a very rich man, and she's fond of me."

Genna, surprised, was wondering if he was now
going to beg for forgiveness. She was forming her
rebuttal as he continued, thinking that had he asked
or been gentle—

"I started at Intel with Shardan, when the agency was formed. We had learned our trade together as agents for the Anglo-European Alliance. My Intel number is four zeros followed by a two. Shardan's number is four zeros followed by a one. Do you follow me?"

"I'm not stupid," she said, and she was feeling slightly ill, for he was telling her that if she voiced a complaint on Ingleside or elsewhere, she would be accusing a man who was intimate with the power elite of the civilized galaxy.

"I have been told as much by Shardan," Soutine said. "Good, then. You see, Darden, false pride has been the Achilles heel of many in our business. Shardan immediately saw that you had great potential, your excellent body and your beauty being potential tools of great power. He told me, however, that you tend to squander your assets without purpose, for ego massage or for personal pleasure. Where were pride and personal pleasure last night?"

Then, as the ship screamed through atmosphere and pivoted for landing, he smiled at her for the first time. "I, too, think you have great potential, and it is my job to help you develop it during this mission."

Without being able to understand, Genna knew that her life had reached one of those points of irrevocable change, and she was lost, confused. She tried to hide the tears that formed and rolled down her perfect cheeks.

Chapter 23

Matt was jerked to a sitting position in his bed by the howl of the emergency call. Teddy rolled sleepily up onto one elbow, saying, "Wha'?" The first rays of the sun were reddening in the eastern sky over the plains.

"You stay here," Matt said. "I'll check it out."

But Teddy, in a hastily donned set of coveralls, was right behind him when he ran across the lawn to the pad where Jack Frost was yelling at others to shake a leg. They managed to pile into the explorer just before the G.D. rumbled and lifted the ship, the hatch clanging behind them when they were already airborne.

"What's happening?" Matt demanded of Cassie. Jack was in the cargo area shouting orders.

"It's Ramses and Nefertiti," Cassie said. "They're down. Dawn shots from a satellite spotted them."

"Down?" Teddy asked.

"Ill, perhaps dead," Cassie said sadly.

It was a short flight. Frost was first out, men rushing behind him with litters large enough and sturdy enough to carry a cheetah. When Teddy arrived on the scene, it seemed to her that Jack was trying to pull an old lion tamer's trick and thrust his head into Nefertiti's mouth as he held it open. The cheetahs were lying limply, sides heaving with their panting. Nefertiti's eyes did not open and she put up no struggle.

"They haven't been eating carrion," Jack said, for his lion tamer's pose had been to smell Nefertiti's breath. "But something's haywire." The animal's breath was not that of a carnivore, made rank by decaying meat lodged in its teeth. There was a sour, bovine smell. He took Nefertiti's temperature quickly, then ordered the team to load the cats aboard the ship.

Teddy went back to quarters to dress. Matt followed the running men into the veterinary lab and watched as Jack jumped and jerked around seemingly aimlessly but actually accomplishing a number of quick tests. A stomach pump produced noxious fluids and sodden lumps of bilious green.

"Grass?" Jack yelped. He jumped about some more and rammed a long, flexible viewing tube down Nefertiti's throat. "Bloomin' damned grass," he shouted. "Her stomach is full of undigested grass."

The stomachs of both cats contained an astounding mass of grass. Jack's team worked swiftly, pulling the clods of grass from the cats with the aid of pumps and flexible tools that looked like automated rakes.

"Get helmets on both of them," Jack said, and it was done. Intravenous feeding was started. An hour later the vital signs of both cats were stable. Jack took advantage of Nefertiti's immobile state to scope her womb and there were two nice little cheetah embryos forming, already moving with new life.

"Grass," Jack moaned, leaning tiredly on the operating table. "A cat might chew a little grass, but pounds of the stuff?"

A meeting with the entire animal staff found no answer to that question. The finest animal behaviorists in the galaxy had never encountered or had never heard of a carnivore eating so much grass that stomach and bowels were impacted with the indigestible mass.

Matt told Teddy about the mystery over a late breakfast. Teddy made no comment, but it was obvious to him that she was thinking.

"Are you all right?" he asked. Since being wounded she had often seemed to go off into a world of her own, her eyes apparently looking at him, but her thoughts far away. He didn't like being lonely, and that was exactly how he felt with Teddy directly across the table from him but so far away.

"I'm fine," she said. "Never better."

"Let's take a day off."

"Can't, Matt. The *Ark's* due tomorrow and there's a lot of planning to be done to get her off-loaded in about ten different spots around the globe. And the tanker will be here in a week or so with whales."

"Well, even I can get a little excited about whales," Matt said.

"Only the plankton eaters. The marine people think there's enough plankton, krill, and small fish such as sardines to support a pod now. I'd like to see the release."

"Suits me," he said. "If you're going to be busy, Earl has asked me to give him a hand with a new gadget of his. He wants to give it a field test and I guess today's as good a day as any if you won't take time off and play with me."

"Give Earl a hand," she said.

Matt left her seated at the table, finishing her second cup of coffee. When he looked back one last time he saw that her face was blank, with that faraway, thinking look. His impulse was to go back, take her in his arms, not let her out of his sight until she was Teddy again.

There were not many things that Teddy was unwilling to discuss with Matt, but she had mentioned nothing about her little dizzy spell after watching the cheetahs at their first kill. She was afraid he'd worry, be an old, mothering pest, and insist that she go for another round of tests with Wells Smith. The incident preyed on her mind. She had to discuss it with someone. She left the dining hall and sought out Kerry Hertz in the botany wing. When Kerry saw her, she tossed aside a paper she'd been filling with notes and smiled.

"Any startling discoveries lately?" Teddy asked.

"Dead bloody end," Kerry said. "Plants are plants, whether they are Earth plants or Beauty plants."

Teddy didn't know exactly where to begin. She looked around at a very exotic collection of specimens.

"There's something on your mind," Kerry said.

Teddy plunged in. "Do you remember what Jack said after he attacked that little zebra? He said: 'We wanted to know why.' I thought it was peculiar, but that it was probably just the result of Jack's embarrassment and confusion. He's a rather excitable man. I thought he'd just lost it for a few minutes in his eagerness to teach fear to the zebras. But when Nefertiti killed the gazelle the other day I was—" She laughed uneasily. "I guess I was being a bleeding heart, or at least unrealistic. I was angry at the cat and full of pity for the dying animal. And it was as if that feeling was shared. I was not alone in my revulsion."

Kerry looked down at her feet.

"I've checked records, notes from every department, looking for another such incident," Teddy said. "I didn't find any."

No, Kerry was thinking, because I didn't have the courage to report a very significant incident.

"There's something out there," Teddy said. "And it can influence the actions of both man and animal.

It made Jack attack the zebra. It caused the elephants to avenge the death of one of their own—''

"That could have been natural behavior," Kerry said.

"And it agreed with me in regretting the death of the gazelle Nefertiti killed," Kerry went on. "To the point where it influenced the cheetahs to stop eating flesh and to gorge on grass instead."

Kerry had heard the alarm, had inquired, and when she found that it was an emergency call for a veterinary team, she had lost interest, thinking it was just another sick animal, or a difficult birth on the plains. She questioned Teddy about the cheetahs. Then she made her decision.

Teddy listened in silence. She assured Kerry that the secret would be theirs. "Thank you for telling me," she said. "I know what it cost you to tell, but it wasn't your fault."

"The devil made me do it?"

"Or Beauty."

"I'm ready to believe almost anything, even an intelligent planet with the brain of a newborn child, learning little by little."

"What if it learns too much," Teddy asked, "and decides that it doesn't like us at all?"

"You're making me want to look over my shoulder," Kerry said.

Teddy was becoming more and more sure in her mind. There'd been one other incident that she'd almost forgotten, had never entered into any record. The first day she and Matt rode on the goats there'd been that unnatural, protesting echo from the cliffs. She had been back there since, and it had never happened again.

She dressed for the sun and sneaked out a side door, found her personal goat and left the compound heading west, circling back to the north when she was out of sight.

The growing herds still seemed to favor the same lush areas of the plain. The hyena pack had killed again, this time a healthy looking zebra colt. The jackals were contesting the hyenas for the remains of the kill.

A vast and aching loneliness settled over her as she rode through the herds toward the far cliffs. She could not see Africa House. She would not have felt more lonely if she'd been thrust back in time to primeval Africa. She kept looking around, checking behind her. With the two cheetahs in the compound there were no large carnivores on the loose, yet still she felt uneasy. She circled far around the last sighting area of the elephants, shuddering with thoughts of how the Russian had been killed. An hour later, she was approaching the cliffs. She tried to remember landmarks by which to choose, to the best of her memory, the area where she had heard the odd echo.

She dismounted and walked a bit farther, until she was directly under the cliffs, standing among scattered, loose rocks and boulders that had been toppled from the cliffs by natural erosion. She felt both lonely and a bit silly. She swallowed, glanced over her shoulder, looked up to see two vultures soaring high. There would be more bird varieties on the *Ark* this time, but still no raptors. In another year, perhaps, the small animal population would have grown to the point of supporting birds of prey.

"Well," she said aloud, "here I am, and I'm not sure why I'm here. I'm here, I guess, to talk to you, Beauty, or to whatever or whoever you are. We must seem very strange to you. We come here in our roaring machines and without so much as a by your leave start building things and pouring the life of Earth out onto you. You've been trying to tell us something. You gave us a message when we tried to cut down one of your trees. And you're trying to learn about us, aren't you? You were curious about the emotions felt by Kerry and Earl, or maybe just about our breeding habits. You wondered why Jack wanted to frighten the zebras, and what it was in his mind regarding something killing a zebra. You saw the cheetah kill the gazelle, and you felt, or shared, my feelings. Did you show yourself to me? Was that you, those small, white globes dancing around the kill?''

She shivered and, once more, looked over her shoulder. Then she sat down on a sun-warmed boulder and, letting her eyes rest on the shadows near the top of the cliff, continued. ''It must have been difficult to grasp—death. I don't think you intended to kill that man over in America. I think you were just trying to warn him not to hurt one of your trees. But you understood death when the Russian shot the elephant, and you influenced the elephants to charge at the slayer and kill in return.

''But you didn't understand why Nefertiti had to kill, probably because my feelings influenced you. You learned quickly that the hummingbirds and the bees were helpful, not harmful. You allow the elephants to eat, as long as they don't kill plants unnecessarily. And you've got still more to learn, because unless you stop us, we're going to fill you with life, Beauty. And it's a pretty odd system.

''Let me draw an analogy. I'm assuming that your plants are just plants. You knew nothing of death. Plants don't really die. Adult plants cease to grow and wither and return to the soil, but their life goes on in seedlings or other form. And yet it's a kind of death, and a simple equivalent of the chain of life in the system we're trying to build here. The dead plants return to the soil and their basic elements are used by the new, in a continuation of life. When Nefertiti kills and eats she's doing basically the same thing, it's just that there's a life at stake. Still, there are those who believe that all life is a part of the same force. It doesn't hold water with me, but the theory is there, and if they're right then the gazelle's life force is continued, not lost, in a baby cheetah, or in the birth of a new gazelle calf.''

She paused. There was only the sigh of the wind to answer her.

"Beauty, bear with us. Learn with us. Carnivores can't live on grass. No peaceable kingdom, Beauty, just the age-old law of eat and be eaten. I hope you can understand that. Let the cheetahs be cheetahs. It would help if you'd reveal yourself to us, communicate with us. Won't you do that?''

She sat in silence. The wind moved her hair against her cheek. The sun moved a fraction of its diameter and got hotter. Sweat rolled down her neck.

"Well, I just wanted to give it a try," she said, rising. "I wanted to tell you how it is. You don't seem to mind our being here, and I think you rather like the animals, or you wouldn't have been upset about the killing of the elephant and the death of the gazelle. We can work together, Beauty. They're your animals now, as well as ours. Help us look after them?''

From far up, from the shadows of the cliffs, they came, two globes of white not more than a foot in diameter. They plunged toward her at impressive speed and her heart began to pound, but they slowed and danced before her, perhaps ten feet away. Then they were gone.

Chapter 24

When Teddy insisted on an early return to their quarters after dinner, forgoing the usual after dinner discussion, Matt was pleased. He put on a film while Teddy showered and donned a cute little nightie, watched with his usual appreciation when she padded, barefoot, to sit on the bed with her legs crossed under her. She used the bedside controls to turn off the screen, and he started toward the bed to join her.

"No, sit over there," Teddy said, indicating a chair.

Matt sat. She began tentatively. As she talked, Matt felt the hair start to stand on his neck, not because of the content of her words, but because he knew that she'd been severely traumatized by the serious damage to her body. But, as she continued, sounding very Teddy like, putting conclusion atop conclusion in a manner that made sense, he became less concerned about her mental condition. When she had finished her account of her experience, her theories, he thought for some seconds.

"That gadget that Earl Fabre was testing today is designed to detect heat," he said. "We set it up, along with an electronic screen, in an area of wild flowers. There was pollination activity going on, but no heat was detected. If those white globes you saw—well, he detected no heat."

"And where there's life, there's heat?" Teddy asked.

"At least in life as we know it."

"There's something," she said. "I talked, and it answered."

"Teddy, you know the long, long history of unexplained phenomena."

"Yes, I know. Sun dogs. Ball lightning. Self-hypnosis. Hallucination."

"Would you object to calling Earl over here, to telling him what you've just told me?" he asked.

"I don't know," she said "I—yes, all right. We have to begin somewhere."

Fabre listened with great interest as Teddy, still seated on the bed but with a short robe covering her filmy nightclothes, went through it all again. He mused for a moment. "There's something I haven't put into the records," he said. "It might have a bearing on what you've experienced, Teddy."

"We know," Teddy said, with a smile.

"Kerry?" Earl said.

"Just today," Teddy said. "I see no reason, Earl, to make it general knowledge."

"I'd appreciate it," Earl said, his face flushed. "Odd, isn't it? There are still things that we can't face with scientific detachment." There was a brief silence. "All right," he said, "something moves pollen. Something, somehow, gets into our heads, or at least reads our thoughts. Those things you've seen twice, Teddy—" He paused. "Well, if it's visible, it should be detectable, either by its own heat or by reflected heat. Apparently, the globes can choose to be visible."

"No one's seen them but Teddy," Matt said.

"Which leads me to wonder if she was seeing them with her eyes or with her mind," Earl said.

"I've thought of that," Teddy said. "After all,

there were three people with me the first time and none of them saw the globes.''

''Assuming it was hallucination,'' Earl said, ''and I choose to think it wasn't, knowing you, then whatever it is chose to reveal itself to you, and could have done so by projecting an image directly into your mind. Be damned difficult to detect something like that. Pure thought? How can a thought be visible?''

Neither Matt nor Teddy ventured an opinion.

''I've checked the movement of pollen in those compact little clumps for emanations in wavelengths running from the hertzian frequencies through infrared, visible, and ultraviolet. And we've been all over this planet with instruments to measure radioactivity. Aside from background radiation slightly higher than on Earth, indicating that Beauty might be just a little younger than Earth, nothing. There's pitchblende and radium beneath the surface, as is to be expected.'' He rubbed his chin. ''I wonder. We're dealing with something entirely beyond our experience here, and I've been approaching the problem from a traditional scientific view, assuming that we know all there is to know about the elemental forces of the galaxy.''

''Are you on to an idea?'' Matt asked.

''Well, at least another approach. The worst that can happen is that we will eliminate the possibility of something that seems to be physically impossible.''

''Want to talk about it?'' Matt asked.

Earl laughed. ''You can laugh tomorrow, when I give it a try.''

The jury-rigged mass of instrumentation was assembled on a high meadow carpeted with half a dozen varieties of wild flowers. It took two trips with an explorer to transport and a day, an evening, and most of the next day to assemble and test. Earl sent word to Teddy and Matt when he was almost ready, and they joined him on the high meadow. Earl and his technicians began to turn on and adjust a scattered grouping of electronic equipment.

"Okay," Earl said at last. "Let's see what we can see."

At first he "saw" nothing. The screen showed pollination activity, and once a tiny, bright hummingbird flitted into the area, a small source of heat. There was no radiation.

"Well, I didn't really expect it," Earl said. "You can laugh. I've been looking for X-ray or gamma sources, high-energy radiation. As I said last night, it is, at worst, a method of eliminating a very remote possibility."

"That's it?" Matt asked.

"I wanta play around a bit more, since we have the equipment set up," Earl said. "It's pretty difficult to focus on the moving clumps of pollen, since we can't see them with the naked eye and can detect them only when they pass through the screen. I'd like to have a way of concentrating on one pollen clump, of following it."

Earl and his technicians went into a huddle. Teddy and Matt took a walk. A pleasantly cooling wind was coming down off the mountains. "Wouldn't this be a great place to build a home?" Matt asked.

"Snows in the winter," Teddy said.

"Skiing. The kids could build snowmen."

"No homesteading on Beauty," she said.

"Somewhere there's another planet with places like this," he said. Then, quickly, "Sorry. I'm not going back on our deal."

"Maybe we should all leave," Teddy said. "Take the animals—"

"Round up all the field mice, the bees?"

"I don't know."

They strolled back. Earl had mounted an odd-looking nozzle on a rotating head and was testing its movements. "I've hooked into the screen," he explained, as Matt leaned over his shoulder. "We're putting a big load on our power source, but I've got a movable screen projection, and when we detect pollen movement—" He grinned. "Ah," he said, moving the nozzle by hand. "Wish we had an automatic tracking system rigged." He tried again. After a few attempts he was able to follow a movement of pollen from one bed of flowers of one variety to another. He and the technicians went into another huddle and he once again took his place behind the movable instrument.

"Here we go," he said. Power hummed. The portable generator's engine lugged down under the load. "Hey, hey," Earl whispered, as he followed movement of pollen with his instruments. "Give me enhancement," he yelled, and a technician did things with the computerized image screen.

It took experimentation with settings to achieve results. Teddy and Matt were watching the screen when the technician yelled, "You've got to see this, Earl."

Earl turned off his instruments and watched the playback. On the screen, a small, white sphere of haze appeared and then the image deepened in intensity. Within the sphere, there appeared a myriad of tiny, dancing fireflies. Earl watched the playback three times in silence. There seemed to Teddy to be a look of awe on the faces of Earl and the three technicians.

"So what are we seeing?" Matt asked.

"I think it's a dance of life," Earl whispered.

The pinpoints of light on the screen seemed to swirl, merge, roil, in some definite patterns.

"What we're enhancing on the screen are the pollen grains," Earl said. "But something is carrying them."

"Earl," one of the technicians said, "you're not

going to believe this, but while you had the instruments on the movement I was getting indications of alpha particle activity.''

"Just alpha?" Earl asked.

"That's it."

"Okay, let's start over." Earl said.

It took several more days, and added equipment, to confirm the technician's observations. Earl made his report to the assembled department heads, with Andrew Reznor present. When the conference room was darkened and the images projected to a large screen, the measured dance and flow of enhanced particles within the globes of activity was mesmerizing.

"You're looking at an impossibility," Earl told them. "With no apparent source, and with no other types of particles, several billion—at best estimate—alpha particles are confined in a limited space that takes the form of a sphere. Even more impossible, the actions of the alpha particles are not random. The moving specks you see are not alpha particles, but alpha particles combined with a grain of pollen. You'll note that some images have more of what Teddy calls fireflies than others. That's because there's a higher concentration of pollen grains in some of the globes. But the most puzzling thing is that there is no release of alpha particles from the confines of the sphere. And we can detect no binding force, no magnetic fields, to hold them in that spherical shape.''

"What is your conclusion, Dr. Fabre?" Reznor asked.

"That we're monkeying around with something entirely different from anything we've ever observed or imagined," Earl said.

"Life force," Teddy said, surprised when the words came from her lips.

"One guess is as good as another," Earl said, not at all amused by Teddy's suggestion.

"What is your interpretation of this mysterious thing?" Reznor asked Fabre.

"I don't have one." Earl said. "I think the next step is to build an electromagnetic trap—"

"No," Teddy said.

"—and capture one of the globes for closer and more detailed observation," Earl finished, looking at Teddy.

"Why did you say no?" Kerry Hertz asked Teddy.

"I don't know," Teddy admitted. "I just thought it wasn't a good idea."

"Would there be any potential danger in doing as you suggested, Dr. Fabre?" Reznor asked.

"There's always potential danger when you're mucking around with an unknown physical phenomenon," Earl said. "I think the danger could be minimized."

"If there's no risk," Jack Frost said, "I don't see why Earl shouldn't take a closer look at one of these things."

"I didn't say there was no risk," Earl said. "I said we could minimize the risk."

"You're talking about experimenting on a living entity," Teddy said.

"We don't know that," Jack said. "It could be a natural phenomenon, an anomaly of the planet's magnetic or gravitational fields. I'm talking in an area outside my expertise—"

"Yes, you are," Cassie said.

"Can you be more specific in your objections to Dr. Fabre's suggestion?" Reznor asked Teddy. "Specifically, why do you say we're dealing with a living entity?"

"Like Jack, I'm speaking in an area outside my expertise," Teddy said. "But, Jack, you should know what I'm talking about. You've had contact with one of these living entities."

"I have?" Jack asked, smiling and raising one eyebrow.

"Unless you're willing to concede that you went temporarily mad and tried to eat a zebra," Teddy said.

"I was influenced by one of these things?" Jack said. He laughed. "I'll have to agree that that is a more flattering explanation than saying I went loony."

Andrew Reznor had presided at many meetings where decisions of greater or less import had been formulated. At that moment, he, himself, had formed no conclusion. He lacked data. He played the gathering of scientists like a musical instrument, drawing each man and woman into the conversation, listening carefully to the play and counterplay of argument, opinion, feelings. At the end of another half hour, he still had no solid grasp of the situation.

Teddy was the last to speak. "Now I know it's fanciful to think of the globes as, perhaps, being elemental life force. First of all, we've never been able to isolate the life force. I remember that once in history there was an opinion that the life force, or the soul, could be weighed. That idea was very popular for a while—I've forgotten whether it was in the nineteenth or the twentieth century— and some respected men of science said that when a person died he lost a minute fraction of his weight at the time of death. I don't even know if that notion was ever tested carefully. I'd guess it was and disproven."

"Disproven." Earl said. "The early instruments were inaccurate."

"So the life force, or the human soul, apparently does not have mass," Teddy said. "Do the spheres have mass?"

"Yes. Difficult to measure, since it's an infinitesimal mass," Earl said.

"So there's something there," Teddy said. "We've had enough incidents of animals and humans being influenced by something outside themselves to make it at least worth considering that there is a thinking *something* here on Beauty. Earl says that there must be some binding force to hold the alpha particles inside the globes. We can't define that binding force, and we can't measure its potential." She paused, and then plunged ahead.

" I have no logical explanation for my feeling that it would be very dangerous to risk releasing such a force. And I have only an emotional assurance that those entities would not take kindly to being trapped in an electromagnetic sink of some sort, if that's the right word. I feel so strongly about it that I would exercise the authority you've given me, Dr. Reznor, to forbid it."

There was a silence. Reznor said, "Very well, Dr. Tinker, I respect your opinion. For the moment, we will treat this phenomenon with the respect due to an intelligent life form."

"I think we should make efforts to contact them," Teddy said.

"By talking to them, as you did?" Jack asked.

"Can you think of a better way?" Teddy demanded.

"I'd feel pretty silly talking to the open air," Jack said, laughing.

"If they can read our thoughts, why talk to them?" Sandy Moore, who had been silent till then, asked.

"I'm not sure they can read our thoughts," Teddy said. "If they could, wouldn't there have been more contact? If they could read thoughts they would have understood what Jack was trying to do with the zebras. Could it be that they sense our emotions?"

"It's your theory," Jack said. "You tell us."

"I'm going to continue to observe them without direct interference," Earl said.

"Yes, good," Teddy said. "Does anyone else have a suggestion?"

"I would like to make one request of all of you," Reznor said. "How many of you are familiar with Pax Five guidelines and regulations concerning the possible discovery of intelligent life in space?"

"I hadn't thought of that," Matt said. "Whoops."

"Briefly, for those of you who have not read the regulations, or have forgotten them," Reznor said, "in the event of any discovery or development team's encounter with an intelligent species or a species that is suspected of having intelligence or is in the process of evolving toward intelligence a full report must be submitted to the Bureau of Colonization. At such time all exploration or development activity is to be halted until a Pax Five Commission can investigate."

"We can't stop now," Jack Frost said heatedly, leaping to his feet. "We've come too far. We have delicate systems under development. There would be serious consequences if we halted our work now."

"For example?" Reznor asked.

"In the seas, for example," Teddy said, before Jack could answer. "We're building the marine food chain and if certain species are not introduced on schedule the species upon which they feed will proliferate without natural enemies or controls and literally fill the oceans."

"That's just one example," Jack said. "We're building an insect population in the jungles. We're due to add insect-eating birds and reptiles within a few months."

"I think it's important, then," Reznor said, "for any speculation or information about our subject today to be confined on a need to know basis. I think we have an excellent team here on Beauty. I hand-picked almost everyone here, and I trust every one of them, but it would be a burden on them and, if you like, it would be involving them in bending, if not breaking, Pax Five regulations. Is there any objection to my request?''

''I think the first thought of a Pax Five investigating team would be to do exactly what Earl suggested,'' Teddy said, ''to trap one of the globes for a closer examination.''

''It may be sheer ego on my part,'' Earl said, ''but I think we're better prepared to follow through than someone coming onto the planet for the first time.''

''I think we're all willing to keep quiet,'' Matt said. ''At least until we have more information about the globes.''

''I must warn you that there is some risk,'' Reznor said. ''If we should be the first people to encounter an intelligent species, you could all be charged with conspiracy to withhold information from the proper authorities.''

''Let's worry about that later,'' Cassie Frost said.

There was general agreement. Not one of them wanted to see his work stopped. Reznor said, ''We're well insulated here on Beauty, and I think we can keep our secret indefinitely. If a time should ever come when we have to go public, I assure you that the full weight of Reznor Enterprises will be behind you, each and every one of you.''

As the others rose, Matt stayed behind. He held up one finger to Reznor, indicating that he wanted a minute of Reznor's time. Teddy stayed as well. When the three were alone, Matt said, ''One thing wasn't mentioned, Dr. Reznor. I assume that there have been no repercussions yet about the Russian general.''

''My son tells me that since the Russians announced that Milyukov was on an extended vacation the media has been oddly quiet about the man," Reznor said.

"I'm in agreement that we can't stop work and tell Pax Five that we've encountered something that might have intelligence," Matt said, "but I'm not sure it's wise to remain silent about Milyukov. He brought on his own death, and if we say nothing until someone traces him here we'd look guilty when we're not."

"We have the records made by your ship," Reznor said. "When the time comes, we can show the worlds what happened. And we can say that it took time to identify the dead man, and that's why we remained silent."

"And if the pilot of the ship that brought him talks first?" Matt asked.

"I don't think he will," Reznor said. "He was, after all, involved in an illegal activity, if, indeed, Milyukov came here on his own. If it was a Russian or a Pax Five operation, those who know that Milyukov died here will keep silent for their own reasons. We know that Intel and other intelligence agencies constantly operate on the dim side of legality, and I, for one, think it's not only permissible but desirable. Intel, for example, has done valuable service many times, in breaking up smuggling groups, in warning of potential trouble spots on Earth and off. But no intelligence agency is going to admit that it's infringing on the privacy rights of the people. And, powerful as Intel is, it would hesitate to tackle Reznor Enterprises head-on, for the giants of the private sector would rally to our side and it would become much more than just Intel against Reznor. Bear with me for just a while longer. I think we'll know within a short time whether or not we're going to be linked with Milyukov."

Matt had not had time to reconcile his doubts about

Reznor's conclusions when word came from Andy Reznor, on Earth, that the Pax Five Council had made formal request to have a survey team visit Beauty to "collect available scientific data already accumulated by Beauty's developers, to assess the properties of this, the newest life-zone world, and to centralize all data so as to make it available to the scientific community."

"It's directly from the book," Andrew Reznor told Teddy and Matt, shortly after the trans message had been received and delivered to him personally. "It's been done on every planet yet settled. If we refuse, it will cause nothing but suspicion. I'm going to have to send an official invitation to the Council."

The invitation was sent.

"If this is, indeed, strictly routine," Reznor said, "we'll have sixty to ninety days before a survey team arrives."

It was, Matt thought within twenty-four hours, not strictly routine. For a trans message came from the Director of the Bureau of Colonization stating that, by coincidence, an advance team of the planetary study group of the Bureau was in the sector of Beauty and, if there were no objections, and if it would not cause undue interruption of important work, the team would like permission to land on Beauty immediately.

After warning his department heads that things were moving more swiftly than he had anticipated, Reznor sent confirmation to the Bureau, requesting the identity and qualifications of the members of the advance team. There was a delay in getting an answer to his request and communications was in contact with a Pax Five ship in orbit, giving landing instructions, when the answer finally came. A priority message to Reznor headquarters on Earth sent Andy Reznor into a frenzy of activity. His message to Beauty arrived as the Pax Five ship was settling on a pad near Africa House. So it was that Reznor, Matt, and Teddy hurried out to the pads to officially welcome to Beauty a Mr. Jeff Soutine and a Miss Genna Darden, nonscientific people, specialists in organization and coordination. However, Andy Reznor's frenzied activity had revealed that both Soutine and Darden worked for Intel.

"This does not mean that they are not exactly what they are represented to be," Reznor said. "Intel and the Bureau work very closely together."

"It's all right if I'm a little suspicious about two hotshot Intel types being advance men for a survey team, and just happening to be in the neighborhood, isn't it?" Matt asked.

"Please be very suspicious," Reznor said. "And very careful."

During preparations for landing, Genna Darden had seen a beauty of a world, lush and green, with vast land areas and fertile temperate zones well suited for human development. Contrasting those unutilized riches with the smallness and starkness of her own home, and picturing the poverty, misery and crowding on Earth, Genna felt a resurgence of her resentment of people who would reserve such a world for animals. She wondered, as the ship settled through atmosphere, where Milyukov had died. His memory was vivid, and although he meant no more to her than several men who had entered and left her life, she made him a promise. His death would not have been in vain. His death would be used—she'd find a way—to force the United States and the Reznor interests to open the planet for settlement.

Both Soutine and Genna were polite, warmly friendly, eager to cooperate with the locals. "I know this is an imposition," Soutine said to Reznor. "We'll try to disrupt the routine as little as possible."

It fell to Teddy, after the official greetings were finished, to show the newcomers to quarters. Genna gushed on about the beauty of the world, and the way the facility seemed to blend unobtrusively into the landscape, as if it had been an original part of it. Teddy found herself liking the striking blonde woman in spite of her knowledge that Genna was from Intel. She decided that two could play the spy game and invited Genna on a quick, private sight-seeing excursion.

"If you're not too tired after the trip," Teddy said.

"I'd love to get outdoors," Genna said, "after being cooped up aboard ship. What should I wear?"

"Pants or shorts, sturdy shoes in case we decide to walk."

"Give me a half hour," Genna said. She went to her room, changed, slipped down the hall to knock on Soutine's door. He was in his undershorts. "The Tinker woman is taking me to see the animals."

"Alone?"

"Alone. Is it too soon?"

"It's never too soon," Soutine said. He opened a bag, triggered the release of a hidden compartment, removed a small, square box. Inside the box was a gaudy ring with a genuine and huge ruby in a bulky, heavy mounting. "You twist the stone, thus," he said, demonstrating. A half inch needle extended itself from the mounting at an angle. "All it requires is a touch." He used his own hand to show her, reaching out to touch her bare arm above the elbow, putting just a hint of downward pressure to compensate for the angle of the needle. "It takes effect within two minutes, and you'll have about fifteen minutes to question her."

"And she won't remember anything she's said while under the influence of the drug?"

"Nothing. She might be puzzled for a few seconds. She might even faint as the drug wears off."

"Too much sun," Genna said.

Genna mastered the operation of a goat quickly and followed Teddy to the plains. To her, the herds

were just so many animals. In Africa some game
farmers bred wildebeests for meat. Settlers on Beauty
would have an available supply of fresh meat, thanks
to Reznor.

To see the elephants required a long ride, almost
to the escarpment. Genna was enjoying the ride. Her
fair skin was protected from the rays of Beauty's sun
by a pleasantly scented sunscreen.

"Can we get up there?" she asked, pointing to
the top of the cliffs, after they'd watched the elephants for a while.

"There's access about three miles south," Teddy
said. "It's a pretty thrilling ride, though. We'd have
to climb some steep slopes."

"Let's try," Genna said.

Teddy and Matt had found the breach in the cliffs,
a series of terraced rock collapses, and had tested
the capacities of the goats there. The fading tracks
of their last ascent were still showing.

"It is steep," Genna said, "but I think the view
from the top will be worth it."

"Stay directly behind me," Teddy said. "And if
you get nervous, yell, and we'll stop."

She had to wend her way around boulders and
avoid slopes of loose scree. The last slope was precipitous and she halted to caution Genna. "You have
to take a run at it. Hit the slope at thirty miles an
hour and keep the throttle wide open. You'll think
the goat is going to topple back on top of you, but
just lean forward and keep the pedal to the metal and
you'll make it."

She was off with a roar of the goat's engine, sand,
dirt, and small stones flying as the goat's wheels dug
and churned. She burst out over the top momentarily
airborne, and the goat slammed to the ground. She
stopped, dismounted, went back to the edge of the
slope to wave Genna up. Once Genna's goat started
to slip sideways and Teddy held her breath, berating

herself for putting the woman in danger, but Genna compensated skillfully and charged over the lip of the slope.

"Wow," Genna said, as she dismounted to stand beside Teddy.

"You had me worried," Teddy said.

"No problem," Genna said, "but I think I would like to sit down for a minute."

They sat side by side on a flat, table-topped rock. The brush country spread before them, sloping slowly to the plains. Individual animals in the herds were mere dots.

"Your planet is warm," Genna said, wiping her brow. "But very nice. It is a fine view from here. I'm so glad we came." As she spoke, she turned the ruby setting on the ring. "You're so nice to show me all this." She reached out, one woman to another, to touch Teddy's arm. She gave her hand just a bit of downward motion. An instantly acting, local anesthetic coating on the needle prevented Teddy from feeling the penetration.

"And now I'm thinking only of the cool water in my canteen," Genna said, withdrawing her hand, moving the ruby back into its setting.

"I'll get them," Teddy said. She walked to the goats, got the canteens, sat near Genna, and they both drank. Lowering the canteen, Teddy shook her head, trying to dispel a sudden dizziness, and then it was gone.

Genna waited another minute, making small talk. Then she looked carefully into Teddy's startlingly green eyes to see her pupils contracted to mere pinpoints.

"Have you heard of General Igor Milyukov?" she asked in a conversational tone.

"Yes," Teddy said, sounding quite normal. "He came here and shot our bull elephant and then the globes influenced the elephants to kill him."

For fifteen minutes Teddy talked almost nonstop, interrupted only by Genna's questions. Genna returned again and again to the manner of Milyukov's death, to the mysterious globes. A mini-sound-recorder mounted between her beautiful breasts taped everything. She was smiling. It was more than she'd expected. Milyukov's death, his murder, could be used. The death of a world reowned man, a valuable man, destroyed by berserk animals would go far in negating the sentimental attitude toward animals among the masses. But the globes concerned her. She was, of course, aware of Pax Five regulations. The presence of the globes, intelligent or not, would ruin her dream of opening Beauty for colonization. Something would have to be done about the globes. Obviously, even if they were sentient, they had done nothing at all with a very desirable planet. Such a planet had to have human life to reach its full potential. She was sure that sensible men like Soutine, Shardan, and Davis Conroy would not let the presence of some goofy things that flitted around acting like bees and pollinating flowers stand in the way of human advancement.

Yes, she was sure. She would talk with Soutine, and he would agree not to mention the globes to the survey team. The planet would be declared suitable for human occupation, and the murder of Milyukov and the conspiracy to keep it a secret would end Reznor's claim to the planet. Even if his hired lackeys in the American government prevented the United States from agreeing to colonization, they would be outvoted in Council and would not risk serious international conflict for one man's dream of a planetary zoo.

As she had been thinking, Teddy, still compelled to talk by the drug, had been dreamily speaking of how she had met Matt Tinker, and of their honeymoon aboard *Tinker's Belle*. But her voice was weakening, her pupils slowly returning to normal size. When she stopped talking, she swayed a bit and quickly put her hand to her head.

"Gee, I got dizzy there for a second," she said. "You're very welcome. I've enjoyed showing you what we've accomplished so far. Of course, you haven't seen the buffalo herds in America. And the coyotes. They've taken to the American plains as if they were born there. And soon we'll have whales in the ocean. Isn't that exciting?"

"Very," Genna said. "Shall we go back now?"

Teddy rose, looked out once more over the view. She was no longer dizzy. She turned toward the goats, then stopped, eyes going wide. "Look, look," she said intensely.

They were there. Dozens of them. Small, glowing whitely, hanging motionless about five feet off the ground. And then others began to materialize.

"What do they want?" Genna asked nervously.

"I don't know," Teddy said.

"They are not living beings," Genna said. "They are reflections. Sun spots. Something that can be explained. They are not intelligent."

Teddy looked at Genna quickly, then back at the globes. "Why do you say that?" she asked. "How did you know we think they are intelligent?"

Genna had no time to answer. A globe flashed toward her, impacting her face in a spray of light that blinded her temporarily. She cried out as another flash of white streaked toward her and then another and another until she was being bombarded with splashes of light that caused no pain except to her eyes, as if a spotlight had been trained on her. She screamed. Teddy started to move toward her, crying out, "Don't. Stop it, please."

In panic, Genna began to run. She slipped on a loose stone, almost fell, changed her direction, and as Teddy tried to grab her, ran into open air like an animated character in an antique cartoon, legs still running as she fell down, down.

Teddy, weeping, looking down over the cliffs, heard the impact of softness on jagged rocks. Some of the glowing white globes had followed the falling woman and now they turned and drifted back toward her. Others were still there atop the cliffs, motionless again.

"Why?" Teddy wailed, turning to face the globes. "Why did you do it?" Strangely, she had no personal fear, only puzzlement. "You killed her. Why?"

The globes faded quickly and she was alone. She used her belt communicator. "Matt, come quickly," she said, and Matt's heart constricted as he heard her sobbing words.

"Are you hurt?" he asked.

"No. Just come. Bring Wells Smith. Without Soutine's knowing."

Matt was running toward her from *Belle* within minutes. It took more minutes to tell him the story. He looked around. "With no warning, no reason, they forced her off the cliff?"

But there was, of course, a reason. Wells Smith found it as he and his team placed Genna Darden's smashed body in a body bag. The mini-recorder had been designed to withstand harsher treatment than falling two hundred feet onto rocks. With Smith an interested participant, they played the tape on *Belle's* sound equipment. They all sat, stunned, as Teddy trailed off into scarcely mumbled words as the drug wore off. Silently, Wells Smith went to Teddy and began to examine her neck, her arms. He found the tiny mark of the needle just above her elbow.

"If it was what I think it was," Smith said, "it wouldn't do any good to run a blood test. Wouldn't find a trace of anything."

"I thought such drugs had been made illegal," Matt said.

"They have," Wells said. "Let's see if we can find how she got it into you, Teddy."

Teddy could not look as Wells and his men removed Genna's body from the body bag and searched it. Aside from a necklace and the ring there was nothing other than her clothing. The ring was caked with dried blood. Smith wiped it off, fingered it, toyed with it, twisted the ruby and the needle extended. Matt took the ring. "I have a feeling we're going to need all the help we can get," he said. "The use of an illegal drug on a citizen of the United States will be in our favor."

Matt and Teddy watched the medical technicians load Genna's body into *Belle's* cargo space. "For the moment, I think we'd better not mention the globes," he said.

"Matt, they've killed. We can't keep that quiet," Teddy said.

"I think they killed to protect you," Matt said.

"But she hadn't really harmed me. I was totally unaware that I'd been drugged."

"To protect Beauty?" Wells Smith asked.

"Against what?" Teddy countered.

Wells shrugged. "Against whatever the sly spy types have in mind," he said. "I agree with Matt. We don't let this Soutine know exactly how this woman died. Can you lie, Teddy?"

Teddy looked around. Beauty basked in the afternoon sun. The elephants were moving away from the cliffs toward water. "I warned her not to get too near the edge," she said. "I turned my head for just a moment, to get the canteen, and when I turned back I cried out to her, for she was standing on the very edge. She started to move back, but the loose rocks gave way and she—she fell."

Chapter 25

For the first time since they had been brought to Beauty, the ever-growing animal population was without human observers. All the people who busied themselves happily in the study of and care of and the hourly observation of newly transplanted species were gathered in the largest conference room at Africa House.

Before entering the room, Andrew Reznor had sent a detailed report to his son on Earth, asking Andy to mobilize the troops, to alert all of the Reznor people on every planet—lawyers, academicians, lawmakers, members of the bureaucracy, business and industrial leaders—to stand ready to come to the support of Reznor and, it was implied, the entire free enterprise system.

No one knew better than Reznor the seriousness of the impending crisis. A man who rarely experienced doubt, he mused for long minutes before going into the room, weighing his options. By far the safest and simplest thing would be to go by the book, to tell Jeff Soutine that certain events that had occurred on Beauty, capped by the death of Genna Darden, indicated the possibility of an intelligent or semi-intelligent life form. But that would mean halting all work and, turning Beauty over to Pax Five. In that event, the planet would soon be swarming with experts in every field, with stultified savants who had been on a government payroll so long that their chief concern was self-preservation. It would take years for the bureaucrats to arrive at any conclusion. Incomplete ecological systems would be distorted hopelessly. The dream would be over.

Matt had taken Jeff Soutine in hand upon his return to Africa House. Soutine took the news of Genna Darden's death with surprising calmness.

"I will, of course, want to question your wife," Soutine said, "and there'll have to be a complete recorded report."

"Of course," Matt said. "We all regret this unfortunate accident, Mr. Soutine. But before you begin your investigation, Dr. Reznor has asked that you be present at a conference of all our people. There are some circumstances involving Miss Darden's death, and previous events, that will be discussed. The meeting will serve to inform everyone at once."

Soutine tried some questions, but quickly saw that Matt was stonewalling. He sensed that something more than an accidental death was involved, and, being alone on Beauty, he knew that he would, for the moment, have to play it Reznor's way.

Matt, Teddy, and Reznor had time for a quick meeting to plan their strategy. Reznor stood before the gathering first. "As some of you know we have with us a Pax Five Representative, Mr. Jeff Soutine. Will you please stand for a moment, Mr. Soutine."

Soutine stood and looked around. He saw curious faces, neutral faces, one or two faces that showed clear antagonism.

"We are all aware of incidents for which we have, as yet, found no explanation," Reznor said. Soutine sat down. "I'm going to ask the Planetary Coordinator and the Planetary Manager to brief all of you on the events that have occurred, culminating today in the unfortunate death of a member of the Pax Five advance team.''

Some of the company had not yet heard of a new death. There was a buzz of talk, then silence as Matt and Teddy took the podium. Matt began, and, more for Soutine's benefit than for those who had been on Beauty all along, he began at the beginning. Soutine had started his mini-recorder. He sat in a relaxed pose, but behind his calm face his mind was racing ahead.

It had been agreed by Teddy, Matt and Reznor to present only evidence that could be demonstrated by physical means, to mention the globes but to omit mention of suspected influence by them. Teddy described the death of Genna Darden and Soutine stood, still calm, relaxed. ''Dr. Reznor,'' he said, ''I hereby invoke Chapter 74, Articles 4-B through 7 to, by authority of the Pax Five Council, order all members of your team to refrain from contact with this entity that has been described. I request the use of your communications equipment to call in a Pax Five task force to investigate a suspected encounter with an intelligent alien species.'' He sat down amid a buzz of startled conversation.

''Your statement is noted and recorded for the record,'' Reznor said. ''However, measures have already been taken.'' Indeed, they had, in the past few hours. The proper reports and requests had been transed quickly to the Reznor home office, all dated one week previously. It was not unusual, in a complex as large as Reznor Enterprises, for important documents to be delayed in the processing. ''I disagree on one aspect of your statement. There is no proof, and not enough evidence to cause reasonable doubt, regarding the potential intelligence of the phenomenon of the moving globes. It is the contention of my staff that they are a natural phenomenon and show random, not intelligent, movement. To this end I have filed an exception, calling for evaluation by a mixed commission made up of representatives from the United States government, the private sector, and, of course, a team from Pax Five. Under Chapter 74, which you mentioned, Mr. Soutine, there are provisions for projects underway to be completed during such an investigation.''

Soutine nodded. The old man knew his space law, but he was hanging himself. So be it. He was, to his surprise, already missing the icy blonde from Iceland. He had never understood her passionate and idealistic desire to force Reznor to open Beauty for colonization, but he had come to like her during the last few days aboard ship, and she had been Intel. Intel stood behind its people. An Intel person did not die without being avenged. He had a feeling that he had not heard all the facts regarding those globes of light that had caused Genna to run off the cliffs.

Soutine was given the opportunity to question Teddy. She told him the same story she'd told before the conference, and Soutine longed for a truth needle. However, he had requested that he be allowed to examine Genna's body and her ring was missing. That was trouble. He decided not to mention the ring. There was the smallest chance that it had somehow been ripped from Genna's finger during the fall, but he doubted it. His suspicion was that the Reznor people were saving the ring as sort of an ace in the hole, to hit Intel with a charge of using illegal drugs at the most damaging time.

He renewed his request to use Beauty's communications equipment. Shardan was, even as Soutine reached him, going through the documents that had just arrived from the Reznor offices through the Pax Five Council. He messaged to Soutine to go along with the people on Beauty until he, himself, arrived with the Pax Five investigative team, and soon he was aboard ship.

One by one, the ships arrived and the numbers of scientists, technicians, bureaucrats and lawyers soon overcrowded the facilities of Africa House so that a temporary row of thermal tents had to be set up to house the least important. While Shardan and Soutine dived into the computerized records, teams roamed the surface of the planet, visiting all the scenes of incidents, carrying ever more and more complicated equipment.

Shardan was impressed by the achievements of so short a time. He puzzled Soutine, who wanted merely to press forward, by taking time to tour the planet with Matt Tinker, to see the buffalo herd, the prairie dog cities, the monkeys of the jungles, the African wildlife. He quickly saw through Matt's casualness to the man underneath and surprised Matt by saying, "This isn't your kind of work, Tinker. You'd be happier on a multiparsec trans into new territory."

"I admit it," Matt said, "but I'm rather proud of what we've helped do here."

Shardan shrugged. "There are more extinct species than living species."

"But extinction, in the past, was because of natural events, planetary change for one reason or the other, not because one species, man, proliferated and simply crowded others off the globe."

"Some think that's what happened to the dinosaurs," Shardan said, "that one species was so well adapted that it spread into the ranges of others, carrying diseases that wiped out entire species. Then they, in turn, were wiped out."

"But can you say what would have happened on Earth in the next million years or so if it weren't for man?"

"No. But I can't be too interested in something that's going to happen long after I'm dead," Shardan said. "Not that I don't sympathize with Reznor's aims. They're admirable, in a sort of impractical way.''

''Are you for opening up the planet to human colonization?''

''I don't think I care one way or the other,'' Shardan said. ''While it's true that a life-zone planet hasn't been discovered in over two years, there will be others. And there's still a lot of room on the discovered planets. There's no crisis for living space. We're moving people off Earth just about as fast as the planets can absorb them, about as fast as transportation and support facilities allow. If it were left up to me, assuming, of course, that those globes of yours are just some insensate natural phenomenon, I wouldn't push for colonization.''

''Where is the push coming from then?'' Matt asked.

Genna's face came to Shardan with great and poignant force. ''Well, the Bureau of Colonization is always greedy,'' he said. But, and it came to him as a mild personal reprimand, the guiding force behind the desire to put a portion of Earth's masses on Beauty had come from one well-formed, beautiful and deceptively strong, little lady.

''We'd like to have you in our corner,'' Matt said.

Shardan laughed. ''I appreciate your openness. I am in the corner of all. It's my job to guard and represent the interests of Pax Five and, in the end, the entire galactic community.''

''I think you'll keep an open mind,'' Matt said.

''I'll try, my friend. I will surely try, but I'd suggest that you think about altering your situation. With the discovery of one good planet under your belt, you'd be welcomed at the Pax Five Exploration Department. The pay is the highest, and the discovery awards are well worthwhile.''

''In an assigned area of space,'' Matt said.

''You can't have everything,'' Shardan said. ''I

think I've seen enough animals to last me for a while. I'd like very much to have a good meal and a good drink.''

Matt wasn't feeling very optimistic. He knew that the rapport he had established almost immediately with Shardan might very well be purely surface with such a man. He had not gotten to his powerful position without command of people skills. Was the advice to check into the Pax Five exploration program a friendly warning that things were going to go to hell on Beauty?

Chapter 26

Earl Fabre was a bit confused. He'd been assigned to work with a team of scientists made up of bipartisan forces. From the records, the team had gotten information about Earl's work regarding the odd method of cross-pollination, but not his work that had revealed a tightly confined globe of alpha particles. The team had now been in the field for a full week with instrumentation that far exceeded Earl's.

"I wonder, Dr. Fabre," said a bearded physicist named August von Bruner, who held the position of director of research at Pax Five, "if there could not have been some problem with your equipment?"

For one week, multiple positionings of instrumentation among various types of blooming plants had shown nothing more than random, wind-blown movement of pollen.

"It's as if she knows she's being investigated by unsympathetic people," Earl told Kerry Hertz, who was also working with the investigative team.

Earl's confusion came from a mixture of feelings. If Beauty laid low long enough, the eggheads from Earth would give up, write the recorded findings off as a stupid series of mistakes by one Earl Fabre, and go home. So he felt relief and a bit of anger that his techniques and skill were being questioned. Well, he could take it. He could ignore the pompousness of von Bruner and the others and when they were gone, he could get back to studying the life form, for he was sure that term could be applied. Still, it rankled a bit when von Bruner, in disgust, tried to wither him with a shaggy eye-browed stare and told his men to start dismantling the equipment. Earl could scarcely suppress a surge of anger and an urge to tell von Bruner that if he'd get out of his plush office into a laboratory or the field more often he might be able to judge a man's work a bit better.

So Earl started walking away, seething in spite of his relief that Beauty had not done her tricks for the visitors.

"Dr. von Bruner," someone said, "I have something."

Earl froze. A sense of excitement came from the technicians as he turned and walked back.

Pollination was going on. The sensitive instruments were showing globular masses. Von Bruner was running from screen to screen, his mouth working without words.

It took only two days for von Bruner to duplicate Earl's work and discover the puzzling nature of the globes, as they went about their work without any apparent notice of the instruments that observed and recorded their movements. A day later, when Earl and Kerry returned to the site after a quick visit to Africa House to report the team's progress to Matt and Reznor, a rather massive array of equipment was being linked by a swarm of men, all teams having been called in from other sites.

"What are they doing now?" Kerry asked.

A quick examination of the equipment caused Earl's brow to furrow. There were powerful magnetic field generators among the gear and it was plain that von Bruner's intention was to trap a globe.

"We will first try to penetrate the entity with a magnetic probe," von Bruner told Earl. "I do not know why you didn't discover the nature of these things, Dr. Fabre. It was quite simple, after all.''

Earl didn't answer.

"If we cannot discover the binding force by other methods, we will bombard it with particles, to observe its actions after penetration,'' von Bruner said.

"Doctor,'' Earl said, "if I were you I'd delay such action.''

"Ha,'' von Bruner said, dismissing Earl by turning his back.

Earl nodded to Kerry, motioning her to follow him to the transporter they'd driven to the site. He contacted Africa House and informed Matt of von Bruner's plans.

"What's going to happen?'' Matt asked.

"I'm damned if I know,'' Earl said, "but I want to be a few miles away when it does. Give me an excuse, on record, to get away from here with Kerry.''

Earl observed the entrapment of a globe. It was, as he had suspected it would be, relatively simple. The globe, held in a powerful magnetic sink, could move minutely back and forth. It glowed white and became visible, then faded again. When von Bruner tried mechanical probes, the globe merely altered shape, sliding away from the probe like an amoeba touched by a tiny needle. Magnetic and electrical force curved around the globe and was dissipated. Earl saw that the technicians were preparing an electron bombardment and was getting a little nervous when his belt communicator buzzed and he went to the transporter with Kerry to hear Teddy asking them to report in to Africa House for a conference of department heads.

"Let's get the hell out of here,'' he said, starting the transporter and sending it speeding away down the slope.

Earl and Kerry were ten miles away from the site

when the sky glared with a white light so intense that Earl slammed on the brakes, momentarily blinded. He found the right button and made the windscreen of the transporter darken and then they saw that the light was so intense there were no shadows and the plants had become transparent. Then the light suddenly faded. The world outside was dark until Earl lightened the windscreen. He called Africa House. "Matt, something's happened at the site. I'd suggest a flyover, high at first, with radiation detectors working."

The transporter's detectors showed no radiation. Earl turned the vehicle and started slowly back toward the site. The vegetation seemed to be unharmed and there was no hard radiation beyond the usual background level. As they came within two miles of the site, they were contacted by Matt, in *Belle*.

"The site is abandoned," Matt said. "No radiation readings. Equipment seems to be intact."

"Okay," Earl said. "We're going in."

"Standing by," Matt said.

The equipment was undamaged, except for some burned wiring. A power generator still hummed. Earl shut it down. Kerry was examining the vegetation for damage. Aside from the harm done by human feet and the placement and movement of equipment, there was none. But there was also no sign of the twenty-odd people who had been on the site. The thunder of a G.D. engine came to them and *Belle* landed in the grass not far away. Matt and Teddy joined them.

"I was inside," Matt said, "and didn't see the flare. It scared hell out of the animals. Those who were outside said it was almost painful to the eyes and that they were blinded for a moment."

"Matt, it was like the flash of an H-bomb, but it didn't damage a blade of grass," Earl said.

"So what do we do now?" Teddy asked, wanting to weep. She saw all their work negated, Beauty in the hands of Pax Five, most probably quarantined. Whatever had happened, it had taken over twenty lives. And yet only one death had occurred among those who loved and understood the purpose of the work on Beauty, and that early on, when a worker was cutting down a tree. All the others could be laid to Beauty's desire to protect herself, as well. Igor Milyukov had demonstrated senseless death to Beauty. Genna Darden had harbored real malice toward all the animals and had stood for colonization, meaning the clearing of forests, the leveling of lands, the uprooting of grass by plows, all the things that went with man's industrial technology. And the von Bruner teams had attacked a white globe directly, by bombarding it with high-energy particles.

"Well, we have to tell them what happened," Matt said.

"Starting now," Teddy said, as low thunder announced the arrival of a Pax Five ship.

Shardan and Jeff Soutine came off the ship and walked swiftly toward the masses of equipment. Teddy wiped away a tear and whispered, "Oh, Beauty, I'm so sorry. So sorry. You welcomed us and I think you had begun to understand us, to be on our side. It's going to go badly now, and I wish that Matt and I had never discovered you. Now they'll probe you and test you and maybe hurt you more and I'm so sorry."

She felt something brush her hair, looked up and saw a white globe just above her head, and into her mind came a feeling of total peace. There were no words, but the message was clear. *Don't worry.*

Shardan did not speak. He walked around, noted the burned wiring. "There were no survivors?" he asked.

"No," Matt said.

"Perhaps someone wandered off into the hills?" Shardan asked.

"No," Matt said. "We were over the site within minutes. We used heat detectors. The closest animate source of heat was about twenty miles away, a family of antelope."

"What do you suppose happened?" Shardan asked.

"Von Bruner penetrated the field of a globe with hard radiation," Earl said.

"Boom?" Shardan asked.

"More flash," Earl said. "And don't ask me why men and women disappeared without damage to the vegetation or the equipment."

There was a pause. Shardan shook his head. Soutine, who had been making his own examination of the equipment, staggered and fell to his knees, then rose, walking over to join the little group.

"You don't call this damage?" Shardan asked, looking startled.

Teddy gasped as a brief wave of dizziness came over her. She blinked and opened her eyes to a scene of devastation. Equipment had been seared. Things inflammable smoked. The vegetation for hundreds of yards around had been burned. Some bushes were still flaming.

"Beauty?" Teddy whispered.

"I'd call that damage," Matt said, looking at Teddy with his eyebrows raised.

"Beauty," she mouthed back at him.

Earl was rubbing his eyes. Kerry, startled by the sudden transformation, clutched at his hand.

"Million to one chance," Shardan said. "I saw something like this once. The engine of a transporter flashed. Looks as if half a dozen of these hydrogen-powered engines went up at one time."

"Looks that way," Earl said, squeezing Kerry's hand.

"Damn," Soutine said. He faced Fabre. "On von Bruner's instructions, I had your equipment checked, Fabre, the instrumentation you used to detect those so-called globes. You had a computer malfunction. It was drawing random images on the screens. Some of them were circles, if you stretch your imagination, globes of white."

"I had begun to suspect something like that," Earl said, "when von Bruner's results didn't confirm my findings."

"A lot of people died for nothing," Soutine said.

No, not for nothing, Teddy was thinking. She looked around. The vegetation was no longer burned. Seeding grass moved in a gentle breeze. She caught the pleasant aroma of the huge purple flowers that grew prolifically on the low bushes. *Not for nothing. Thank you, Beauty.*

"Dr. Fabre," Shardan said, "I'd appreciate a report from you, in detail. There'll have to be an investigation, of course, but it looks pretty clear-cut to me. Von Bruner's been behind a desk so long that he goofed, someway."

"I'm afraid I can't speculate on the exact nature of the accident," Earl said, "but I'll record what knowledge I have about the setup von Bruner was using, and what I knew of his plans."

"Thank you," Shardan said. He turned to Soutine. "Well, Jeff, let's get back and make our own report and start the postmortems."

The others lingered. The Pax Five ship thundered off and up. It seemed, at first, that no one wanted to be the first to speak. Teddy took a deep breath and started it. "Obviously, Shardan and Soutine were not aware that they'd seen two different views of the site. I was. Were the rest of you?"

"Damned well aware," Earl said. "When I blinked my eyes and saw the equipment charred and the vegetation crushed and seared I came pretty close—to be crude—to needing a change of underwear.''

"Those massive pieces of equipment torn to bits, scattered all over—'' Kerry began, then paused when Earl gripped her arm.

"Torn up and scattered? It was in place, but charred and burned by heat.''

"Discolored and some damage and still smoking,'' Teddy said.

There were more comparisons of what each had seen.

"We all saw it a bit differently,'' Matt said. "We saw what we would have imagined, based on our own individual experiences, to be the results of a fire or an explosion. But each of us saw something different.''

"They can make us imagine that we're seeing something they want us to see,'' Kerry said, with a shudder.

"But we knew,'' Teddy said. "We knew the truth, and Shardan and Soutine didn't.''

"This is getting just a little too weird for me,'' Kerry said. "I don't like the idea of something getting inside my head and making me hallucinate.''

"But they like us,'' Teddy said. "They like the animals. They want things to stay as they are.''

"Teddy, those things have now killed a lot of people,'' Kerry said.

"Enemies,'' Teddy said. "Enemies of life, and of what we're trying to accomplish here.''

"Maybe they've only killed three people,'' Matt said, "the workman, Milyukov and Genna. Maybe von Bruner killed one of them when he bombarded it. Have you thought of that?''

There was no immediate answer. Kerry sighed and looked and tensed. "Hey, hey,'' she said.

Pollination was going on. The globes were clearly visible, in white, glowing, dancing and soaring from flower to flower like supernatural butterflies. The humans watched for a long, long time and then, with the globes still visible, boarded transporter and ship and headed back to Africa House.

Chapter 27

Andy Reznor was a puzzled man. For weeks now he'd been getting communications from all over the settled galaxy requesting more information on an impending crisis that had not materialized. Girded for battle as he was, there was, perhaps, an element of disappointment in the eldest Reznor son, for he hated waste, and all his precautions and preparation had been wasted. No crisis came. There'd been a serious accident on Beauty when a bumbling bureaucrat misused potentially dangerous equipment and blew himself and twenty-three others into so many pieces that it was only necessary to notify the next of kin and have a commemorative service.

Meanwhile, a Pax Five exploration ship had found a fine planet close to the inner flank of the fan-shaped area of colonization. The Bureau of Colonization was happy, and its large flocks of field workers were charting and surveying the plane. The media was saying that it was the finest yet, even better than the animal planet, Beauty, which was not really ideal for colonization because of its remoteness.

Andy sent a brief message: "Dad, what the hell happened out there?"

"Read the reports," Andrew Reznor answered.

The reports said, among other things, that a malfunctioning field-portable computer had given false information to Reznor scientists but that Pax Five experts had quickly pinpointed the problems. There were lengthy and technical explanations for the hydrogen explosion that had killed von Bruner and twenty-three others, a brief report on the accidental death by falling of an Intel employee.

There were technical reports on Beauty's weather, geology, tectonics, her biota—or was that the correct use of that word when Beauty had no animal or insect life except that which had been imported from Earth—and all the other subjects that were studied when a new planet was first surveyed. There were minerals on Beauty, but nothing to get excited about. Her radioactives could stay where they were and good riddance, there being no need for them. Her gold was not enough to raise greed when the plentiful supply from the mining asteroids of dozens of systems was under Pax Five control with an artificially supported price.

Over Andrew Reznor's signature was a document outlining future plans to allow limited public visitation, but not until Beauty was filled with life. So that particular plan could easily be put on ice for decades.

Little by little, Andy relaxed the alert, sent his thanks to all those who had been standing ready, along with not a few checks that added up to considerable sums. Things were very much back to normal when his secretary announced that a Mr. Shardan, from Intel, was waiting in his outer office but did not have an appointment and should she tell him to call for one.

"I think we'll allow Mr. Shardan a bit of latitude," Andy drawled. "Please ask him to come in."

Shardan was dressed in a business suit. His lips were smiling under his bent nose, but his steel gray eyes were piercing. He had allowed his grizzled hair to grow a bit and it made him look somewhat younger. He glanced at an elegant, simply designed watch as he sat down, after shaking Andy's hand.

"A pleasure, Mr. Shardan, to see the legend in person," Andy said.

"You have two sound cameras and two sound-only recorders going," Shardan said.

Andy was only momentarily hesitant. "The watch?" he asked.

"Something new," Shardan said.

"Made by Reznor Technical on Ingleside," Andy said. "I thought I recognized it."

"Turn the cameras and the recorders off, please; this is not an official visit."

"Done," Andy said, moving his hand under his desk. He noted that Shardan did not look back at his watch.

"I had some interesting talks with your father while I was on Beauty," Shardan said. "He's an admirable man. I told him, as I am telling you, that after seeing what he's trying to do on Beauty I, and my agency, will stand behind him."

"Mr. Shardan, I thank you," Andy said.

"The old man—" He paused and smiled. "Excuse me, Dr. Reznor—"

"That's all right," Andy said. "Everyone calls him that, including me."

"He asked me to convey to you personally that he's having the time of his life, and that he wouldn't object to having you and your family spend some time on Beauty. I'd recommend it. It's a fine world, and quite peaceful."

That's it? Andy was thinking. There had to be more to Shardan's visit. Perhaps he'd have the room swept electronically when Shardan left. But, on the other hand, he couldn't quite see the Director of Intel personally planting bugs.

"I have a personal favor to ask," Shardan said.

"I'll do my best," Andy said.

"One of my people lost, for lack of a less incriminating word, an object on Beauty. I'd like it back."

Andy made his decision quickly. All his adult life he'd been forced to make snap decisions occasionally based on nothing more than his personal perception of the character of an individual.

"An item of jewelry, I believe," Andy said.

"Yes."

Andy pushed a button and checked the *Ark's* schedule. "One of our ships will be returning from Beauty within a week. I'll have it sent over by personal messenger."

"Thank you," Shardan said. "I've always found it a pleasure to work with members of the private sector."

"As opposed to governmental units?" Andy asked, with a wry smile.

"On the other hand," Shardan said, "the new system of checks and balances that has evolved in the past hundred years, although far from being perfect, should not be scorned." He spread his hands. "I don't think I'd particularly like living in a galaxy run by a board of directors."

There was still something on Shardan's mind, in spite of his relaxed posture, his easy talk. Andy could be smooth, too. "If all governmental units operated as efficiently, and with as much good sense as Intel, I would be pleased."

"Thank you," Shardan said. "I appreciate that." He looked up at the ceiling for a moment and lost himself in a realistic light painting of a summer sky. "Your father offered me a position with Reznor."

"We could always use a man of your caliber," Andy said.

"I was flattered, but I told him I rather enjoyed my work."

"A man should be happy in his work," Andy said, wondering where Shardan was heading.

"Not that it doesn't get frustrating at times," Shardan said. "But it has its moments. In our capacity we often make enemies simply by doing our duty. I feared, at first, that things were going to get rather unpleasant on the subject of your planet. While I was, basically, in sympathy with your father's desire to make Beauty a paradise for all of Earth's animals, we'd never been nose to nose with an intelligent alien species before and it was clear what had to be done."

"Fortunately," Andy said, "our own observations were faulty."

"Yes," Shardan said. "All's well that ends well." He paused and his eyes belied the relaxed expression on his face. "However, I don't like unanswered questions. I don't mind a little dig from the media now and then regarding the unsolved disappearance of General Igor Milyukov. I can stand the heat from the Russians. My report has been made. It is the conclusion of Intel that General Milyukov, for reasons of his own, set off on a long trans voyage. We traced him to three planets and then he disappeared, along with the civilian ship and its pilot. We have no choice but to conclude that an accident in space destroyed the ship and those aboard. I trust that you know enough about me to know that once I make a judgment it takes more than logical proof to reverse it?"

"So I've heard," Andy said.

"Missing from Milyukov's collection of antique weapons were three items, one of them an antique, British-made weapon which fired a powerful projectile, a weapon once used to hunt the big game of Africa. Milyukov once used a similar weapon to kill a polar bear, and he was obsessively interested in material concerning big game hunting in the past. I know of only one planet where there would be big game to hunt."

Andy stared back at Shardan without blinking.

"You said that this was not an official visit," he said, after a long, tense, eye-locked pause.

"Your privacy screen is up," Shardan said. "I am not on duty."

"Information in exchange for information?" Andy asked, ever the seeker of value for value.

"Within the limitations of secrecy," Shardan agreed.

"Milyukov landed on Beauty by transing directly into atmosphere, stalked and killed a bull elephant with the weapon you mentioned, and was killed by the other elephants in the herd. His body was, of course, heavily damaged. It is being preserved on Beauty."

Shardan nodded. "Burn it," he said.

"A good suggestion," Andy agreed. "There was at least one man aboard the ship, a converted yacht, painted black and silver. He fired missiles against one of our ships and severely wounded a woman."

"Matt and Tedra Tinker?" Shardan asked, with quick interest.

"Yes. Since Tedra Tinker recovered, with no lasting effects, I have advised Matt Tinker to forget the incident. He is reluctant to do so. The information I'd like to have is the name and present location of the man who fired the missiles."

"I don't see Matt Tinker as the mad avenger," Shardan said. "And he'd be out of his class going against this man. However, the question is academic. We've been looking for the pilot, ourselves. I think it's safe to say we have a better chance of finding him than Tinker would have, even with Reznor help."

"Still, I'd like his name."

"Jake Jordan. A self-styled mercenary. His usual activities included diamond smuggling from the mines beyond Valhalla."

Andy made a note of the name.

"There is one other thing," Shardan said. "I think it's only fair to tell you that I'm going to try to hire Matt Tinker away from you."

"He's done a good job," Andy said. "If he goes his wife goes with him, and we'd miss her, too."

"Fair warning," Shardan said, rising.

Andy did order a sweep of the office and the reception areas. There were no planted devices. He was not surprised. He had spent an hour studying the Reznor intelligence profile of Shardan, who was described as being an old-fashioned man in many ways, with an almost quixotic sense of honor.

But Andy was still puzzled, and he didn't like being puzzled. He had been certain in his mind that Shardan's visit had been to delve deeper into the fact—even if no one seemed to realize it other than a small group of Reznor people—of a native intelligent species on Beauty. He went back to the massive accumulation of reports on Beauty, but try as he might, he could not understand how the highly skilled investigative teams had failed to detect the odd, living globes of light. The survey teams had sped through their work routinely, gathering their material quickly, seemingly eager to leave the planet. The questions—a dead Russian general, indications of intelligence in the globes, a dead Intel agent, an accident that had killed a score of skilled people— all were brushed over so quickly that it was as if Andy's father had written the reports himself.

"Andy," Denise Reznor told him when, for the third time in an evening, he brought up the subject, "count your blessings. If it was a whitewash job it was done by the authorities, not by your father. Don't worry about the good news. Save your worry for the bad news when it comes."

"But there's something missing," Andy said, before dropping the subject once and for all.

Chapter 28

Actually, many things had been left out of the reports originating on Beauty. Only two people, Matt and Teddy, knew just how much information had not been included.

On a night not long after the departure of the last survey ship, with whales swimming Beauty's ocean and over a hundred new species in place to begin their long, long expansion to fill their environmental niches, Teddy suggested a moonlight ride. It seemed almost sacrilegious to intrude on the perfect night with the sound of goat engines, so they drove slowly, enjoyed the breeze in their faces, and spotted one of the new prides of lions. The lionesses had killed early and the entire pride was feasting.

Teddy, in the lead, found herself heading for the cliffs, past the stream where the elephants watered, up the gradual rise. Moonlight glinted on the sheer face. She had chosen not to arrive near the spot where Genna had fallen. She stopped her machine, got off and sat on a flat boulder. The odd, laughing howl of a hyena came from the plains below. Matt sat beside her. They were both silent, listening to the night, to the wind, to the cough of a lion.

"Why are you smiling?" Matt asked after a while, entranced by her moonlit face.

"Oh, just a little something," she said.

"Bigger than a breadbox?" he asked idly.

"Not yet."

"Smaller than a baseball?"

"I dunno. How big is a three-month-old embryo?" she asked, looking up at the moon and smiling musingly.

"Wanta run that by again?" Matt asked.

"Men are so darned unobservant," she said. "I haven't menstruated in over three months."

Matt put his arms around her and pulled her to him. "Are you telling me that the good old single ovary came through?"

"Would you like a boy or a girl?"

"We've gone over that before." He kissed her lightly.

"You're taking it calmly," she said.

"Oh, yeah?" He leaped to his feet, whooped a great whoop, and did a little dance.

"Better," she said.

He sat down again.

"I'd like to have our child born on Beauty," she said. "And then I think it'll be time to go."

"We can come back now and then," he said. "Bring our little girl to see the animals."

"That will be nice," she said. She leaned her head against him. The lonely hoot of an owl echoed softly from the cliffs. And then a solitary globe began to descend, slowly, seen immediately by both. Teddy sat up straight. No one had seen globes since their appearance at the sight of the von Bruner accident. The globe did not bob or weave, seemed not to be in a hurry, came directly toward them, halted five feet off the ground and a few feet away.

"Hello, Beauty," Teddy whispered.

For perhaps a full minute, they watched the motionless white globe. "Do you see movement in it?" Teddy whispered.

"I think so. Can't tell, really."

Silence.

Then, "Matt?" a note of fright in her voice.

"I feel it. Shush."

Loneliness. A tortured, burning, fuming land-scape, boiling lava, noxious atmosphere, sulfurous, acidic, unbreathable. Slow change and a sense of being suspended in time. Rains. Rains needing an adjective in multiples of torrential. Great and thunderous discharges of lightning. A gradual clearing to leaden skies and silt-filled, soupy seas and still the loneliness until, in muddy, silted darkness, there was an awareness of life, tiny, insignificant. Swift movement and again that feeling of being lost in time and there were green things, odd, primitive, but living, and a sense of peace, of fulfillment that saw change after change to giant, fernlike plants that grew and faded and then the blue skies of beauty and clouds and familiar scenes. Familiar vegetation and a languorous feeling of pure contentment, slow movement, the hint of something, the smell of flowers, a sense of mission. The work. The work was all, and plenty, and simplicity, and euphoria. A jar. The far off, lonely thunder of a G.D. And with a shock, she was looking at herself, and at Matt.

"Matt?"

"I see. I see. Be quiet."

Sorrow, pain. A dead, pollen-covered body beside a huge tree. Understanding and such joy as had never been known, a feeling of vibrant life unlike anything experienced and the herds, living, breathing, rich, red blood coursing, a feeling of completeness and a yearning never to be lonely again.

Pain again, frustration. Jack's intense desire to teach a zebra colt to run for its life. Puzzlement, and a mental wail that hurt the head. The musky feel of sexual arousal and a rather embarrassing view of Earl and Kerry. She understood. Subconsciously they had wanted just that, but would not admit it and we

*made it possible to know why they were unfulfilled
and why it hurt us so, for we are not prepared for
such powerful emotions and the rich, red blood
draining from the lifeless form of the big animal and
an outside feeling of shock and hatred and the desire
for punishment coming from above.*

"From us," Matt whispered.

*The incredible pain of knowing that Beauty's an-
imals could be slaughtered for, unthinkable, food,
and the trees pushed down by huge machines and
millions of the pain sources, humans, ripping, tearing, killing animals, and—blackness.*

The globe was motionless, no movement visible
inside.

"Oh, Beauty," Teddy said, "how it must have
hurt you to do what you felt you must do."

In her head was a moment of agony and she
gasped.

"It's all right now," Teddy said. "We'll explain.
The numbers of humans on Beauty will always be
limited. There'll be more and more animals."

Pleasure.

A feeling of finality, of good-bye, and yet the
sphere was still there.

"Good-bye?" Teddy asked. "Because Matt and I
will be leaving in a few months?"

More.

"I don't understand," Teddy said.

"They've found a way to block contact with humans," Matt said. "There will be no more contact,
ever."

The globe bobbed up, down, and then was streak-
ing for the cliffs, disappearing before it reached the
top.

"Well," Matt said, "we *have* encountered our
first intelligent alien species."

"So beautiful," Teddy said. "No hint of how they
came into being, but they were here when the planet

was young, when the surface was still molten, when the oceans formed, for how many billions of years alone, and then the first life, the tiny, primitive plants of the ocean and more billions of years and now the animals. And all they want is to help, to do the work. They pollinated everything, Matt, what a massive work, and now—''

''How will they help the animals?''

''I wonder,'' Teddy said. ''It gives them great contentment just to feel life. What will they do?''

''If they protect the grass eaters, they'll kill the carnivores,'' Matt said. ''If they choose only the old and feeble for lion or cheetah food they'll interfere with the process of natural selection.''

''No, they won't. They understand now.''

''We could learn so much from them. How a solar system is formed. How a planet develops. How life comes into being.''

''But the human mind, its emotions, they're too strong for them,'' Teddy said. ''It hurts.''

''Maybe they'll change their minds in the future, contact someone again,'' Matt said.

''I don't think so. It was so final.''

''Do we tell the others about this?'' Matt asked.

''No,'' she said quickly, and wondered if that was her own thought or if— ''No.''

It was an exciting time in the development of Beauty. Before the birth of Teddy's baby there were bird songs in the mornings, the buzz of insects. Andrew Reznor compromised, for the moment, on one of his pet hobby horses and introduced only nectar-drinking mosquitoes. On flowering Beauty, there was never a shortage of nectar. Matt caught a five-pound bass from a little lake near Africa House. Seal herds were to be seen at specific places along the continental shores, but one had to know where to look to find any of the animals, for it would be many years before the natural birthrates raised the numbers of any species enough to fill their habitats.

Beauty became a favorite stop for galactic officials and Reznor's private sector friends and acquaintances. Several times a year the animals of Beauty starred in documentaries broadcast on one world or another. Scientists from all the settled worlds waited in line to study and observe. And Cassie Frost's chimps, flourishing in Africa, began to build woven shelters to keep them out of the rain.

Matt, helping a tummy-swollen Teddy walk through some brush-littered chimp country, took one look at the shelters and said. "I think the next few centuries are going to be very interesting."

Chapter 29

Andrew Reznor made a brief speech. Jack Frost toasted Teddy, Matt, and the new addition to their family, now one year old. Kerry cried. Cassie said, "You'll be back. You won't be able to stand not knowing what my monkeys are going to do next."

It was time to go. The new ship, called *Tinker's Belle*, waited on the pad. She was state of the art. She had a built-in nursery and Teddy had had to limit the number of gifts, lest the room be packed solid. The first human children born on Beauty had been spoiled and pampered by dozens of self-styled aunts and uncles and younger cousins.

"We'll have small but nice schools here," Cassie said. "So when you're through transing around the universe and want to settle down—"

"There'll always be a place for you," Reznor said, which was not a worthless promise, since applications for resident work on Beauty outnumbered vacancies by the thousands, even with the facilities designed to study and tend the animal life growing.

Matt was slightly hungover next day when he and his little family boarded *Belle*. Teddy had prolonged their leavetaking until Beauty's sun was ducking below the western horizon. Twilight came quickly as Cassie and Kerry said one last good-bye to the child. Night came while Matt, with a new life for which he was responsible, was being extra careful with the take-off check lists. *Belle* lifted into the darkness, before the rise of the moon.

"Matt, hold at about five thousand feet and drift over the plains," Teddy said.

"One last look?"

"You don't mind?"

Belle's lonely thunder swept, growling, over the plain. Resting herds didn't bother to move. The thunder reverberated from the far cliffs.

"Matt," Teddy whispered, "Matt, look."

He had already seen.

Below, like thousands of stationary fireflies, the white dots hovered over the standing, grazing, dozing animals.

"Each of them has one," Teddy said. "Each of them has an animal, and they're not lonely anymore."

"They showed themself to us, to you," Matt said. "Will anyone else see it, ever?"

"I don't know." Teddy scurried to the cradle at the rear of the bridge, loosed restraining straps, pulled the child from the cradle and held her up to the port. "Look, Beauty," she said. "You're so young, and I'm sure you'll never remember, but look."

A globe, far below, dashed into motion and for a moment she was puzzled. Then, judging by the speed and the abrupt halt, Teddy realized that she'd witnessed a kill, perhaps by Nefertiti or one of her cubs. She felt only a momentary sadness. Life went on, and it would grow and develop and fill Beauty as it had once filled the Earth.

She put her child back into the cradle. Matt said, "Up we go." *Belle* rose smoothly. The child laughed at the sensation and then, only minutes later, while the ship was clicking and purring as Matt programmed a trans, she was asleep.

Teddy used the viewers on maximum magnification. She could see only the infrared shadows of the herds. She could not see the globes.

"Ready?" Matt asked.

"Ready," she said, taking her seat. "I can't see the globes."

"No. Here we go."

Belle transed. As the stars appeared again, in unfamiliar patterns, both Matt and Teddy looked back toward the cradle to see how their child had taken her first trans.

The one-year-old girl named Beauty Tinker slept peacefully. Neither her mother nor her father could see the globe that hovered one foot over Beauty Tinker's auburn head, from which emanated the sweet, uncomplicated, nonpainful life force of a child.

DAW

A GALAXY OF SCIENCE FICTION STARS

DAW

Science Fiction Masterworks from
C.J. CHERRYH
THE ALLIANCE-UNION UNIVERSE

The Company Wars
- ☐ DOWNBELOW STATION   (UE2227—$3.95)

The Era of Rapprochement
- ☐ FORTH THOUSAND IN GEHENNA (UE1952—$3.50)
- ☐ MERCHANTER'S LUCK   (UE2139—$3.50)

  The Chanur Novels
-   ☐ THE PRIDE OF CHANUR   (UE2292—$3.95)
-   ☐ CHANUR'S VENTURE   (UE2293—$3.95)
-   ☐ THE KIF STRIKE BACK   (UE2184—$3.50)
-   ☐ CHANUR'S HOMECOMING (UE2177—$3.95)
- ☐ VOYAGER IN NIGHT   (UE2107—$2.95)
- ☐ PORT ETERNITY   (UE2206—$2.95)

The Mri Wars
- ☐ THE FADED SUN: KESRITH   (UE1960—$3.50)
- ☐ THE FADED SUN: SHON'JIR (UE1889—$2.95)
- ☐ THE FADED SUN: KUTATH   (UE2133—$2.95)
- ☐ SERPENT'S REACH   (UE2088—$3.50)

The Age of Exploration
- ☐ CUCKOO'S EGG   (UE2083—$3.50)

The Hanan Rebellion
- ☐ BROTHERS OF EARTH   (UE2209—$3.95)
- ☐ HUNTER OF WORLDS   (UE2217—$2.95)

NEW AMERICAN LIBRARY
P.O. Box 999, Bergenfield, New Jersey 07621

Please send me the DAW BOOKS I have checked above. I am enclosing $_____
(check or money order—no currency or C.O.D.'s). Please include the list price
plus $1.00 per order to cover handling costs. Prices and numbers are subject to
change without notice.

Name _____

Address _____

City _____ State _____ Zip _____
Please allow 4-6 weeks for delivery.